The Detective Joanna Best Mysteries
Book 6

A Murder is Denounced

Cenarth Fox

The Detective Joanna Best Mysteries
Book 6
A Murder is Denounced

First published in 2019 by Fox Plays
www.foxplays.com
www.cenfoxbooks.com

Cover design by Oliviaprodesign

ISBN 978-0-949175-40-3

Dictionary of Australian words

Here are some of the mainly Australian words/sayings in this novel.

biscuits - cookies
blower - telephone
blue - a mistake or a fight
bollocking - a severe reprimand
brown bread - rhyming slang for dead (UK)
carks (carked) it - dies
CBD - Central Business District, Downtown
Chinese Whispers - game called Telephone in the USA
Coat hanger - nickname for Sydney Harbour Bridge
footy - Australian Rules football
full stop - period
GST - Goods and Services Tax, UK's VAT
hanging black crepe - telling bad news as it is, no sugar coating
IBAC - Independent Broad-Based Anti-Corruption Commission
jocks - male underpants
kays - kilometres
Man from Ironbark - character in a Banjo Paterson poem
Mummy/Mum - Mommy/Mom
nark - annoying person or thing, to annoy
nature strip - grass/lawn between road and sidewalk/footpath
pit stop - toilet break
sangers - sandwiches
Shanks's pony - on foot, walking
sheila - a female, often a girlfriend
shellacking - in sport it's a heavy defeat
Sin City - Sydney, Australia
socks - sox
Springvale - Melbourne suburb with vast cemetery
tacker - toddler, young child
torch - flashlight
Triple 0 - emergency number, 911 in the USA, 999 in the UK
turps - turpentine, the grog
tyres - tires
wedge - an amount of money (UK)

For
Kevin Trask and Kevin Holman
Supporters of Theatre and Magpies

1

IT WAS CALLED THE COCAINE CESSNA. The plane flew so low and so fast over the Venezuelan jungle, a tribe of angry monkeys protested to the World Wide Fund for Nature. But for drug dealers, the nine-seater aircraft was perfect. It helped them avoid radar, cops, the Drug Enforcement Agency and armies.

The Columbian cocaine was flown to a homemade runway in Venezuela, then, on a fast boat, it sped up to Florida. There it was dumped overboard at an agreed time and place on a moonless night before finally being fished out of the sea. Yessir, the floating nostril-eating powder made it to the United States.

Occasionally the drug runners screwed up and the coastguard won the lottery. When that happened, heads rolled within the Mob, and the DEA officers took selfies with the captured contraband. Of course everyone knows 93% of the cocaine leaving Colombia arrives safely on the streets of Miami, Manchester or Melbourne, and in the war on drugs, the cops cop a shellacking.

The Cocaine Cessna did a flyover to check the situation. The guy in the control tower was on a lunch break. The control tower! What control tower? What runway? It was a bulldozed strip in the dense rainforest where even 4WD vehicles tied a white flag to their aerial. Half of Venezuela is forest, and leaving aside the Howler Monkeys and their mates, this part of the jungle was sparsely populated; no humans.

The pilot was "Punky" Brewster, a seasoned airman running crack for the Mob. His sole passenger was Vladyslav "Vlad" Davydenko, a former army vet from Eastern Europe, now a US citizen, and a happily married family man. The Mob values family.

Vlad was the go-between. Fabio in Colombia made the stuff, and Camilo in Florida bought it. Meet Vlad the middle man.

He scanned the ground with powerful binoculars and saw men waiting for the drugs. Their 4WD vehicle was parked on an overgrown track, God knows where. 'That's them, Punky. Take her down.'

The pilot made a cracking living flying coke. He flew the snow in and the cash out. This was the key exchange. Eric was on the ground with the folding stuff, Vlad in the air with the snorting stuff. They did a swap. Eric took the drugs to the US. Vlad took the cash to Colombia.

The Cessna needed an expert pilot. The homemade runway was surrounded by virgin rain forest, more dense than dense. Take three steps into this jungle, if you can, and you're lost.

In favourable weather, the Cessna needed at least 2000 feet to land and take off. Forget the dangers of being caught running drugs. One pilot error and you scored a rainforest burial. Punky was good but as the plane came in over the treetops, Vlad felt his gut tighten.

On the ground, the men with the money turned their backs as dirt, leaves and twigs swirled around.

Punky made his usual expert landing, turned the plane and taxied for take-off. Vlad pushed the bundles of cocaine to the door.

Once upon a time, ships carried tons of the stuff but those bloody coastguard narks got lucky a few times, and so drug lords reduced their risks. Vlad's US boss, Camilo Gonzales, settled for smaller packages and today's lot totalled a mere 300 kg, enough, mind you, to keep Cam in socks and underpants till Thanksgiving. This delivery of coke was worth a mere 10 million on the streets.

Punky kept the engines idling. This was no stopover where a cab took the crew into town to the nearest Travelodge. It was dump the drugs, grab the cash, and piss off—pronto.

The plane door opened and Vlad shoved out the first bundle of coke. He looked at the money man he'd dealt with many times before. Eric was a Texan with skin handcrafted by the sun. Taciturn was Eric; a grunt about as garrulous as he got. He opened the first attaché case. Bundles of bills were crammed in like sardines. He tried to make eye contact with Vlad who was too busy to notice.

'Have you counted it, Eric?' yelled the grinning Vlad as another bundle of cocaine landed on Venezuelan soil.

The second attaché case was opened, and Vlad saw another pile of 100 dollar bills. He grinned again, pushed out the final bundle, started to step forward to collect the cash but froze because Eric went mad.

He spoke. The tough Texan with a penchant for privacy went all talkative. It wasn't so much Eric's verbosity but rather what he said and how. A theatre director would have asked for better projection but the audience—Vlad and Punky—certainly suspended disbelief.

'It's a trap,' was all Eric got to say as weapons behind him opened up. Eric pitched forward, Vlad fell back and Punky hit the throttle. The Cessna jerked forward. Vlad flattened himself on the floor and Eric was already flattened on the dirt runway now turning red.

Bullets sprayed the plane as it gathered speed. It was like aiming at the side of a barn. Punky had landed and taken off in some pretty hairy situations but this was a doozy.

The Cessna was not the fastest at getting airborne. This one didn't.

Punky copped a bullet or three; the plane swerved hard left, ploughed into the brick wall of a jungle and stuck its nose in the air. The gunfire stopped only when the plane exploded. The executioners chewed grass as the plane spewed heat and bits of metal. The only good news being the cash and the coke were safe.

Everything was collected and the crooks who robbed the crooks set off through the jungle to their vehicle and then to the beach. They steered well clear of the remains of the plane and its medium-rare, barbecued occupant—singular.

When the plane hit the jungle and stuck its nose in the air, Vlad the Invincible was thrown out, copped a mouthful of pristine Venezuelan vegetation, and slithered into the jungle. He stayed there. The flames roared above him. He lay still and only when the voices of his attackers fell silent did he lift his head. He could have murdered a beer.

He thought about Eric and Punky. Talking was tough due to his leafy lips and pointless as Punky and Eric were deaf, permanently.

Great. If I survive the crocs, jaguars, monkeys, snakes, spiders and sloths, how the hell will I survive the Mob? "It was like this, boss. These pricks started shooting and ..." Nah, f'get it. Cam and Fabio will never believe me. I am a dead man. The only way to stop being killed by the Mob is to kill myself. Where's me gun?

Back in Florida, Cam grew anxious. Fabio less so because of the upfront payment in case of a disaster such as just happened. Cam knew the drop-off time. He expected a coded message confirming the successful swap. Niente. Eric and Vlad went all shy. No message.

Camilo Gonzales was new style Mafioso. He hated the malarkey about gangsters loving blood, bullets and broads. Cam was a member of various clubs and professional associations. He was a Freemason for Chrissake. He owned six retirement villages each with a wing for seniors holding a hot ticket to heaven.

Who would have thunk it, the Mob running healthcare? And why not? Going legitimate was all the rage. There were benefits. Cam could hold his head high in the local golf club. He could make a killing out of killing—legitimately of course as senile seniors were "helped" on their way. "We need the beds, y'know." And there was always the added bonus of dabbling in good old-fashioned crime on the side. Cocaine.

Drugs were a sound investment. The demand for coke was on the rise. Vast areas of South America were becoming coca plantations. Climate change? What's that? Rip up the Amazon Basin and fill y'boots, my son.

Of course there were risks from the guys in white hats but Cam rode his luck—until now—and to lose both cash and coke was a real kick in the cashews. And it all happened because one of his trusted henchmen double-crossed him. Vlad, you are a very naughty boy. Or was he?

In fact Vlad was a victim with Cam the villain. The drug lord shot himself in the foot—feet. Cam caused the jungle hijack and massacre.

Shipping large quantities of cocaine from South America to the United States is a complex operation. Drug lords need staff; lieutenants for decision making and worker bees for muscle.

One of Cam's worker bees was Kris Palmer, a twentysomething lad who dropped out of Florida State University wanting a lot of money yesterday. Drug running was his route to instant wealth. Working for a drug lord paid damn well so Kris joined Eric's crew racing up the coast of Venezuela in a fast boat.

But despite being far from home and living the criminal life, Kris kept in touch with his Mom and her folks, his family. Pop was his best pal and Kris was shattered to hear the old guy suffered a stroke and landed in a nursing home. Kris rang home. The news was good. Pop recovered enough to get up and walk and talk. Kris made plans to come home and see the old guy.

Kris rang a week later. 'What?' he screamed at his Mom.

'I'm so sorry, son, but your Granpaw passed last night.'

'But you said he was recovering. You said he was getting better.'

'He was,' blurted Mom, herself now crying. 'We can't believe he could go so sudden like.'

Kris took the news real bad. He wanted to know what happened. He investigated and discovered the nursing home where his Pop resided was one of several owned by his boss Eric's boss, one Camilo Gonzales. Kris kept digging and heard rumours of certain practices at Cam's nursing homes. Extra doses of morphine were allegedly given to those who were deemed to be close to death's door. It was the "we need the bed" policy passed from Camilo to his managers. It only took one conscience-free nurse and a doctor willing to sign the death certificate to make the whole thing legal, unsuspicious and definitely economically beneficial—for Camilo Gonzales.

But it got worse. Worse? Yes, because murder was only part of Cam's wickedness. He instructed his lawyer and managers to coax patients into making a "small" bequest to the nursing home which cared for them in so loving (read lethal) way. Grieving relatives were outraged.

'But Mrs Jones,' explained the manager, 'your dear father insisted on thanking the staff who cared for him by making this bequest in his will. Who are we to go against his wishes?' Who indeed?

Meet Camilo the bastardo.

Kris fumed and planned revenge against Camilo. He knew other drug lords shipped drugs so he offered one of Cam's rivals a chance to smash the man who he believed murdered his Pop.

Kris pretended he was double-crossing for money, and took a nice wedge. For that he divulged details of when the cocaine was moved, the plane, pilot, middleman, destination, runway, ETA, the lot. Kris legitimately cried off the fatal run having a Florida funeral to attend. Cam's rival, fellow drug lord Larry "The Bitch" Connolly, ran the show.

Eric and his team were surprised and killed with Eric spared to maintain the ruse. Then he and Punky were slaughtered. Had Vlad been killed, Cam would have had no obvious guilty party. Vlad's luck ran out when he has wrongly blamed for the double-cross.

Cam's kill-the-old-folk policy meant Kris's Pop died from a morphine overdose and boy, did that come back to bite the Mafioso.

With the murderous crooks gone, Vlad crawled out of the jungle. The plane smouldered and a whisper of smoke wafted up from Punky's charred remains. The lifeless Eric sunbathed on the runway. Both were listed on tonight's menu for the local wildlife. Being well-done, Punky's spare ribs were on the Specials' board.

Vlad searched the plane. In the blackened fridge he found apples, cheese and beer. He stuffed his pockets. He explored where the killers once stood and found cigarette butts and footmarks—not only thieves and murderers but litterbugs. He looked to the heavens. The Sun was sliding below the trees leaving about an hour of daylight. It was close to impossible attacking the jungle by day. By night it *was* impossible.

The murderous thieves escaped along a path marginally better than the jungle. Vlad followed. With no idea where he was going, as soon as he couldn't move, he knew he was off the path.

It got darker. Different animal sounds spooked him. He dared not stop. Resting on the jungle floor would be petrifying. Climbing a tree would be dangerous and worse. What's a nice snake like you doing in a place like this?

As his desire to go on faded, he stumbled upon the so-called road where the 4WD vehicle had been parked. He looked along the track and in the gathering gloom saw nothing but jungle. He was somewhere but nowhere. Darkness crept up behind him. His gun on the plane was destroyed. With it, he'd be safe; not to shoot the wild animals but himself.

Then he heard a new sound. It was the sea, waves breaking on the shore. He couldn't see it but to reach it meant attacking the dense, almost impenetrable jungle. How far was the ocean? He had no idea.

It was either walk on the overgrown 4WD track and hope it led to somewhere safe before nightfall, or attack the jungle to reach the sea he could only hear. Some choice.

He fancied a swim so stepped into the jungle and grabbed vines. His arms and legs were scratched, his face cut. Spiders dropped on him. Monkeys sprang from branches above, screeching at the intruder. He felt weak. Darkness fell but the sound of the sea got louder.

He tripped and fell, not landing on the jungle floor because the undergrowth was so thick. He looked up and in the darkness saw the eyes of a snake poised to strike.

'Jesus,' screamed Vlad and ran. Well, tried to run. But where? Anywhere. A fanatical desire to survive drove him on and it worked as he crashed out of the jungle and collapsed on the beach.

When Cam heard nothing, he sent men to investigate. It was two days before his goons hacked their way into the jungle and found the burnt out remains of the plane. The grisly discovery meant the pilot and the paymaster were accounted for.

'Two bodies?' screamed Cam, not caring about his language on an open line. Listening, the FBI agent took notes.

To Cam it was obvious. Bastard Vlad pulled a sting. He killed the pilot and bagman, and fled with the drugs and the money. Cam almost self-combusted. He created a new project. Whoever finds, tortures and kills Vladyslav Davydenko will earn a cool million. Bring me the head of John the Baptist. Spread the word, boys.

Get Vlad.

2

BERYL WAS A YOUNG GRANDMOTHER with an old name. Her daughter, Christine, had two pre-school kids and a marriage not so much broken as shattered. Gran minded the kids to give her daughter a break. It was past 9 pm when she drove into Christine's drive.

Christopher, 4, was awake and busting to be unbuckled from his child seat. 'Wait, Christopher,' said Gran. 'I need to help Kirrily.'

The little girl, 2, slept a deep sleep. Beryl carried her granddaughter to the front door with Christopher there first. He reached up and pushed the doorbell. They heard it sound inside. Kirrily stirred.

Christine didn't answer the door. Christopher gave the bell another push. Again it sounded. Still Mummy didn't respond.

Beryl worried. The police had served not one but two restraining orders on Christine's estranged husband, Kevin Grande. The man was a brute. So the non-appearance of her daughter pushed Beryl's fears into the red zone.

'Mummy,' called Christopher and went to push the bell a third time.

'No, Christopher. Come back to the car and I'll ring Mummy.'

Unhappy, the boy obeyed. Beryl put the sleeping granddaughter back in her seat, and her protesting grandson in his.

She grabbed her phone and rang her daughter. It went to Voicemail. Beryl stepped out of her car and rang the local Frankston police, their number on speed dial.

'Have you been inside?' asked the officer.

'No and I don't want to. If she's been bashed again, I do not want the children to see her.'

'We'll have someone there as soon as possible.'

The police were true to their word. Thankfully Christopher took a shine to his Tablet and watched a cartoon for the umpteenth time.

Beryl saw the cop car arrive and stepped out to meet the male and female uniformed officers.

'Here's the front door key. She would normally have the porch light and other lights on. I'm scared. She might be unconscious. He's ignored restraining orders before.'

'Okay Mrs Lemon, we'll have a look. Hopefully she's nodded off. You stay here and mind the kids.'

The police opened the front door and called. 'Christine, hello, it's the police.'

No reply. They flicked light switches. The house was eerily quiet. They called again then split, moving through the house turning on lights as they went.

In the kitchen, the female constable made the discovery and called. 'Brett, here, in the kitchen.'

It wasn't pretty.

This was one of those moments police hate; telling family members their loved one is deceased. The cops notified their station, checked the house was empty then walked out to inform Beryl.

'I'll tell her, if you like,' said the female.

'Thanks,' replied her colleague, 'but don't let the kids hear.'

They approached the car, and Beryl was out and knew before a word was spoken.

'She's dead isn't she?'

'I'm sorry, Mrs Lemon.'

'Was she bashed?' The police hesitated. 'I want to see her.'

She started to head inside but was stopped.

'No, Mrs Lemon. It's a crime scene,' said the female.

'You don't want to remember your daughter like this,' said the male.

Then Kirrily cried and Grandma helped the living. Her daughter was beyond help.

Not all killings are murders, and not all murders are the same. Some have no planning, no premeditation. An argument starts, someone loses their rag, grabs a kitchen knife and thrusts, or they swing a fist and the person who is struck, falls and hits their head. Done. Other murders involve meticulous planning, and a long, cruel and torturous execution. Christine's was one of those.

Her enraged husband, Kevin, seethed for months at having his wife leave him, and the police serve him with restraining orders. He'd been locked up after one threatening outburst.

During the marriage, he became more violent. His drinking didn't help but it was his masculine pride (if that's what it's called) which tipped him over the edge. Being denied access to his children, unless supervised, drove him nuts.

'I'm their father for fuck's sake,' he roared at Family Services and the police. His best mate—his only mate—supported him throughout and boosted Kevin's belief he'd been wronged by the authorities and that woman. Kevin couldn't beat the authorities so, being a coward and a bully, he beat the woman.

He watched and waited. He knew his mother-in-law would often babysit the kids. When his mate, on spy duty, rang to say the old bitch had taken the kids away, the brute did his thing.

If I can't have my kids, neither can she.

His brutality was stomach-churning. This was no quick kill, and the quality of mercy was definitely strained. Christine begged in vain.

Towards the end, she wanted to die. Her sorrow at the impact her death would have on her children now and forever was horrendous but the physical and mental torture Kevin applied meant death became a welcome friend.

He planned to kill her, wanted to kill her but delayed his version of a coup de grâce knowing once she died, he could no longer hurt her.

He kept saying, 'And this is for stopping me seeing my kids.' Not their kids or our kids, *his* kids.

His maniacal mood didn't prevent him thinking about escape and detection. He'd watched TV cop shows where forensic officers dressed for the occasion. He did the same although bike clips and galoshes over crocs, and a shower cap on his nut were not usually worn by crime scene professionals. His unusual clothing only made Christine's pain more intense. She was the tiny mouse to his feral and ferocious cat. He toyed with her, taunted and teased her then, having bashed her senseless, watched her choke on her own blood. Sadly, there are many men like Kevin Grande.

The Frankston uniformed officers who discovered the body called local detectives. They were told the violent family history and, in turn, informed Homicide.

DI Rose, DS Billy Hughes and Detective Senior Constables Stephen Payne and Charlie Baldwin arrived. The long-serving pathologist, Dr Gabrielle Strange, was absent. A new pathologist, the quietly spoken and humourless Dr Petr Laudi (rhymes with Audi) who, because of his silent behaviour, would become known as Rowdy Laudi, and later just Rowdy, arrived and donned the required clothing. Some would later speculate he wore same to bed.

'It has to be the ex, ma'am,' said Baldwin. 'This was no break and enter gone wrong.'

'Thanks for the bleeding obvious, Senior,' said Rose. 'Have DS Fletcher take some uniforms and arrest the gentleman in question.'

'Not DI Blunt, ma'am?' asked Billy.

Rose simply looked at Hughes and all three detectives got the message. Callum Blunt was the black sheep of the family, the relative not invited to Christmas.

Laudi was joined by several officers from Forensics. They got busy and the Homicide detectives moved outside.

'What's happened to Dr Strange?' asked Baldwin.

'She's retiring or at least working less hours,' said Billy.

'Fewer,' replied the DI. The others looked at her. 'Sorry, when I first joined Homicide, DCI Robertson moonlighted for the Grammar Police.' More stares. 'Right, we need to talk to neighbours, the local police and the mother. Who else?'

'Neighbours and colleagues of the main suspect,' added Charlie.

'The only suspect,' said Payne.

Rose didn't like that. 'Open mind, gentlemen, if you please. You two get knocking on doors in the street. Billy you get what you can from the test tube team. I'll go and see the grandmother.'

'And the kids,' added Billy.

Rose shook her head. 'And the poor little kids.'

3

MICHAEL CHAN WAS A GOOD FRIEND. He survived the trip to France and England with his pal, Jo Best. He helped rescue her colleague and lover, DI Pierre Richelieu. Fighting crooks and crooked cops in Paris gave Michael a real buzz but seeing firsthand how Jo and Pierre were serious in their love for one another gave his heart another type of buzz. It hurt. Unrequited love usually does.

Jo loved Michael as a brother, which was not his preferred relationship. Still, she helped him recover funds stolen from his parents, and took him on mind-boggling adventures, so the computer guru would forever be grateful. He flew home without Jo; two's company and all that jazz. Then, from Paris, Jo sent him a strange text.

> *Hello Michael. About to board Qantas at CDG Paris. Can you please collect me at Tulla? Love and thanks.*
> *Jane Eyre*

Flying home, Michael wondered when, or even if, Jo would return to Melbourne. Richelieu was wealthy, presumably inherited his mother's enchanting Parisian home, and he and Jo could set up their love nest in Rue Cremieux. Why come back to Hicksville? Why return to what former PM Paul Keating called, "the arse end of the world"?

Richelieu had wealth and real estate, and passion for Jo. She once enthusiastically returned serve. But reading between the lines of Jo's text, Michael reckoned all was not well in Paradise; it seems the lovebirds were not exactly lovey-dovey.

Why is she coming home so soon? Why have me collect her? Why no mention of the Inspector? And what does she mean by signing off as Jane Eyre?

He checked Jo's flight details and arrived at Melbourne Airport on time. In the arrivals area he hung back. He thought about pretending to be a driver waiting for a passenger, and holding up a sign with the word GODOT. But something told him jokes were not required now.

He saw her before she saw him. Being a detective, she was looking without looking and spotted her quarry. Their eyes met across a crowded room and soon they stood face to face. She put down her rucksack and kissed him. Michael forgot to bring his anti-confusion pills, meaning his emotions started squabbling.

'Welcome home, Detective,' he said.

'It's lovely to see you, Michael,' she said, giving him extra thoughts.

He picked up her luggage. 'Good trip?' She nodded. He was about to say, "How's Pierre?" when she got in first.

'The bastard is married, Michael. Can you believe that?'

Now if her comment had involved LAMP stacks, petascale data storage infrastructure or processing large datasets from drones, Michael would have waxed lyrical. But the marital status of his friend's colleague or lover or both stumped the IT specialist.

As they walked to the carpark, Jo continued. 'I fly half-way round the world, risk my neck and get him out of a lifetime in jail and then, by chance, discover he's got a wife. He said zip. No kids so far but nothing would surprise me. What is it with men, Michael? What's with this romance and secrets crap?'

He stopped. She kept walking then stopped and turned back to look at him. He was blunt. 'You're asking me; seriously?'

She smiled and he instantly felt better. She went back to him and took his arm. They continued walking.

'Sorry. So tell me, how are you? How's Alan?'

Michael was now on safer ground, and gave Jo a description of his cat, and its ongoing research into salmon fishing in the River Tay.

The duo made it to Michael's car, he took out a second mortgage to pay the parking fee, and they headed to Jo's flat in Clifton Hill, the suburb next to Northcote where Michael and Alan lived.

'So what's on the Best agenda?' he asked, fishing.

'Did you understand my literary reference about Jane Eyre?'

'Not at first,' he said driving onto the freeway. 'But doing a spot of research, I came up with the eponymous young woman falling in love with a married man who kept his deranged wife in an attic.'

'That's exactly what Pierre's done.'

Michael's eyes widened. 'He keeps his wife in his mother's roof? Is that what those thudding sounds were?'

Jo ignored his joke. 'Apparently she has schizophrenia, stopped taking her meds, stabbed a neighbour, was convicted of manslaughter, and today lives in a secure institution at Her Majesty's pleasure.'

'I think *Les Misérables* did away with the French monarchy.'

'Ha bloody ha,' scoffed the angry detective.

'And being a good Catholic, Pierre won't divorce her,' said Michael trying to unscramble the data.

'But dearest, brave Pierre chose not to tell me. I found out from someone else.'

'Hooray Henry.'

She looked at him, impressed. 'Now you're showing off, Michael. How the hell did you know that or was it a wild guess?'

Michael explained. 'Easy. Eliminate the impossible. Antony would know or could easily discover the Inspector's legal affairs. The lawyer was jealous of Monsieur Richelieu's romantic attachment to your good self, and so, out of spite, told the lady who rejected his advances.'

Jo exhaled. She never failed to be struck by Michael's logic and deductive thinking. 'I've said it before, Michael, Victoria Police would welcome you with open arms.'

Ah, but would you? thought the driver.

They drove in silence with the odd question and answer. When they reached her flat, he hopped out to help. She felt guilty and it sounded in her voice. 'Coffee?' she asked.

'Thanks but after your long flight, I recommend an early night.'

She nodded her appreciation. He was a good friend. Again she kissed him and again his emotions squabbled. He waited till she opened her front door then tooted and drove home.

On the other side of the world in Paris, her colleague and would-be lover prepared for appointments with two solicitors from the same firm. One was Monsieur Arbert, the senior partner, an elderly man who had handled Pierre's mother's legal affairs for decades. The other was a criminal lawyer, an aristocratic Englishman, the Honourable (more like dishonourable) Antony Heron-Royhay known to some as Hooray Henry.

14

'Bonjour Inspector,' said Monsieur Arbert.

'Bonjour Monsieur Arbert,' replied Pierre.

'Please take a seat and tell me how you are getting on since your dear mother's passing.'

The small talk continued until the business began. 'Now Inspector, to business, s'il vous plaît. How can I help?'

'I 'ave three issues which require your legal expertise, Monsieur. The first is my will. Obviously my dear mother is no longer a beneficiary. I 'ave a number of changes and all the information is listed in this document. Perhaps only a codicil is required but I will leave it to you.' Pierre handed the solicitor an envelope.

'Merci.' M. Arbert opened the envelope and read the document. In all his years as a solicitor, he rarely argued against a client's wishes although in this case, he was sorely tempted.

'I will leave the wording to you,' said Richelieu.

'Merci, Monsieur Inspector. Now you mentioned three issues.'

'Oui. The second concerns the agreement I 'ave to care for my wife. As you may recall, my wife's brother, Monsieur Florent Droid, 'as power of attorney over my wife's affairs, and I make a monthly payment into an account over which 'e 'as control.'

'I am aware of the arrangement, Monsieur. What change or changes do you wish to make?'

'None.'

'None, Monsieur? Then why raise the subject?'

'Because of the third issue.' Pierre paused. 'I wish to divorce my wife.'

Should M. Arbert ever decide to become a poker player, he would excel. His expression remained neutral. 'I see.'

'I wish to maintain the financial support for my wife even when we are no longer married. This support is to continue until 'er death. If I predecease my wife, or my ex-wife, my new will must stipulate that the financial agreement continues until 'er passing.'

Again the solicitor showed no emotion. 'I understand, Monsieur.'

'And as a sign of good faith, I will give my wife the property in Rue Cremieux as part of the divorce settlement.'

'Are you sure, Monsieur? I mean, you are making a generous and ongoing financial settlement. Why include your mother's home?'

Richelieu took a deep breath. 'Those are my wishes, Monsieur.'
Arbert nodded. 'So 'ow soon before the papers will be ready?'

'Ah, the wheels of legalese, Monsieur, as you well know, turn at a
snail-like pace, and that on a good day.' Richelieu frowned. He
understood. 'May I enquire where you plan to reside, Monsieur?'

'For the moment, 'ere in Paris, so as to sign the various legal
documents; after which I return to live and work in Australia.'

M. Arbert nodded. 'I shall give these matters my immediate
attention, Monsieur.'

They shook hands and Pierre departed. He walked along the
corridor and stopped at a door with a sign, *The Honourable Antony
Heron-Royhay*. Richelieu knocked.

'Come in,' called the English lawyer. Richelieu entered. 'Ah,
Inspector, bonjour. Please take a seat. How are you and the beautiful
Mademoiselle Best?'

If Pierre knew it was his lawyer who blabbed to Jo, and helped
send the lovely female fleeing from France, Antony would no longer
be Pierre's lawyer, and might even have copped a well-deserved slap.

'She 'as gone 'ome to Australia, Monsieur.'

'Oh?' queried Antony. 'Nothing serious I hope?' He did hope and
rejoiced in the troubled romance but turned the conversation to their
legal challenge.

Antony represented Pierre when the detective was framed in a
powerful revenge attack by criminals, corrupt Parisian police and
former police. The lawyer did little to help free Richelieu; that was
down to Jo Best and Michael Chan.

But the aristocrat milked the release, and painted himself as some
kind of gung-ho legal genius. Now, on behalf of his client, Heron-
Royhay's plan was to sue the authorities for wrongful arrest, wrongful
imprisonment and slander aiming for massive damages with his hefty
fee being a part of the settlement—*naturellement*.

'Here is our court application, Inspector.' Antony handed Pierre a
sizeable document. He had mixed feelings. If he won, it would mean a
sizeable windfall but he was already wealthy, still mourning the loss of
his mother, and unhappy about his girl fleeing France. Pierre finished
reading the document.

'Do you understand, Monsieur?' Richelieu nodded. He felt flat. 'Do you have any questions?' Richelieu shook his head and returned the document. Heron-Royhay bubbled with excitement.

He handed Pierre a second much shorter document.

'I have a simple contract to confirm our terms,' oozed the lawyer, wanting a signature as quickly as possible. One small part, buried on the penultimate page, gave Heron-Royhay control of any media product such as a book deal, film or TV documentary which might flow from the compensation claim. He was a devious bugger, the Hon Pom.

Pierre gave the contract a cursory study before signing. The lawyer subtly placed same under lock and key and offered coffee. Pierre declined the hospitality.

'I 'ope, Monsieur you can attend to these matters in my absence. I will remain in Paris for a short time until Monsieur Arbert has completed some legal matters for me.'

'Oh?' asked the lawyer, fishing, desperate for any news.

Richelieu paused before explaining. 'I 'ave made some changes to my will and to other personal matters. Once the paperwork 'as been signed, I will fly 'ome to Australia.'

Heron-Royhay pretended to have no interest but was in fact frantic for any information. Having made himself a literary agent to Richelieu's claim for compensation, he wanted any gossip going.

But worse, far worse, the lawyer had recently met with Monsieur Florent Droit, Pierre's brother-in-law. Droit wanted advice on the financial agreement which existed between his sister, Margaux, and her husband, Inspector Pierre Richelieu. Heron-Royhay ignored the obvious conflict of interest and was happy to advise both brothers-in-law. He willingly told Droit about Richelieu's affairs yet told the Inspector nothing about his dealings with Droit.

Pierre departed oblivious of this skulduggery.

4

JO CONTACTED family and friends. Her mother was pleased but seemed distracted as she entertained her new beau, now referred to as Antonio, his "proper" Italian name. *Did I interrupt anything?*

Jo's sister sounded friendly, her improving health helping. Her boorish husband demanded the phone wanting to speak with his dear sister-in-law. *Has Caitlin's cancer turned them into human beings?*

Her grandfather was thrilled to hear from his favourite detective but seemed reserved. When Jo asked about Nan, Pop's voice dropped in pitch and volume. *What's he hiding? I'm afraid to push him.*

Dr Gabrielle Strange took an age to answer. Jo was about to hang up when the pathologist spoke. Instead of the gothic sounding medico whispering, "I'm Strange," there came a curt, 'Yes?'

'Good evening pathetic pathologist, this is ...'

'Oh it's you. Decided to join us after all have you?'

Jo couldn't speak. Where was the cheery, cheeky conversation from the woman she respected and loved? Before Jo could reply, Dr Strange jumped in.

'I can't talk now. Later.'

The line went dead and Jo thought about pinching herself. *Was this a dream? I'm out of the French frying pan and into the Aussie fire.*

She looked at her list. Two names remained—Dr Jack Carr and her boss, DI Elly Rose. *What's the worst that can happen with those two? Jack's daughter's health has gone backwards, and my place at Homicide is under threat?*

'Bloody hell,' she whispered thinking depressing thoughts. She rang her boss and this time, hallelujah, the response was much more to Jo's liking. Rose saw the caller ID.

'Good evening, Senior Constable and welcome home.' Jo's sigh was audible. 'And I believe congratulations are in order.'

'Thanks ma'am. It's good to be back.'

'DI Richelieu rescued by his brilliant colleague.'

'Colleagues plural, ma'am; Dr Chan was his usual invaluable self.'

'And I hope you're keen to be back at Homicide in the morning?'

'Definitely, ma'am; 0800 hours or sooner if you wish.'

There was a pause. 'And I also hope I won't have to ask if you and DI Richelieu have become an item during your overseas junket?'

Jo grimaced. 'It certainly was no junket, ma'am, and I can swear on the *Guidelines for Police and Legal Practitioners* that DI Richelieu and I are most definitely not an item.'

'I think you're supposed to say, "We're just good friends".'

'More like "just friends", ma'am,' said Jo with feeling.

Silence. Rose was trying to interpret that last bit and Jo was shocked at her bitter retort.

'Right,' said Rose. 'Well we've got a tricky homicide where we reckon we know whodunit but are struggling to prove same. We need a bright young thing to crack it. I'll see you in the morning.'

'Thanks ma'am, goodnight.'

Jo enjoyed mixed feelings being thrilled to hear something positive from her boss but worried she said too much in denying any intimacy with Pierre. And what was worse, he still didn't know she knew about his incarcerated wife. *When will I confront him?*

Right now it seemed, as her phone rang and she saw the caller ID. It was the French detective with the heroic eyes and silken tongue.

'Pierre,' she said trying to sound neutral.

'Bonjour ma chérie. 'Ow are you? 'ave you arrived safely in your flat?'

'I'm fine, Pierre. I've just spoken with DI Rose and she is expecting me in the office first thing in the morning.'

'So soon? But surely you must 'ave a break. Take an 'oliday.'

'Thanks but I'd rather crack on.'

'I wish I could take you away for a few days. We could finish what we 'ad to abandon in Paris.' Jo didn't speak. Pierre worried. 'Ma chérie, are you there?'

'Oui but I'm tired, Pierre. The jet lag is kicking in.'

'Of course, forgive me. I will call again, tomorrow. Sleep well, my darling. Au revoir.'

'Bye,' she said in a soft voice, and tossed the phone on the sofa. 'Bugger,' she whispered. 'This is getting messy.'

There was one more name on her list. Dr Jack Carr was someone she liked, no, more than liked. His parents and kids were fabulous people and she wondered if her feelings for the GP were formed or helped because of his family.

She needed a lift and knew a brief chat with Jack would do the trick. She rang and he answered. His voice hit the spot.

'Is it true? I'm speaking with the lovely Detective Jo Best?'

Jo struggled as a lump formed in her throat. 'Good evening, Doctor.'

'Welcome, and as the poet said, "Home is where the heart is".'

Jo remembered her first meeting with the GP. Then he quoted one of his favourite poets, Tennyson. Jo assumed this latest quote was again by Lord Alfred. 'Ah, I'm guessing it's by Tennyson.'

Jack laughed. 'Possibly, but I think it was Elvis.'

Jo laughed. She felt better and wanted to keep chatting. 'So how are you, Jack and your folks and your kids?'

'Fine, we're all good.'

'And Grace? How's she going?'

'I'd like to say fantastic but it's more like pretty good. Her speech is improving all the time but getting back to Little Aths will take time.'

'She'll make it. I know a winner when I see one.'

Jack was touched. They paused. Then the sound of children's laughter bounced down the line.

Jo smiled. 'That sounds like your lively lad.'

'He's playing with a friend he hasn't seen for ages.'

'Great, please give him and all your family my love.'

'Will do and I hope we get to see you soon, Jo.'

'Me too. I'm back at work in the morning but I'll ring once I've found m'feet.'

'Look forward to it. Thanks for calling, Jo.'

'Bye Jack.'

She ended the call, scratched her head and made a mental list. 'Family okay, job okay, Strange friend not okay, lovely GP okay, and the lover situation *definitely* not okay.' She undid her rucksack. 'Washing, Joanna, time to soak those smalls.'

She suffered from the type of jet lag where she was tired but couldn't sleep. Her mind raced until finally it pulled over and quit.

She slept like a log on Mogadon, woke, looked at her clock radio and swore. The alarm didn't work and Jo promised her boss she'd be at work at 0800 hours. It was now 0710.

It is possible to shower, dress, swig fruit juice, apply makeup and get dressed in nine minutes. Jo ran to the Clifton Hill station, raced onto the platform and squeezed into a carriage as the doors closed.

She remembered her day at this station heading towards her first Homicide interview. What a disaster. Forced to make an arrest, her hair was wrecked, her uniform ripped and her face bloodied.

Do I look any better today?

She knew all Homicide eyes would be on her. Off to Paris to rescue a fellow officer and the trip a raging success. Well yes ... and no. DI Richelieu was set free but the Titanic romance hit an iceberg.

What should I say? Can I fool my colleagues?

The main issue was Richelieu's return. Jo knew she must speak to him before he fronted Homicide. If he rocked up full of romantic dreams and got the cold shoulder in front of the squad, there would be one massive embarrassment spill.

She alighted at Southern Cross and hurried to work. The incident room was full and DI Rose began to speak as Jo appeared. A raucous cheer went up, clapping followed and the boss could hardly reprimand the brightest detective on her team.

Jo took a seat with back-slapping officers giving her heaps. Rose called for order.

'Okay, let's leave the welcome for later; business before pleasure.'

The room groaned. Billy Hughes chimed in. 'Come on, ma'am. We want the inside story on how the DI was rescued by Wonder Woman.'

Others added their support and Rose didn't want to kill the enthusiasm. She gave Jo the come-here finger movement. Jo stood and moved to the front as the room cheered and applauded. Rose spoke.

'Let's have the truth, Senior, the whole truth and ...'

Everyone finished the sentence. '... nothing but the truth.' More laughter which quickly settled. Talk about a rapt audience.

Jo forced a grin. She captivated her audience. 'Once upon a time,' she smiled and the room filled with laughter. So much so, office staff wandered in to listen.

Without trying, Jo became a brilliant storyteller. She explained the backstory of how, years ago, DI Richelieu arrested a corrupt cop who swore revenge. She ran through the planted drugs, the fake step-sister, the second corrupt cop and evil crime boss. She omitted the attempted seductions by the English landed gentry but related the business of writing a blog accusing the police of arresting the wrong man which turned Paris upside down. Most were impressed, some seriously so.

'You used the media to set the DI free?' asked Billy Hughes. Jo shrugged. 'But you hate the media.' That prompted a huge laugh.

Then Charlie Baldwin called. 'And is it true Frenchmen make fantastic lovers?'

Another laugh which quickly died as the hope of gossip appealed. Pause. Jo milked it. 'No comment, and I want to see my lawyer.' That got the biggest laugh.

He gave her the thumbs up and Rose took control. 'Okay, enough.' Jo sat. 'I'm sure we're rapt Jo was able to help DI Richelieu and we hope he'll be back with us next week.'

DI Rose was doing well in her new role with her ability to mix and join the troops while being able to steer them back to work when necessary. Now was one such time.

'Right, back to the Frankston homicide. We arrested our sole suspect last night, the victim's ex, and I want a ton of information before we interview him this morning. So, what's the latest? Billy?'

DS Hughes stood and pointed to material on the display board. 'There's still only one suspect, the ex-husband, Kevin Grande with an *e*. He's a tram driver working out of Preston with a list of priors involving violence towards the victim. He was arrested for breaching an AVO taken out by his wife. He did time for assault. His anger at being denied custody of the kids seems to be the obvious motive. If I can't have them, neither can she.'

'What about forensics?' asked DS Justin Fletcher.

'Nothing yet.'

'Send Jo Best, she'll get them moving,' said Charlie Baldwin.

Jo ground her teeth at this old joke which fizzled.

'What about someone other than the ex?' asked DI Blunt, Mr Unpopular, now trying to crawl back into everyone's good books. 'Could it have been a burglary gone wrong or a druggie who lost it?'

'All possible but unlikely,' replied Hughes. 'Mr Grande had motive and opportunity, and the awful injuries to the victim means it must have been someone with an anger problem. This was personal.'

That killed the conversation.

Rose continued. 'We may get something from the PM and Forensics but his alibi is crucial. Whatever he says, if he says anything, we need to test and quickly.'

DS Fletcher responded. 'He's living with a mate, Cooper Yale, in North Melbourne. After we arrested Grande, we interviewed Yale who swore blind his mate was at Yale's place from about 1800 hours until tram driver Kevin left for work next morning on the first shift.'

Billy Hughes spoke. 'The new pathologist, Dr Laudi, estimated death between 1900 and 2100 hours so if Grande was in North Melbourne as his mate claimed, he ain't the killer.'

Jo observed. She was tickled pink to be back working on a case, especially a tricky homicide, and her first question was about Dr Laudi. *Who is he or she and what has happened to Dr Strange?*

The meeting ended and Charlie Baldwin apologised. 'Sorry about the smartarse remarks, Jo.' She gave a wave dismissing the matter. 'And it's great to have you back.' He winked and she smiled.

Billy Hughes approached. 'Right, Senior, you're with me.' Jo grabbed her bag and followed DS Hughes.

'Why am I always the bridesmaid?' called Baldwin which got a good response.

5

VLAD SLEPT ON THE BEACH, close to the water, the safest place he reckoned to avoid sharks and crocodiles. He ate the food from the plane, the first time he ate a whole apple; peel, flesh, pips, stalk, the lot. Apple and beer for breakfast was a first but would it be his last supper? There was golden sand aplenty but no Golden Arches. In the night he heard many scary noises and kept moving.

He stopped worrying about Cam. Survive Venezuela first.

Back in Florida, Vlad lived with his wife and young son in Orlando. He loved them but lied about his job telling his wife he worked on the oil rigs in the Gulf of Mexico. He made a fortune from cocaine but lived in a modest house. Neighbours thought he was a regular guy.

In Venezuela he watched dawn break with the rolling waves in front and the mysterious jungle behind. By plane, Caracas to Miami was a two and a half hour flight. Walking would take a bit longer. He started.

After an hour he rounded a headland and struck gold. A fishing boat rested on the sand, and on it sat three men repairing nets. Vlad fell back. His Spanish was basic and, as a former soldier, he could handle himself. He carried a few grand in cash. He put $300 in his back pocket and the remaining few thousand inside a sealed bag in his jocks. If he and the money survived, the cash to be laundered might need to be laundered. He worked out a story, walked around the rocks, waved and called.

'Hola!'

The fishermen were surprised but one seemingly unarmed person caused them no concern. They watched him approach and stopped work when he arrived. He smiled and spoke slowly.

'Do you speak, English? Inglés?'

The men shook their heads and observed the gringo.

Where did he come from, what's he doing, and what does he want?

Vlad ramped up the sympathy routine. 'I, me, lost. I go Cuba,' he said pointing north, 'Cuba.'

'Cuba,' they all said, laughing. Vlad tapped their boat and pointed to himself and the boat. 'You take me to next town. Si?'

The oldest man waved a hand and spoke in Spanish. 'We only fish here.' He indicated the sea in front of them. 'Here.'

Vlad was losing. 'I have money.' He looked at them. 'Dinero?' They knew what that meant. Did they ever? He produced the money from his back pocket. US dollars looked good to the fishermen. 'Here,' he said giving a $100 bill to each man. They took it quick smart. 'Take me to next town, where you sell fish. Comprende?'

Heads nodded. 'Si, next town.'

Vlad was rapt. *Day 1 and I'm rescued.*

Eventually the nets were back on board and Vlad helped shove the boat into the sea. The ancient motor chugged. The men knew their routines, and Vlad relaxed when they gave him bread and cheese and a flask with something homemade and alcoholic. He sat at the bow.

The men chatted with lowered voices. Vlad picked up the odd word. He pretended to be admiring the sea views but spotted them looking sneakily at him and tooling up with knives they used to gut fish. This looked bad. *Day 1 and I'm murdered.*

Vlad stood and looked at the mighty jungle. It was back there somewhere. He could fight and be killed. He could fight and kill but could he steer the vessel? Yes, but in which direction? He could go for a swim. *Do I want to be stabbed and thrown overboard or jump overboard and become a shark sandwich?* Some choice.

Two of the men approached slowly from different directions. Vlad couldn't believe he survived the plane massacre, and the perils of the jungle only to be murdered and, wait for it, *after* he paid 300 bucks for a mini ocean cruise.

One man fiddled with a rope pretending to work. Another came at Vlad holding fruit. This was a ruse. 'Hey, Gringo,' he said.

The old trick failed and Vlad waited for both to lunge before stepping forward causing the attackers to almost stab one another. The third fisherman saw all this from the cabin. Vlad used his military combat training and for the crew, this didn't go as planned.

Vlad had the first two backing away. From the cabin, the skipper produced his party piece, the ship's artillery. It looked like a "hand gonne" carried by Christopher Columbus in 1498. Was it loaded? Would it fire? Vlad didn't wait to find out, so snatched a wooden crate and leapt overboard.

The victorious crew jeered and watched their passenger bobbing, drifting away in the choppy sea. Vlad tried to calculate the direction of the jungle. It's wild and spooky creatures and choking vines now appealed. Forget this drowning caper. He opted for direction A—the wrong one—and began dog paddling.

After an hour, his body was reasonable but his mind came under pressure. *Give it up, my son.* His body prepared to follow. Then he heard an unusual sound. Could it be a speed boat? *What the hell?*

Hearing someone yelling, and in English, did wonders for his soul. Do drug runners have a soul? As he bobbed up on the latest swell, the rescue craft slowed as it approached. He was fished out of the ocean, wrapped in a protective blanket and sped away to the mother ship.

This was a Caribbean cruise liner sitting low in the water, packed with obese seniors. The captain was off course in search of exotic fish.

'You were very lucky, my friend,' said Captain Verholven, a Dutchman. 'We sent out a drone to find the big fish and we found you. So tell me, how did you get to go swimming in the Caribbean?'

Vlad gave a truthful but disingenuous tale about falling overboard from a fishing boat. He was given a shower, change of clothes, medical check and a slap up meal.

The first mate reported to the skipper. 'Well, am I right?' asked the skipper. 'Our visitor is involved with drugs?'

'Has to be, Captain. He even had money in his underpants.'

'So we can say he was swimming in cash.'

The first mate groaned, and the captain radioed the authorities in Barbados and Florida. A West Indies rendezvous was agreed.

Vlad was treated with respect and advised he would need to clear Customs when they arrived in Barbados. Being sans passport didn't faze Vlad with his gift of the gab and a stash of cash in his bum crack.

He didn't know the Americans enjoyed a good working relationship with the authorities in the Windies who were happy to hand over drug-running escapees. Welcome home, Mr Cocaine.

Vlad got thinking. *If the DEA jail or release me in Miami, Cam's men will get me and gut me.* Having survived the jungle massacre, the jungle, and the ocean, Vlad reckoned his 9 lives were up. He needed a way out. *Help me, Mr DEA, please.*

Vlad woke in a clean Florida cell and reckoned he was in Paradise. He got breakfast in bed and when the "butler" mentioned a chat with the DEA, Mr Cocaine worked on his elevator pitch.

He knew he was in deep shit with Cam who would believe Vlad planned and executed the coke bust, and any guy who robbed the Mob was a dead man walking. Looking over his shoulder for the rest of his life was now Vlad's default position. He needed help.

The DEA guys got chatting and Vlad rolled over. His thinking was simple. *With Cam, I've got no chance. With the DEA, I might, just might make it to old age.*

'I wanna make a deal,' he said.

The DEA officers knew every offer going. 'No promises, no guarantees, buddy, but we're listening.'

Vlad let rip. 'I've been running drugs from Colombia to the US for years. I've just survived a mini war between drug lords. My boss thinks I stitched him up.'

'And did you?"

'Oh sure,' said Vlad with sarcasm. 'I've got ten mill in me jocks and a ton of coke up me arse. Great stitch up. Look, there's already a price on my head. If you guys help me disappear,' he hesitated, 'I mean get a new start with a new ID, I'll give you the works on one of the most successful cocaine dealers in the US. Deal?'

The cops smiled. 'Not so fast, ah, how do say your name?'

'That's not my name. You guys are gunna give me a new one.'

They smiled, liking his attitude. 'We offer nothing and give you less until you tell us everything, and even then, we may pass.'

'But that's crap,' protested Vlad.

'Take it or leave it.'

Vlad shook his head. The DEA would love to nail a drug lord but no way would they do Vlad any favours unless he came up with some pretty impressive intel. He did.

He spilt the beans, peas, pumpkin and potatoes. He gave names, dates, places, distribution networks, and even Cam's golf handicap. The DEA nominated Vlad for DEA Snitch of the Year.

He was given a choice. Get a new ID, extensive plastic surgery and a large wad of cash but hang around and keep feeding the DEA new data, or, get a new ID, minor plastic surgery, 500 bucks and a plane ticket to anywhere other than Mars. Vlad made his choice, Option 2, and Cam became top of the DEA's most wanted list.

So the DEA wanted Cam almost as much as he wanted Vlad. And that's interesting because to date, nobody who crossed Camilo Gonzales has survived.

6

BILLY HUGHES DROVE with Jo beside her. 'Thanks for inviting me, Sarge, but what's wrong with the others who've been on this case from the off? Or do you want a woman's touch?'

'I want a smart detective's touch. Now tell me the real story of what happened in Paris.' She was serious. Whatever else you got from Billy Hughes, there was never any bullshit.

'As I said, Sarge, it was scary, but Michael Chan was his usual brilliant self and I got lucky with the article I posted online.'

'Ah, luck,' said Billy. 'Some wise person once said, "The harder I work, the luckier I get".' Jo felt good. 'So you and the DI; all good is it?'

That hurt. *What does Billy know?* 'Fine, why wouldn't it be?'

Hughes paused and the tension got busy. 'Tread carefully, Senior,' she said and left it there.

North Melbourne was a short drive from Homicide. They parked and Hughes explained the situation.

'The murder suspect you heard about, and he's the only one, claims he was in this block of flats when his ex was brutally bashed and murdered 70 kays away in Frankston. If his alibi holds, we're in trouble. We interviewed his mate who lives here and who supports the suspect's alibi. So now we're working through the other flats to see if anyone can give us anything to prove or disprove the mate's story. There are still a few residents to interview. I'll lead but you can do your magic routine any time you like. Are we good?'

They looked at one another. 'I have a magic routine, Sarge?'

Hughes gave a forced grin and led the way. They entered the block of flats and knocked on doors. Most residents were at work and the two who were home didn't recognise the suspect from the photo.

On the third floor, a door was opened by a woman, 30s, plus size figure, attractive and half asleep. The cops showed their ID and explained their mission. 'May we come in?' asked Billy. 'It's important.'

The woman turned and walked inside. The detectives followed and sat in her lounge. It exuded taste. Hughes ran through the usual questions, showing the photo. The woman offered nothing.

Jo chimed in. 'Do you live alone, Dani?'

She looked surprised with Billy intrigued. 'How did you know my name?' Dani was more angry than curious.

'The letterbox downstairs says "D. Walsh" and the birthday card in your hall says, "Happy birthday, Dani".'

Hughes purred and Dani settled. 'Yes, I live alone.'

Jo nagged. 'So no visitors on the 9th between 6 pm and midnight?'

'No.'

'You may not have seen the man we're talking about but any visitor coming or going might help us.'

Dani got short. 'I told you, I live alone and don't have visitors.'

'What, never?'

Jo went too far. Dani got nasty. Hughes took over. 'Here's my card, Dani. If you hear anything about the man we're investigating, or remember something later, please give me a call.'

They stood to leave. Unseen by Hughes, Jo looked at Dani and placed her card on the hall table. Outside, Hughes reprimanded Jo. 'I see the overseas trip hasn't stopped your ability to push too hard.'

'She's lying, Sarge.'

'Of course she is but having a secret lover or hosting a baby shower on the night in question may tell us nothing about our killer.' Pause. 'And yes, I did see the cigarette butts with and without lipstick.'

'And the man's shirts hanging in the bathroom.'

'Bugger,' said Hughes. 'I missed them.' They drove to see the pathologist. 'Look, Jo, we need help with this, and rubbing a possible witness up the wrong way doesn't help. If anyone saw our suspect or sees or hears something tomorrow or next week, then we want their help. Telling someone they're lying about a boyfriend, about anyone, even if they are, doesn't make you popular.'

Jo wanted to ask, "Do we want to be popular or effective?" but didn't. She liked DS Hughes for many reasons, one of which was she never pulled her punches.

As they drove, Jo remembered her strange Strange phone call. She didn't mention it to Hughes, and they entered Pathology to find two pathologists examining the injuries suffered by the battered Christine.

Strange looked up. 'Well, well, well, the prodigal daughter returns. How was the overseas sex jaunt, Detective?'

Jo was shocked and embarrassed. Hughes simply took it as typical banter from the woman who called a spade a forkin' shovel.

'Good morning, Doctor,' said Jo. 'I trust you are well.'

'I am but she's not.' She nodded at the corpse being examined— again. 'Have you met Dr Laudi?' Jo and the new pathologist nodded. 'I've conducted a further examination, Detective Sergeant, as per your request, with nothing new to report. The attacker was right-handed as are about 90% of humankind, and could not have done what he, and you'll note I said "he", did in less than fifteen minutes, possibly longer.'

Jo took her first look at the body and felt nauseous. The deceased suffered multiple wounds and was seemingly attacked post mortem.

'No other evidence under nails, inside the body?' asked Hughes.

'I do thorough the first time, Detective. What I found is in my report which went to Forensics. Them's the ones to hassle.'

Hassle? The detectives were confused and disappointed. Why were they being attacked for doing their job? Why was the pathologist being exceptionally sarcastic, beyond even her normal level of rudeness?

Hughes kept her cool. 'Thank you, Doctor. I appreciate you going the extra mile. We're frustrated because we reckon we have the killer but can't crack his alibi. We'll leave you to it.'

Hughes left. Jo looked at Strange who nodded at her. 'Chop, chop, Detective, run along,' she said and Jo felt sick.

'What's eating her?' asked Hughes as they went to Forensics.

'No idea, Sarge. I rang her last night and she gave me short shrift then hung up. She was fine before I went overseas.'

'Any chance you can do some snooping?'

Jo looked at Hughes. 'Snooping? Are you joking, Sarge?'

'You're the only Homicide member who has a relationship with her. She's a brilliant pathologist and we need her fit and firing. If she's gone off the rails, we need to have her put back or put out to pasture.'

'Am I a Homicide detective or a psychologist?'

'Well you're bloody good at sorting murders. Why not give the mystery of the loopy pathologist a spin?' Jo didn't have an answer, and Billy's raised eyebrows spoke volumes.

They entered Forensics where Jo spotted the love-struck scientist, Alastair Dean, the poor sap she once led on, only for him to seek revenge and embarrass her. He saw her and felt an urgent need to pass water. The scientist handling the Frankston material had nothing new, meaning nothing to report. This case was grinding to a halt and fast.

That night, Jo changed and headed out. She bought some expensive dark chocolates and parked in North Fitzroy. No phone call, and no prior warning before she gave the door a knock.

Mumbling rumbled down the hallway. Gabrielle opened the door, saw her visitor, turned on her heel and headed back to the kitchen. Jo took that to mean she could enter. She did. Not a word was spoken.

In the kitchen, an open bottle of red and a glass of wine stood ready. Gabrielle placed a second glass on the table. Jo worried. Gabrielle's recent drinking problem meant she lost her licence. She claimed to have given up the grog but clearly was now back on the turps.

'I brung some choccies,' said Jo, placing the box on the table. Gabrielle wanted to smile. She poured wine in the second glass and pushed it to Jo who said, 'Thanks,' and raised her glass. 'Cheers.'

Gabrielle acknowledged Jo with her glass but remained mute.

They looked at one another. Jo opened the box of chocolates, helped herself and pushed the box across the table.

Gabrielle selected her favourite and chewed. With chocolate in mouth she finally spoke. 'I get it. He's thrown you over, hasn't he?'

That hurt mainly because in one way it was true. Jo copied her companion and stayed silent. Finally she spoke.

'Tell you what, Doc, I'll give you chapter and verse on my sordid saga provided, when I finish, you do the same.'

More silence. The tension became rich and the pauses would've made a Pinter play feel rushed.

Gabrielle swallowed more wine then topped up her glass. 'Deal,' she said. 'Only I want every sexual position and all the dirty talk.'

Jo worried. Of graphic sex, of *any* sex with Pierre was there none. *She'll think I'm holding back. She'll reckon I cheated and that means she won't feel obliged to tell me her situation.*

32

'He's married.'

Gabrielle was surprised, was expecting gossip, and immediately lost interest in matters prurient feeling sorry for her friend.

'I bet he told you *after* he had his wicked way.'

Jo shook her head. 'Two things; he didn't tell me, and he didn't have his wicked way.'

'What? But I know you fancied him.'

'I did and was ready, willing and able.'

Gabrielle panted. 'Well come on, don't keep me in suspenders.'

That further broke the ice. Jo's vision of the plump pathologist in lingerie tickled both their funny bones.

'Tell me,' insisted Gabrielle.

'We wined and dined in a romantic Parisian restaurant, flirted like teenagers, then arrived at the love nest ready for action only to be swamped by screaming journalists with flashlights. I fled. End of romantic interlude. Fade to black.'

Gabrielle became her old talkative self and bombarded Jo with questions. 'Right, from the top; I want the *whole* story.'

Jo nodded. 'Okay. Michael and I exposed the police corruption and how Pierre was set up. We got him released and naturally he was over the moon. His lawyer fancied me so I hid in a priest hole to escape his evil clutches. He was mightily pissed.'

Gabrielle shook her head. 'You're making this up.'

Jo ignored her. 'Michael has always fancied me and when Pierre was released from prison, the lawyer and Michael stood there while Pierre and I kissed, and being in France it was clearly a French kiss.'

'I like it,' whispered Gabrielle.

'Michael took off and came home, and the lawyer, in a fit of pique, told me his client was married.'

'I'm shattered there's no sex but it's still bloody fantastic.'

'You haven't heard the best bit yet, Doctor.'

Jo paused, milking the expectation.

'Well go on,' snapped Gabrielle.

'Years ago, Pierre's wife killed someone, was found not guilty by reason of insanity, and today resides in a psychiatric institution.'

'Edward Fairfax Rochester,' exclaimed Gabrielle. 'Hello Jane.'

They high fived. One of the reasons Jo and Gabrielle got on so well, was they were keen on tales written by Jane Austen and the Brontës.

'It gets worse or better. I know Pierre's married but he doesn't know I know. He's coming home soon and from his latest phone call, I reckon he's expecting to pick up where we left off.'

'He wants to marry you.'

Jo hesitated. 'That, madam, is not an unreasonable assumption.'

Gabrielle snorted. 'What's with the double negatives? You cops are obsessed. Just say, "That's a reasonable assumption".'

Gabrielle's grammatical rant killed the storytelling. Both were unsure what to say. More wine sipping. Then Gabrielle remembered.

'Did you say you hid in a priest hole?'

Jo laughed, 'I did.' She explained the father and son's pathetic, some would say sordid, attempt at seduction. Now it was Gabrielle's turn to laugh but her cackle stopped instantly when Jo spoke.

'I think it's your turn, Doctor; we have a deal, remember?'

The temperature in the cosy kitchen dropped sharpish. A chill set in. Jo sensed it. Whatever caused Gabrielle to start drinking again and be rude to Jo must be bigger than big.

'Don't speak until I've finished,' said Gabrielle. 'Understood?' Jo nodded. Gabrielle spoke. 'My parents are dead. Only my sister is alive although she's dying. My mother shared a secret with my sister and made her promise to tell no-one. But because my sister is soon to cark it, she decided to tell me.' Jo was hooked. 'She has.'

After a dramatic pause, Gabrielle raised her glass then put it down without taking a sip or, in her current condition, a gulp.

'My dying sister is my half-sister. The man who is her father is not *my* father although I always thought he was. I think he did too.'

Jo's breathing changed. This sounded scary. It got scarier.

'My biological father is dead. He was someone I knew and liked and who helped me become a medico.'

'That's sad,' said Jo who copped a blast.

'I told you not to speak until I've finished.' Jo winced. Gabrielle paused and made another failed attempt at wine consumption.

'Apparently my mother and biological father enjoyed a fling when my mother was married to my in-name-only father. My sister doesn't know if her father knew my mother was with child by another man and it's something we'll never know. And we'll never be sure if my real father knew he was my father, and that really hurts.'

Gabrielle paused again and this time the wine did pass her lips. Jo thought the pathetic pathologist was about to cry.

'My parents died years ago but last year I went to the funeral of my real father. I wept because I loved him for all he did for me. I wept not knowing he was my father.'

Now she did weep. Jo moved to Gabrielle and hugged her friend. She convulsed. Her sadness ran free. Time was irrelevant. She recovered and turned away from Jo pulling free some paper towel. She wiped her eyes and blew her nose causing the paper towel to cringe.

Jo decided to break the ice. 'I thought my situation was bad but it's nothing compared to yours.'

Gabrielle picked up the wine bottle and tipped the remaining contents down the sink. She rinsed and dried her glass and put it away. Jo took her glass to Gabrielle who looked at her visitor. They were good at talking with their eyes. Jo's wine chased the disappeared wine.

'Coffee?' asked Gabrielle.

'Please,' said Jo. The coffee was made.

'So what's the plan with Maurice Chevalier? You know when you joined Homicide, I reckon Inspector Richelieu sang *Thank heaven for little girls.*'

Jo felt great they were back being normal, and even smiled at Gabrielle's gag. But Jo didn't know how to handle her tricky situation.

'So in my case, oh wise one, what do you recommend?' she asked.

Gabrielle scoffed. 'You're asking a woman who couldn't make a relationship last longer than a politician's promise. You're on your own there, kiddo.' Jo felt sad. 'Who else is in your little black book?'

Jo grinned. 'Mind your own bloody business.' They both laughed and felt better. 'So what's this I hear about you retiring?'

'All true, my dear. I'm being eased out the back door. You'll soon have the pleasure of working with Rowdy Laudi. He's good without being great but don't expect any lengthy sentences. Rumour is he's a Quaker and speaking's a sin.'

They finished their coffee and a good chunk of the chocolates.

'I'll get going,' said Jo and Gabrielle followed her up the hallway. At the front door, they embraced and said nothing. Jo stopped at the front gate, looked back and saw Gabrielle with tears on her cheeks. Clearing the air and making confession was good for both their souls.

Jo sat in her car and rang her grandfather, the retired Detective Chief Inspector and former head of Homicide, John "Robbo" Robertson. 'Hi Pop, it's Jo. How are you?'

His voice sounded excited, even jubilant. 'Fantastic now I've heard from my favourite copper.'

'Are you up for a visit? I know you need your beauty sleep.'

'The kettle's on. Get moving.'

Jo laughed, told him she'd be there in half an hour and set off.

Fitzroy North to Glen Iris was about 12 kilometres and as Jo drove, she thought about a detour via Mont Albert and a quick hello to Dr Jack Carr and family. The kids would be in bed but to see her favourite GP seemed a good idea. Her heart agreed.

She turned into the Carr street and pulled over. She killed her lights, was about to get out when two people came out of Jack's drive. The streetlights were good and so was her eyesight. She recognized Jack but not the woman with him. They seemed friendly.

Jo watched. Jack opened the door for the woman who turned to face him and they kissed. It wasn't a passionate kiss of two lovers but it wasn't a polite peck on the cheek either. Jo felt like a peeping tom.

She watched as Jack stepped back and the woman set off, her car's headlights shining on Jo. Instinctively she ducked and her car was lit with Jo lying across her passenger seat.

What the hell am I doing? Then a terrible thought occurred to her. *What if Jack saw my car and is right now walking towards me?* She heard footsteps. "Oh hello, Jack. Yes, I'm looking for my phone which has fallen under the passenger seat. I'll be with you in a minute."

Then the person walking towards her car spoke and Jo sighed. It wasn't the good doctor. She sneaked a look and the Carr driveway was empty. She did a quiet U-turn and drove to Glen Iris.

'I was worried,' said Pop. It was 45 minutes since Jo rang him.

'Sorry Pop, traffic.' Liar. 'How's Nan?'

'Fine, fine. Now I want to hear all about your brilliant detection in French France. Is there nothing you can't do?'

Jo laughed. *Has Pop given up on his grammar standards?* They drank tea. Pop put out a plate of biscuits then, from a pocket, produced a chocolate frog.

Another burst of happiness for Jo remembering how she and her sister scored a treat when they visited their grandparents as little tackers. Having just helped the pathetic police pathologist devour a chunk of dark Belgian chocolate, Jo decided to save the frog for later.

She gave a redacted version of her Parisian adventure. Certainly the budding romance with the dashing DI disappeared. Pop asked questions and seemed to be tiring. Jo showed concern.

'You seem tired, Pop, and you haven't told me how Nan is going.'

Pop went from tired to depressed in pretty quick time. Jo was out of her chair and sitting beside the old man. He rarely, read never, cried but now didn't try to hide his feelings.

'Oh Pop, I'm so sorry. Now I'm back, I'll come with you to see Nan. And if you can't go, I'll go for you. I'll ask Mum and Caitlyn. We'll all go.' She rubbed his arm and waited for him to speak.

'I don't like going anymore.' He wiped his eyes. 'She's convinced I'm her father and wants to know why I don't bring her mother with me.'

Jo didn't know what to say. She picked up the cups and plate of biscuits and headed for the kitchen. 'I'll fix these, you stay there.'

When she came back, he was standing and holding an A4 envelope. 'I've made a few changes to my will and have sorted the funeral arrangements. It's all in here.' Jo hesitated. 'Go on, take it.' Jo did. 'Read it when you get home.'

'Okay. Does Mum know about this?'

'Not yet. And I've made you my power of attorney. If something happens to me while your Nan is still alive, you're the one who'll make the decisions.' Jo felt pressure. She wasn't in the best of moods anyway but this only made things worse. 'Sorry to do this to you, Jo, but your mother and sister will never rise in the ranks, whereas you've got promotion written all over you.'

Jo sort of smiled as she cried. They hugged and he walked her to the door. Once he would've walked to her car; now, a trip too far. She gave a short tap on her horn as she drove home, crying most of the way.

Life was not too flash for Jo of late. Her love life was a mess. Her grandparents were both in a bad way. Her friend, Gabrielle Strange, copped a real kick in the guts and was back on the sauce. All she needed now was to cock-up a homicide and her life would be complete.

She arrived home, checked her emails and prepared for an early night. Her phone rang and the dreaded number appeared. It was the married gendarme with the velvet tones and kissable lips. Could she ask him if he was married? Or ask why he didn't tell her? Or ask if he ever would? She sat on the sofa and answered the phone.

'Pierre, bonjour.'

'I am terrible,' he said and Jo worried. 'What's happened?'

'I am suffering the 'eartache being apart from the woman of my dreams.' Jo felt sick. 'I miss my favourite Senior Constable. 'ow is she, s'il te plaît?'

'She's a bit under the weather, Pierre.'

More concern hurried out of Paris. 'But that is not good. What can I do to you make you better?'

Tell me about your wife would do for starters, thought Jo.

'Listen ma chérie, I still 'ave some legal matters to attend to 'ere but then I will be coming back to 'omicide and of course to you.'

'When, Pierre?'

She kept her answers short and there was zero emotion in her voice. Was it the distance between them, or love blinding his thinking? Who knows, but he continued his sweet nothings.

'Soon, my love, and when I am by your side, Joanna, I 'ave something important to ask you, n'est-ce pas?'

Oh shit.

'Take very special care of yourself, ma chérie and I will call you soon with the date of my arrival. 'ere is a kiss for your adorable lips.' He made a kissing sound. 'Au revoir, sweetheart.'

She whispered 'Au revoir' and ended the call. Leaning back on her sofa, in frustration, she screamed.

7

CAMILO GONZALES TOOK OFFENCE AT ANYTHING; innocent comments became insults. He demanded his wealth be acknowledged. He fancied himself as a non-royal royal. Punks who disrespected him only did it once. Cam was a road rage incident waiting to happen. If someone took his parking spot at the golf club, he'd seriously consider having the driver's car incinerated.

So when his order of 300 kg of quality cocaine wasn't delivered and the cases of cash he coughed up in payment for the drugs were nicked, Cam became incandescent with rage. When it happened to him, theft was evil. Far worse was the disrespect shown to the Mob boss.

How dare they was his logic.

But Cam, having killed the grandfather of one of his own mules, triggered the heist. Without knowing it, he friendly fired himself.

A huge reward was offered for the return of the drugs and money, and a staggering amount for the capture of Vlad.

Cam hired a PI. The guy was good and charged accordingly. Donny Jones, DJ, checked out Camilo Gonzales before accepting the luncheon invitation at Cam's Florida mansion. Donny knew he was dealing with the Mob but hey, they pay unbelievable money.

Over an entrée of Chinese shrimp and broccoli stir fry, Cam laid out his proposal, and finished with a short summary. 'You screw me and I'll break both your fuckin' legs. You find me this guy and you can retire tomorrow. Do I make myself clear?'

DJ was more wary than scared but wanted to retire and go fishing, and here was his chance at a fantastic boost to his pension fund.

'I do, Mr Gonzales, and these shrimps are to die for.'

Cam craved respect and this guy ticked all the right boxes.

'Now to make sure everything goes down okay, I'll have one of my guys tag along with you. He'll be your gofer. Call him Scruffy.'

'Much appreciated, sir,' said DJ knowing the muscle would be reporting to his boss, would kill DJ without hesitation if told to by his luncheon companion, and wouldn't lift a finger to help the PI.

The search for Vlad just got serious.

DJ began with Punky whose boss ran an airline freight company and claimed to know nothing about drugs. 'We're strictly legit, buddy, and I know nothin' about what happened to Punky. He wasn't even supposed to be in Venezuela. I made sure his wife got all his back pay.'

Mrs Punky was more forthcoming. 'He told me he was working for some heavy dudes, and I told him to stop but he said the money was way better than flying coffee beans.' When asked if she knew who attacked his plane, Mrs Punky shook her head. Even if she did know, her survival depended on keeping her trap shut. Scruffy got angry.

Eric worked for Cam. Eric was entrusted to hand over the money in exchange for the cocaine and oversee its passage up to Florida. The fact Eric worked for Cam for years and never put a foot wrong, and now was dead meant DJ was making zero progress in locating Vlad.

Eric's family thought he was a used car salesman in Michigan. They couldn't understand why he was in a Venezuelan jungle being used for target practice. DJ bombed again. Scruffy got angrier.

The tricky task was investigating Vlad because he too worked for Cam, again with an impeccable work history. Why would he make the suicidal switch and stitch up his boss? Why rip off the Mob?

With a loving wife and kid in Orlando, Vlad was smart. Money from drugs was huge. He made more in a day than he would in a month working 9 to 5, and though the dough was plentiful, Vlad never flashed the cash. He bought properties on the quiet but he and his family lived in a modest bungalow. He was Mr Average.

DJ and Scruffy came a calling. Mrs Vlad, Carrie, suffered big time. She suspected hubby worked with drug runners as he was away for days at a time. But she loved her husband and because she asked no questions, she heard no lies.

DJ quizzed her but always with respect. His polite manner got nowhere causing his gofer cum bodyguard, Scruffy Nolan, real name Brian Gazitsky, to quietly seethe.

This PI is supposed to be shit hot. He's being paid mega bucks and getting nowhere fast.

When DJ seemed to have run out of questions with nothing to show for it, Scruffy cracked. He produced a Glock 43, grabbed Carrie and Vlad's 8 year-old son, and held the weapon to the boy's head. Screams bounced around the room. The most worried person was DJ. He was about to go from highly-paid PI to an accessory to murder.

'Tell me where Vlad is or the kid gets it,' snarled Scruffy.

Carrie begged, DJ pleaded. The kid wet himself with tears and pee.

'We don't know,' cried Carrie. 'He rang and said he was going away. Please, we don't know where he is.'

'You're lying,' screamed Scruffy, his anger primed to explode.

'Scruffy,' whispered DJ offering a hand. The gun shifted from the boy to DJ. To save himself and his job, DJ turned to Carrie.

'Let me see your phone, please.'

This threw Scruffy. He reckoned violence was not so much the best way to get results as the only way. Carrie handed her phone to DJ. He worked through its history, photos and texts. He took out his phone and punched some numbers.

'Just take the fuckin' phone,' yelled Scruffy. DJ hesitated and slipped Carrie's phone in his pocket.

'We can use this,' he said to Scruffy whose boiling blood dropped to simmering. DJ prepared to leave. Boy did he want to leave without any bloodshed. 'Come on.' He nodded at Carrie, then Scruffy, and left.

Scruffy shoved the boy at his mother and stormed out knocking a vase which smashed.

Their car was parked around the block and DJ was kept waiting until Scruffy got behind the wheel and revved the engine. DJ tapped on the window to be let in, shifting from wary to worried.

This guy's nuts. He'll shoot me then say I ran into his gun.

The car took off leaving DJ to stand there and swear. Alone in a suburban street in Orlando, Florida, he reckoned his best chance was to find an alien spaceship and get the hell out of here. He fumed.

A screech of tyres made him look up as Scruffy exhibited his masculinity using a car. He blasted the horn and DJ walked, no way was he going to run, back to the car and got in. Cancel those aliens.

'If you wanna survive, pal,' snarled Scruffy, 'you'd better start makin' progress. Your next move might be y'last.' The men looked at one another. 'So where to, arsehole?'

'Jacksonville.'

'This better work, pal.' They drove. There was not a lot of chit-chat on the two-hour trip although Scruffy threw in the odd burp.

DJ sat on the bed in their mid-town motel. Scruffy was drinking in a bar across the road. DJ had a theory. Vlad betrayed the Mob and cleared off with both the drugs and the cash. Something went wrong and Vlad rolled over. Or, Vlad had nothing to do with the heist and rolled over to stop Cam's assassins killing him. Whatever, Vlad was now working for the DEA and, if true, would need a new look. DJ found a text Vlad sent to his missus, Carrie.

I'll find you, Babe, real soon, tho u may not know me. Luv u

The *u may not know me* bit suggested a visit to a plastic surgeon. To survive the Mob, Vlad would change his appearance.

In the photos on Carrie's phone were many family shots taken at Surge Adventure Park in Jacksonville. There were different dates, and years. Vlad and family spent a lot of time in this part of Florida.

From Google, he found a mighty big DEA building right here in town. DJ figured Vlad, being a Florida boy and with the DEA being big in Vlad's favourite holiday town, Jacksonville was as good as anywhere to start looking.

He searched online for plastic surgeries in Jacksonville. 'Jesus,' he murmured, 'I'm in the wrong game.' Tummy tucks, liposuction, breast implants, Botox, Rhinoplasty and much more were freely available. *What the hell is a fat injection?*

DJ reckoned Vlad would want a low-key surgeon, a one-person operation, someone unlikely to ask questions but take double the fee in cash up front. No names, no pack-drill. Vlad began cold calling.

Of all the gin joints in all the towns in all the world, she walks into mine. Call it coincidence, luck or happenstance but DJ got lucky with his third plastic surgery. They were closing and the receptionist was in a hurry to leave. The owner of the business appeared, sent the receptionist home and addressed his visitor.

'How can I help you, sir?'

'I'm looking for one of your clients.'

Shaking his head, the plastic surgeon killed the conversation. 'Sorry, no can do. We're super strict on patient confidentiality.'

DJ said nothing, took out a chunky roll of hundred dollar bills and placed them on the desk. The men looked at one another. The surgeon moved to the cash and examined it using a pencil. He was in no hurry.

'Gotta photo?' he asked.

DJ placed a snap of the old Vlad on the same desk. The surgeon took one look, pocketed the cash, and walked into another room with DJ following. A file was handed to the PI. He opened and examined it.

'Take it,' said the surgeon. 'I keep no digital records and lose paperwork when the customer has the bill paid by the DEA. But you already know that.'

DJ didn't but did now. He nodded to the surgeon and left, feeling fantastic. He returned to the motel in eager anticipation of a bumper payment from Cam. Stepping inside his room, he copped a smashing blow to the back of his head.

Down but not out, he looked up to see a belligerent Scruffy holding a half empty beer bottle. 'I told you to stay here. I'm callin' the boss and he'll tell me to knock you. No Vlad, no money, no life, Shithead,' he roared. 'Now stay there.'

Holding his phone, Scruffy keep watching DJ as he called Cam.

'Boss, it's me. This useless prick just tried to clear out. He's bleeding you dry. Do you want me to ...' Scruffy stopped speaking then held out the phone to DJ. 'The boss wants to speak to you.'

With one serious headache, and while bleeding on the cheap carpet, Donny spoke to his employer. 'Hello Mr Gonzales.'

'What's happened?'

'All done, Mr Gonzales; I've found your missing package here in this fine city.'

'Great,' said Cam.

'Fuck,' gasped Scruffy.

'I'm chasing the new label but I have a photo of your former and now new-looking product. I can email it to any address you like.'

'Great. Do nothing. I'll be in touch. How is Scruffy treating you?'

'Scruffy?' DJ looked up at the now worried thug. 'Oh he's fine. Treating me like a brother.'

The call ended and Donny held up the phone. Scruffy took it and also DJ's hand helping him to rise. 'Sorry, man' he whispered and backed off pronto.

Cam felt great. Vlad was found; sort of. Word had spread about Cam being shafted which infuriating the drug lord. Now word would spread about Vlad being hung, drawn and quartered which made Cam glow.

'Excuse me, Mr Gonzales,' said his Spanish-speaking housekeeper. 'There are some gentlemen to see you.'

'What? Who? I have no appointments.'

'They say they have a warrant.'

Cam went back to being furious. 'What!' He headed out of his main living-room into the freeway-type hallway leading to the massive front door of his mansion, in another zip code. There stood four uniformed officers from the Drug Enforcement Agency of the US Justice Department. Their senior officer held out a piece of paper.

'Mr Gonzales, we're from the DEA and this is a warrant to search your property.'

Cam's joy at learning that Vlad had been found, or at least a trace of him, died. Cam's lawyer was on speed dial.

8

NEXT MORNING, HOMICIDE DETECTIVES were addressed by their hands-on boss. DI Elly Rose led from the front.

'I know all murder investigations are equal but in this case, some are more equal than others, and the brutal death of Christine Grande is a perfect example. This case *must* be solved. The dead woman must get justice as must her young kids, her family and friends. Let's nail the bastard who did this. No mistakes, missed witnesses, or lost forensics—let's build a rock-solid case and charge this killer.'

She would've made a good football coach or motivator. There were no comments or questions as the detectives awaited her instructions.

'Kevin Grande is a bully and a thug with a violent record. This was a premeditated and callous murder. He knows the system and will admit nothing. We must break his alibi. It's the only thing stopping us from charging him. So, questions?'

'Anything new from Forensics, ma'am?' asked Charlie Baldwin.

'DS Hughes?'

Billy spoke. 'We've heard the assailant knew what he was doing and must have worn protective clothing. The knife, never found, was used only to wound and torture. The suspect's prints are in the house but then he used to live there. This was a prolonged and brutal murder.'

'What was the cause of death?' asked DI Blunt, still being sidelined after his cock-up trying to arrest a war veteran in a wheelchair.

'Asphyxiation,' replied Rose. 'She was deprived of oxygen due to blood and mucus in her airwaves. She choked on her own fluids.'

Detectives cringed, some groaned. Rose didn't pull her punches. 'There were no bruises on the roof of her mouth but just about everywhere else, and the killer wore gloves.'

Blunt continued to try and make a name for himself rather than catch the culprit. 'So no prints, shoe prints, hair, clothing fibres; nothing left by the killer?'

Rose snapped. 'Forensics reckons he could have worked for them.'

The room fell silent. Jo got thinking. It was hard to push Gabrielle Strange, her grandparents and her love life to one side but try she did. 'If the suspect refuses to co-operate, ma'am,' asked Jo, 'can we get something out of his mate?'

'We can try. He too is in custody and DS Fleming and your good self, Senior, will soon brilliantly unpick his lies. DS Hughes and I will have first crack at the suspect.'

Other detectives were used to the lowly Detective Senior Constable Best getting handed important tasks although DI Blunt, being new, raged inside. His dislike for Jo Best kept growing. Hatred beckoned.

Before they entered the interview room, Rose asked Billy to lead. Grande chose not to have a lawyer. He'd been around the block and knew how the system worked, although he'd never been arrested on suspicion of murder. With a confidence which unsettled the detectives, he grinned across the table at Rose and Hughes.

'Two ladies,' he said, 'I'm impressed.'

'You seem to have a fondness for women, Mr Grande,' began Billy. 'Women on their own, slight of stature, and worried about the welfare of their helpless children. Is that a fair comment?'

Grande kept grinning. He ignored the sarcasm exuding the air of a man confident he wouldn't be charged. 'No comment.'

'Why did you ignore the AVO taken out by your wife?' asked Billy.

The grinning disappeared. 'What's that got to do with anything?'

'Motive and attitude; you've got a violent streak and don't give a toss for authority. The fact you were charged with assaulting her reinforces your propensity to torture and brutalize.'

'Propensity? Listen, lady, I'm a bloody tram driver. You'll have to speak English if this is gunna continue.'

'Don't undersell yourself, Mr Grande. The killer was so smart he dressed so as not to leave any fibres from his clothing. We reckon he wore a shower cap and gloves with covers on his shoes, and such behaviour takes a clever person, Mr Grande. Don't sell yourself short.'

'I'm impressed.' He paused. 'Oh, was there a question in there? Sorry, I must have missed it.'

The interview made zero progress. Rose shifted her position and Billy passed the baton to her boss.

'Kevin,' began Rose and the mood changed. There was no subtlety in this good-cop bad-cop routine.

'Ah,' replied Kevin, 'the good cop speaks.'

'How well do you know your kids?'

He knew what she was trying to do but took the bait anyway.

'Nowhere near well enough because the bitch told the court lies about me, and they stopped me from seeing them.'

'You say lies, she points to bruises.' Billy wished she'd said that as Grande didn't have an immediate reply. Rose continued.

'Do you want to see your kids, Kevin?'

He turned nasty. 'Oh, what is this? Confess to killing the slag and we'll let you watch your kids through a two-way mirror for ten minutes on the fifth Sunday of the month? You'll need to do a lot better than that, girls.'

The word "girls" was smeared with oil of pejorative.

'What do you suggest Mrs Lemon tells your kids about their mother?'

'That evil bitch.'

'It's a serious question, Kevin. You claim you didn't kill Christine. Someone did—and in a brutal way.' Rose opened a folder. 'We have photos.'

He pushed back. 'Not interested.'

Rose placed them in a row facing Grande. He looked at her and not the pics. 'Someone who hated your wife did this.' She paused. 'Can you help us catch the bastard?'

'You want me to do your job?'

'We want your kids to grow up knowing their father didn't kill their mother.'

He shouted and slapped the table. The photos jumped. 'I didn't kill her. I sure as hell wanted to but I didn't, and you can't prove I did.'

Rose attacked in kind. 'You hated her. You still hate her. You threatened and bashed her.' She slapped the photos. 'The person who did this is a loser filled with hate, a coward who thinks he's brave because he can bash a helpless woman.' She mocked him. 'A Mister

Toughness who, when faced with a fair fight, runs a mile.' She paused and looked at him. 'Ring any bells, Kevin?'

Grande glared at the detectives, ready to lash out then, in a second, went all calm and smirked. 'Nice try, ladies, close but no cigar. I had nothing to do with her murder so charge me or let me go.'

The interview ended. Rose and Hughes met with Fletcher and Best in the adjoining room with the monitor which featured the interview.

'You saw all that?' asked Rose.

'Yes ma'am,' replied Fletcher and Jo. 'He's right. We've got motive but no forensics and his alibi clears him. But a chain is only as strong as its weakest link. If Grande's buddy breaks, we've got him. Okay?'

'No pressure then,' said Fletcher as he and Jo went off to war.

Justin told Jo he would open the bowling but she could share the new ball. Cooper Yale was 40, a driver delivering sand and screenings and who lived alone in an apartment in North Melbourne. His mate, Kevin Grande was crashing on Yale's sofa till he found new digs.

Cooper was not under arrest, and Justin explained his rights. Cooper waved a dismissive hand.

'Let's start, Cooper, by telling us how you first met Kevin Grande?'

'We ran into each other.'

'What, literally?' Cooper nodded. 'Where?'

'Ah, corner of St Georges and Arthurton Roads. He had right of way, passed me, braked suddenly and I clipped the end of his tram.'

'You crashed into his tram?'

'We agreed to have a beer and get our stories straight and found we had a bit in common.'

'Like what?'

'Like both having a bitch of a wife who shafted us in the Family Court meaning we got ridiculous restrictions on seeing our kids.'

Jo cleared her throat and Justin pulled back. She attacked.

'Kevin's been arrested for beating his ex.' Cooper shrugged. 'Have you ever been arrested, Cooper?'

'Never,' he boasted.

Fletcher couldn't believe Jo would ask the next question but she did.

'So, Cooper, when did you stop beating your wife?'

He nearly fell into the dumbest trap. 'Ha, bloody ha,' he sneered.

Fletcher copied his boss and produced photos of the wretched victim. Justin and Jo worked as a team. He spoke. The photos were facing Cooper who couldn't help but look, although from a distance.

'Kevin's ex, Cooper. I guess you haven't seen these. They're not pretty. She was tortured before being murdered. Take a look.'

He pushed back from the table. 'Get lost.'

'Come on, have a close look.' The photos were pushed closer.

Cooper leant forward and snapped. 'Okay, I've seen 'em, all right?'

'Only a sick bastard would do this to another person.'

Cooper shrugged. 'So?'

'We reckon we know who killed Mrs Grande, and there's only one thing stopping us charging the killer.'

Jo jumped in. 'Making a false report to police, Cooper, is a serious offence. How does 15 years inside sound.' Cooper went quiet.

'Ever visited anyone in jail, Cooper?' asked Justin. Cooper kept quiet. 'Can you swear an oath in a court that Kevin was in your flat all that time?'

'He was there.'

'Answer the question,' said Jo.

Justin increased the pressure. 'So you were in your flat the whole time and Kevin stayed with you?

'That's what I said.'

'What did you have for tea?'

Cooper got angry. 'I don't know.'

'Did you eat in or out?'

'Can't remember.'

'Cooper,' said Jo, 'it was two days ago. You were with your mate. Did you go to the pub?'

'Yeah.'

'Which one?'

'Me local.'

'What did you order?'

'Steak.'

'What did Kevin order?'

Cooper shook his head, his stroppy attitude accelerating. 'Dunno. Ask him.'

'We will and then we'll ask you again.'

Cooper was close to shutting down. He hated his ex and the Family Court and the ruling it made against him. If he could have killed the judge, sanctimonious prick, he would have done so without hesitation. Kevin was the only person who understood. They were in the same boat and must stick together.

Justin was guessing but attacked again. 'So we can go to your local pub, check their CCTV, and see you and Kevin having fish 'n chips?'

Cooper leant forward. 'I hate fish 'n chips.'

'And you were with Kevin at the pub and then back at your place the whole time until 3 the next morning?'

Cooper paused. 'Did you say I was free to leave at any time?'

'Only if you're not arrested.'

Cooper's mind was working overtime. 'So tell me, when did his ex get killed? What time, *exactly*?' He was taunting them now.

Justin and Jo knew they were stuffed—for now. They ended the interview and Cooper was free to go.

The four detectives discussed the two interviews. 'Cooper's the weak link,' said DI Rose. 'Well done you two but we need to attack from another angle.'

'What about his family?' asked Jo.

'His mother and sister are here in Melbourne but his old man shot through to North Queensland,' added Billy.

'Bags interview the old man,' volunteered a grinning Fletcher.

Rose kept probing. 'What about his work colleagues?'

'They may not tell us anything helpful,' said Hughes, 'but if Cooper knows we're snooping around, we could get right up his nose.'

'Good,' said the DI. 'Do it. Justin, you tackle his family and Billy, you ruffle his work mates. Choose your teams.'

Hughes and Fletcher spoke as one. 'Jo,' they said, both wanting the best player on their team.

The detective sergeants were a tad embarrassed. Jo was pleased as was Rose who liked to see her players tackling one another hard on the training ground.

'Sort it out,' she said and left.

9

VLAD TOOK THE CHEAPER OPTION. He gave the DEA a detailed dossier on Camilo Gonzales, and in return got a nose job, plumper lips, some cash, a new name, a Canadian social insurance number, an Australian Medicare card, and two passports. Plan A was to rescue his wife and child, leave drug running, and start a new life in Canada.

He flew to LA where he lived when he first arrived in the US, and where people knew him. If he survived there, he could rescue his family and start again. He booked into a motel, dyed his fair hair dark, bought a pair of weak glasses, and changed his wardrobe.

Nervous, he set out to test the new him. He entered a bar where he used to drink. Sure enough he spotted a couple of former drinking buddies. This was the test. If his disguise failed, the Mob would find him sooner rather than later.

The barman scared the shit out of him because Vlad forgot about Freddie Mercury, real name Ian Walker. Their families were friends.

'What'll it be, pal?'

Vlad stared at him. 'Beer.'

Freddie went to grab the drink but stopped. 'Do I know you?'

This was it, the moment of truth time. Other drinkers, including Vlad's old pals, looked to see who Freddie was talking to.

Vlad went for a slower and deeper delivery. 'I'm new in town.'

Freddie decided he was mistaken and Vlad's pals lost interest. For Vlad, that beer never tasted so good.

From his new phone he sent a coded and short text to his wife. Minutes later he got a reply and froze. The innocent short message from his wife was oh so wrong. Was it ever?

Vlad panicked. His wife knew the code. The fourth word in any text she sent him must start with the letter *k*. *hi babe luv u* was all it said.

Somebody had pinched Vlad's wife's phone; somebody called Scruffy. He gave it to Camilo Gonzales in Florida. Cam got excited when Vlad sent a text to Carrie his wife. Cam replied without using the code. For Vlad, it was time for Plan B where the first step was to lose his phone.

Cam's feelings for his former lieutenant went beyond hate. This non-person stole Cam's money and drugs, and ratted on him to the DEA. Both acts were unforgiveable. The mobster raged.

The DEA search of the Gonzales "bungalow" took forever basically because it was so big. Cam was "invited" to take a trip downtown for a formal chat. Cam had his swish lawyer, A. J. Hurschenfeld III, by his side. AJ's attire was worth more than Cam's housekeeper's annual wage. His scarf alone had its own valet.

AJ earned his keep. Cam was so far removed from any link to his drug dealing it would take a team of forensic accountants consulting daily with Sherlock Holmes to even guess at Cam's involvement. There were no records of his drug dealing full stop. Cam was a cleanskin. However, his legit business interests were an open book. And why not? Cam was a New Age Mafioso.

The DEA let him go.

'How did this happen?' asked AJ in Cam's palatial car as they drove to freedom. Cam explained about the heinous Vlad who, unbeknown to his former boss, was no longer called or even looked like Vlad.

'I'll find that shit if it's the last thing I do.'

'Be careful, he may be a trap set by the DEA,' said the lawyer.

Cam looked at AJ who regretted speaking. The hatred festering inside Cam gave off an odour impervious to any gent scent.

Vlad, now James Lawrence Anderson, pondered his next move. Did he want to reach old age? Yes. How badly? Very. Were his chances better with his wife and son or on his own? He needed time to answer that. He'd read about men who walked out on their families. He reckoned returning to his family would not only put him in danger, (read face certain death), but his family as well. Cam would torture Vlad's loved ones in front of Vlad before killing him. For Vlad, it had to be Plan B.

He prepared to leave the US and to never see or communicate with his family again. He day-dreamed about being a secret guest at his son's wedding in 20 years' time. So it was ciao Vlad and hello James.

Where would he go? Canada was too darn close to the US which gave him little choice as the second fake passport supplied by the DEA was Australian. The passport was aged to pretend that James left Oz many years ago to live and work in Canada. Now he was under a witness protection scheme, and set to be born again Down Under, although not with the good folk at Hillsong.

He searched online for the ideal city. Australia boasted many immigrants, reeked with prosperity, had English as its main language, and beaches with babes.

The proximity of Bondi and its bikinis to the business hub of Sydney sealed the deal. Sin City it was.

And speaking of sand, Jo and Billy Hughes drove into the yard of *Melton Sand and Screenings,* and approached the door marked *Office*. It was opened by a corpulent gent who would not normally get off his arse. Two females grabbed his attention. *Unusual,* he thought. *Could they be cops?*

Right first time, Russ. 'Police,' said Billy as she and Jo flashed their ID. 'Are you the boss?'

They retired to his dump of an office and chose not to sit. Cleaning here was a dirty word. 'What's this about?' he asked.

'One of your drivers, Cooper Yale.'

Russ groaned. 'Oh he hasn't done it again has he?'

The detectives came alive. 'Done what again, Mr ...'

'Gravel, Russ Gravel.'

Jo wanted to laugh and thought he was winding them up. 'Is that *your* name or the name of the business?'

Russ was over the jokes and ignored Jo. 'He uses the truck to dump rubbish for cash. It's illegal and obviously against company rules. I told him if he's caught again, he's history.'

Billy remained calm. 'Rubbish is not our priority, sir. We're homicide detectives investigating a murder.' Russ gasped. 'Apart from fly tipping, what else can you tell us about Mr Yale?'

Russ was mortified. 'Cooper's wanted for murder?'

'Is he reliable? How long has he worked here? Any disputes or fights with customers? What's his history?'

Mr Grovel gravelled. No, Mr Gravel grovelled. He didn't want the police anywhere near his books though Homicide had zero interest in dodgy GST accounts.

'Look, he's usually okay. Customers don't complain which is all I ask. Can't tell you no more.'

Billy persisted. 'Where is he now and when's he due back?'

Russ checked an old monitor. 'He's gone to Gisborne. Won't be back till at least 4. Look, do I have to answer these questions?'

'Not at all. But we're trying to solve a brutal murder, Mr Gravel, and your co-operation may help us catch a killer.'

'I can't believe Cooper's a killer.'

'He's not a suspect,' said Billy.

Russ fumed. 'Well why didn't you say? And why are you here?'

'Because he knows someone who is.'

'Kevin,' said the boss without hesitation, and the detectives got excited. 'I bet it's his mate. They're thick as thieves. Both have wife worries, and trouble with access to their kids. Cooper craps on about the rigged system and how he and Kevin are fighting for men's rights. But that's all I know. So, who's been murdered?'

'You've seen this mate, Kevin?' asked Billy.

'Now and then and I reckon they're only mates because of their wrecked marriages. I don't think they even like each other.'

Billy pulled the plug. 'Well thanks for your help, Russ. And you can do us a favour. Tell Cooper two Homicide detectives were looking for him and asking about his movements.' They left and drove away.

'Nice tag, Sarge,' said Jo. 'Russ will be all over Cooper when he comes back.'

'Grande is strong. We'll only get him if Cooper cracks.'

Jo mused. 'So let's hope DS Fletcher winds up his family.'

'He will. Now, where can I drop you?'

DS Justin Fletcher and Detective Senior Constable Charlie Baldwin went cold calling in Ringwood, to interview the sister and mother of Cooper Yale, Mr Alibi in the Christine Grande murder. The ladies were given no warning. This was a brutal homicide, and the desperate position of the investigation demanded smart thinking.

Jocelyn, Cooper's sister, opened the door. She was her mother's fulltime carer and led the men inside. 'It's the police, Mum.'

The elderly Mrs Yale only looked worried because she was. 'What do they want?' The detectives entered the lounge where the matriarch sat in a corner chair watching the racing channel. She liked a punt. 'You don't look like police,' she said.

Justin switched on his charm routine. 'We're detectives, Mrs Yale.' He introduced himself and Baldwin. Jocelyn dragged magazines and knitting from the sofa, and the cat excused himself. 'Thank you,' said the DS and the men sat. 'No need for alarm, we're not here with any bad news.' Justin smiled. 'Your son, Mrs Yale, ...'

'What's he done? He's never been in trouble with the police.'

'Cooper is helping us with our enquiries.'

'You always say that,' blurted Jocelyn. 'What sort of enquiries?'

'We're homicide detectives.'

'Murder,' yelled Mrs Yale sounding like the bloke in *The Man from Ironbark*. Jocelyn was distressed about her Mum's distress.

The police fought to restore order. 'Please, there's no question Cooper is involved.' *That's not true.* 'He's given an alibi for someone and we want to find out a bit about Cooper.'

'He's got a horrible wife,' said his mother.

'A total bitch,' added his sister.

'We know he's had issues with the Family Court,' added Fletcher.

'And it's so stupid,' said Jocelyn. Police ears pricked. 'Chloe said she'll stay with her Dad if he stops being rude to her Mum.'

'Who's Chloe?' asked Baldwin who should have known.

'His daughter. She told Cooper if he's nice again, she'll tell the judge she wants to stay with her Dad.'

DS Fletcher took this in. 'Does Cooper know what Chloe thinks?'

Mrs Yale answered. 'Of course but he's too damn stubborn to ...' She suddenly burst with joy. 'Yes, yes, go, you little beauty.'

She stared at the TV as her horse flashed home to win. She bubbled. Fletcher looked at Baldwin. The police thanked Cooper's family and Baldwin led the way out. The DS lingered.

'Ladies, there's no need to mention our little chat this afternoon. We'd hate to upset Cooper. Bye.'

Outside, Charlie spoke. 'Nice one, Sarge. I bet they tell him.'

'That's the plan, and we can use that info about little Chloe. I reckon we've found our weakest link.'

At home, Jo made herself a snack, and switched from solving murders to sorting sweethearts. The business with DI Richelieu needed fixing. Why did he woo, wine and dine her without announcing he was married? Their relationship moved from the casual to the careful and was approaching the colossal when Jo got the married news, but not from lover-boy.

She wanted to know why he didn't tell her but wanted to ask him face to face. None of this explanation by phone business. This must be up close and personal. And if the seductive Frenchman didn't have the right explanation, they were no more. The would-be lovers would be colleagues only.

Her phone rang and she smiled at the caller. 'Good evening Dr Chan. How lovely to hear from you.'

'I rang to see if you're okay? How are you handling your latest romantic disaster?'

'You're a kind man, Michael Chan.'

He ummed. 'Kind is good. Unbelievably attractive is better.'

Jo laughed. She would always want Michael as a friend and colleague but not as a lover. She knew his unrequited love hurt.

'I have a new homicide, nasty and tricky.'

He ignored her switch of topics. 'What about the GP who fancies you? They make good money, doctors.'

'Michael, enough.' She paused remembering her recent visit to Jack Carr's abode and his goodnight kiss with a mysterious blonde.

'Oh don't tell me you've thrown him over too.'

'Thrown him over? Michael, you must stop reading Barbara Cartland. Now tell me, how is Alan?'

'Well and up for a chat any time you're passing.'

'Sounds good, and Michael, thanks for the call and your concern. You'll be the first to get any breaking news.'

He thanked her and rang off. She looked at her silent phone.

Why has the debonair Detective Inspector not been on the blower? Is he expecting me to call him? Does he know I know about his missus? Is he worried he blew it by not coming clean when he had the chance?

She ran a bath and finished the last bit of unpacking from her trip to Paris. Her new shoes and boots gave her a tingle. The water temperature was a smidgeon above perfect and the bubbles beckoned. She slipped beneath the suds and Murphy's Law kicked in.

She screamed. People wait till you're on the loo, in the bath or closing the front door on your way out, and then ring. Being a cop got her going. Being courted by a delicious detective helped as well.

So out of the bath and dripping everywhere, she wiped her hand and looked at the caller ID. 'Bugger,' she said and picked up her phone. 'Hello, Mum.' Nobody spoke. Jo worried. 'Mum? Is that you?'

'... had a stroke.'

Jo panicked. 'Mum? What's happened? Are you okay? Mum?'

A croaky voice responded. 'Mummy's had a stroke.'

Jo felt sick. She thought of a million questions. *Where are you? Did Pop tell you? Does Caitlyn know? Where is Nan? Is she alive?*

That night, a luxurious bath and matters of a romantic nature went out the window.

10

JO TOOK OFF. In the car, she rang her mother who kept crying. 'I'm on my way, Mum. I'll be there in fifteen. Where's Nan?'

'I don't know,' gasped Shirley.

Jo wanted to ask her to ring Pop but did so herself. 'Hi Pop, it's Jo.'

His voice struggled. 'Have you heard?'

'I'm driving to collect Mum. Where are you? Where's Nan?'

'She's here with me at Box Hill. I'm not sure which ward.'

'We'll find you; won't be long. Chin up Detective Chief Inspector.'

She didn't know what more to say. The man who inspired her to join the police and then Homicide, the man who stood up to bullies and murderers and witnessed gut-wrenching scenes was facing his toughest case. She heard it in his voice. Next year would be his and Ida's diamond wedding anniversary. Now his world was under attack. Despite her full-blown dementia, his girl was still his girl. Losing her would be a hammer blow.

Jo rang her sister. Caitlin knew. 'I'm not up to going, Jo.'

'No problem. I'll take Mum. How are you?'

'Good.' Jo found her voice and words unconvincing. 'Give Nan and Pop my love. Please explain I just can't make it.'

'Of course. Put your feet up. I'll ring once I have some news.'

Jo reached her mother's place. Shirley was an emotional wreck. If it's true the closest relationship is between a mother and daughter, then Ida and Shirley were a perfect example. They often argued and complained about the other but underneath was a deep and solid love.

Jo drove her mother to the hospital and did all the talking. Shirley struggled to speak. 'Have you heard anything else, Mum?'

'She had a stroke and the ambulance took her to Box Hill.'

'Well let's get there and find out. How is Antony, sorry, Antonio?'

Shirley gave a quiet whimper of despair and Jo wondered if he'd suffered a stroke or worse, broken off their relationship.

Now is not the time to ask, Joanna.

They parked and found their way to the right ward. The nursing staff explained. 'Mr Robertson's with his wife. I'll tell him you're here.'

Pop came out looking shattered, unsteady on his feet. He hugged the two women. Jo, though desperately sad, tried to keep matters normal. Her grandfather was not only sad but suffering from guilt.

'If only I'd been there. If only I'd stayed,' he chastised himself.

'Pop, enough.' Jo shocked her mother and startled her grandfather. If Jo wept and despaired, they could understand. But no, here she was acting like a grown-up while her elders blubbed and lost it. 'We can't let Nan see us like this.'

Some might call this tough love and the two "adults" could see how serving as a detective in Homicide helped Jo behave calmly in this tricky, difficult situation. She guided her family to seats and told them she would speak to the medical staff.

The doctor she found believed in hanging black crepe. 'To be blunt, Jo,' she said after names and positions were exchanged, 'I think it's just a matter of time. It wouldn't matter if your grandmother was fit and well, the severity of her stroke is such she would be just as incapacitated, probably more than she is with her Alzheimer's.'

Jo closed her eyes fighting tears. 'Have you told my grandfather?'

'Not in as many words. He blames himself for his wife's situation.'

Jo nodded, tried deep breathing then asked for more straight answers. When she reckoned she knew the facts, she thanked the medico and headed off as the bearer of terrible news. The look on Pop and Shirley's faces made the task a hundred times harder. They hoped for good news while dreading her words.

Jo made her mother and grandfather proud by explaining the facts in a sympathetic way. Her news wasn't news, it was something they either knew or suspected.

'It's a massive stroke,' said Jo. 'They believe Nan will not recover.' Jo let the fact sink in. 'There's nothing the hospital can do except keep her comfortable. She's unconscious and not in any pain.'

'I want to take her home,' said Robbo. Shirley discovered more tears and Jo looked at him. He understood. 'Then I'm staying.'

Jo paused. 'I think we should all say our goodbyes to Nan now because she may not survive the night.' More silence, tears and restricted breathing. Pauses between sentences seemed natural. Jo stood and held out a hand to her elders. 'Come on, let's go in together.'

They did and moving farewells began. Jo struggled to speak to her grandmother and worried in bending to kiss her, the pillow might cop a soaking. Jo whispered. 'Thanks for the chocolate frogs, Nan.'

After the farewells, Jo took her mother's arm and guided her outside. *Is this the right thing to do? Am I preventing my mother from being with her mother when Nan dies?*

Shirley went without resistance. She and Jo sat in the corridor and held hands. Only a few minutes passed before they heard a groan. Pop held his wife's hand as Ida died. Outside the room, the women wept.

Going home wasn't easy. Which home and in whose car? Jo wanted to drive the others but Pop had driven himself to the hospital. There was no way Jo would allow him to drive but before she could figure out a solution, a stranger appeared. Well, not a complete stranger.

Jo's father, Shirley's former husband and Robbo's one-time son-in-law strode towards them. Shirley's nightmare was complete. She called him Malcolm X, and the fact he married a child bride and sired two children after their divorce only rubbed salt in her wounds.

'Robbo, I'm so sorry,' said Malcolm offering his hand.

'She's gone,' said the widower. Malcolm grimaced and looked at the women. He kissed his daughter's cheek and Shirley drew back in case he planned a similar move with her.

'Caitlyn rang me and I came to do whatever I can to help.'

'Thanks Dad,' said Jo. 'I'll drive Mum and Pop. Can you please drive Pop's car to Glen Iris?'

'Sure. Keys please, Robbo. I'll meet you there.'

Malcolm left and the trio of mourners headed off to Jo's car. Pop froze. 'I haven't done anything about the funeral.'

'All under control, Pop,' said Jo. 'I gave my card to the nurses in Reception and told them to pass it to the funeral director you chose when Nan went into care. Remember you gave me your instructions.'

Shirley was too upset to ask questions and the elders looked at their flesh and blood and both hugged her. 'Come on,' said the detective, 'let's get you both home.'

Malcolm drove Pop's car to Glen Iris but didn't stay. He called a cab and headed back to his car. Inside, Jo and Shirley argued over who would make the tea. Jo yielded and sat with her grandfather.

'I don't want you on your own, Pop. I'll stay in the spare room.'

He nodded. He wanted to speak but found it easier to say nothing. Jo struggled and figured a change of subject might do the trick.

'We're got a tough homicide, Pop.' That took his mind off his misery but only just. 'Did you ever have a case where everyone knows the killer but can't get the evidence to charge?'

Again he nodded. 'A few,' he said. 'What's the problem?'

'We can't crack the killer's alibi. Any ideas?'

Robbo ignored the question. 'We have to tell Ida's family. They'll be upset they couldn't see her.'

'Auntie Gwen and all those nephews live interstate, Pop. They couldn't have been there even if they wanted to.'

Shirley entered with the tea and Jo helped her get sorted.

'I'll stay with Pop tonight, Mum.'

'No you won't. I will.'

She surprised the others. Shirley and her father often nagged one another. Now they were united in grief. Over tea they talked about the funeral, and what Ida would want.

Jo made her move. She kissed her grandfather and told Pop to stay where he was. Shirley walked Jo to the door.

'Call me if you need me, Mum. I'll ring in the morning and we'll plan from there. I'll come over and drive you home.'

'No you won't. Antonio will.'

'Right,' said Jo, who hugged her mother and drove home. She felt doubly sad, not just because her Nan was dead but because those close to her were heartbroken.

Once home, she wondered about telling people. She didn't get the chance because her phone rang. It was the boyfriend from Paris.

She spoke in a neutral voice. 'Bonjour Monsieur.'

'Bonjour Mademoiselle. 'ow is my favourite detective?'

'Not well, I'm afraid.'

'Oh?'

'Pierre, my grandmother died this evening.'

Richelieu's tone changed instantly. 'Oh ma chérie, I am so sorry. Please accept my deepest condolences.'

'Thank you.'

'This lady was the wife of the retired DCI Robertson, oui?'

'Oui.'

'I 'ope you and your family will celebrate 'er life and remember all the good times you shared. I do not know your grandmother's name.'

'Ida.' Jo felt better, softer due to Pierre's words and sincerity.

'As you know I 'ave 'ad a similar experience in losing a loved one recently so I know a little of what you are experiencing.'

There was a connection between them. 'Merci Monsieur.'

'I find life seems to pass too quickly. I find if we do not take the opportunities when they appear, they disappear and do not return.'

The atmosphere changed. Jo knew he was now talking about them.

'Possibly, Pierre but taking opportunities always depends on being honest and, as we require of witnesses, to tell the whole truth.'

There, she'd done it. She didn't plan it. It just came out. Silence. He had worried about mentioning his wife ever since they grew close. It might have been shame he felt for his wife's actions, or fear Jo would reject him because he was married. He was unsure. But now he knew she knew.

'I 'ave thought, Mademoiselle, you 'ave become a little, 'ow you say, distant of late. Something 'as 'appened between us and I am so sorry.'

'The problem, Pierre, is nothing has happened. You could have told me the truth and you chose to say nothing.'

More silence. Finally he spoke. 'Well, Joanna, my failure will not change my feelings. I know I 'ave been a coward but I also know 'ow I feel about you.'

Jo hesitated. She tingled and her anger at his silence melted. She whispered. 'Merci Monsieur.'

'I 'ope to return to 'omicide in the next week and 'ope you will permit me to fully explain my life.' He paused and she didn't speak. 'If so, Joanna, I will explain everything. Au revoir, my darling girl.'

Jo wanted to speak but couldn't because Pierre ended the call. She coughed as her throat hurt. *What a night.*

11

VLAD TOUCHED DOWN in Sydney. His "old" newly-created Aussie passport passed muster. 'Coming home?' asked the Border Force officer approving the document.

'Sure thing,' replied Vlad.

'And you've lost your accent,' she said handing him the passport.

He grinned and worried. He needed to blend in, and sound more Aussie and less like an American with a tinge of Eastern European. He acquired local currency, found a cab and headed to town. He bought a phone with a plan, booked into a modest hotel in Paddington with wi-fi, and hit the real estate and job vacancy sites.

A flat appealed so he took a cab to the address in Surry Hills, met an estate agent, and liked the first flat he saw. 'Not so fast, James,' said the agent. 'I guess from your accent you've been away a while.'

'I have.'

'Well here flat owners get to choose the tenant. They don't want some idiot holding all-night parties.'

'Hey,' said Vlad opening his arms, 'do I look like I do drugs?' If only the agent knew. So Vlad completed the tenancy application and divulged his personal info. With phoney work references created by the DEA, and his healthy bank balance, he impressed.

But Vlad needed digs *and* a job. He was good for cash but he needed, as they say, to get a life. He tried to find both a flat and a job from the same source. Worth a try; nothing ventured.

As Vlad the drug runner, he soft-soaped drug dealers and now employed his charm on the unsuspecting agent. It worked. Vlad hopped in the agent's car and, back at the real estate office, was introduced to the boss. According to his false referrals, Vlad worked in real estate in Canada. Now he was keen to work in Sydney.

Luck was on the new arrival's side. The real estate company was always on the lookout for good sales reps and Vlad with his rugged good looks—recently adjusted—and gift of the gab, landed on his feet.

He returned to his hotel having found a flat and a job which came with a car. Driving on the left hand side of the road would be a challenge, and he was on probation with his new job, but hey, Day One Down Under and Vlad was off to a flyer.

Cam got serious. He could survive the cash he lost, the plane and the manpower, and there would be more drugs but the pain, the screaming agony at being made to look a fool gnawed at his insides. His burning hatred towards Vlad gave cancerous cells the boost they needed. He contacted Donny Jones, DJ the PI he paid to find Vlad the first time.

'Sorry, Mr Gonzales,' said Donny. 'I've retired thanks to your generosity.'

'So who can you recommend?'

'I know a couple of local guys but if your man's overseas, which is where I reckon he'll be, I can't help you; sorry.'

Cam ended the call sending his blood pressure higher. He knew what Vlad now looked like but not his name or location. Having Vlad's wife's phone proved useless; it died.

Scruffy paid another visit to Orlando again threatening to torture the son unless Vlad's location was revealed. The terrified mother and child said nothing because they knew nothing. Cam's rage continued.

Desperate, the drug lord did something he swore he would never do; he asked for help. He arranged a meeting with other Mob bosses. Some thought it was a plot to kill them. Their "seconds" triple-checked the venue and their opposite numbers.

The meeting went ahead and Cam pushed his pride aside and explained his problem. God it hurt. The mobsters shook their heads, expressed outrage but wallowed in schadenfreude, and loved hearing about Cam's misery.

No offers of help were made until, right at the death, Larry "The Bitch" Connolly spoke.

'I can help, buddy,' he said, 'but it's gunna cost ya.'

'Try me,' replied Cam prepared to go to any lengths, literally.

Larry made his offer—the pitch of the bitch. It was massive. 'You owe me nothing unless I find and off this prick—agreed?' Cam nodded. 'If my man finds and kills him, you give me 50% of your coke once it lands stateside.

Wow. The offer shocked everyone especially Cam. 'What, forever?'

'Nah,' scoffed the Bitch. 'Let's say, five years.'

'Two,' haggled Cam.

'Three,' haggled Larry.

Cam didn't hesitate. 'Deal,' he said and extended his hand. There was no blood or spit involved, nothing Masonic, but this deal had secrecy and treachery written all over it.

Cam would never pay. Once Vlad was found, Cam would kill Larry. What deal? Cue internal laughter for Cam. But Cam didn't know Larry was the cause of his problem in the first place. Larry ran the Venezuela massacre and heist. Cue louder internal laughter for Larry who, once he found Vlad, planned to tell Cam the truth before shooting the speechless owner of retirement homes. It was Larry's way of eliminating a rival.

Talk about pacts with the devil. For now there was bonhomie and toasting but if either discovered the truth, then ring the bell for WW3.

Cam was about to be screwed by the guy who screwed him before. And it all happened because greedy Cam "legally" murdered one of his mule's grandfather by morphine overdose. How dumb is Camilo?

Larry could find Vlad because Larry had a contact inside the DEA, a snitch. Simon was dirty, and life for him was super dangerous but oh so financially rewarding. The snitch worked in the DEA Miami office.

The Bitch loved opera and whenever a DEA favour was required, Larry posted a review on an online opera blog.

Simon knew that whenever Joseph Green (Giuseppe Verdi) posted his musical thoughts online, the DEA criminal, was to meet his paymaster during the first interval in the *Gents* on the First Tier in Miami's Ziff Ballet Opera House on the Saturday after the blog review appeared. Mind you, Joe Green hadn't seen the opera until the night of the meet but based his comments on what others wrote. Sneaky.

The Bitch and Simon shared a silent rendezvous where money and instructions were unobtrusively exchanged. Once Simon collected the required data, there was a dead-letter drop for the info Larry required.

The FBI and DEA both had an interest in the Bitch but stood their teams down whenever the opera-loving mobster slipped on his tux. Nothing to report that night, and the music, well, enough said.

It took Simon a few days of digging but he was able to tell the Bitch about a certain James Lawrence Anderson (picture enclosed) who moved into the DEA witness protection program and received Canadian and Australian passports. Where he is now was anyone's guess but it probably wasn't Vladivostok. Ha, ha; Vlad in Vladivostok!

So when Larry lunched with Cam in a Miami restaurant for those with money, the Bitch now knew Vlad's new name, face and likely destination. The drug lords were observed by undercover feds. Two Mafiosi dining together in public was always worth a look.

Larry spoke. 'You're right about your man rolling over to the DEA. He's had plastic surgery and got himself a new name and passports.' Cam was delighted.

'Bastard,' hissed Cam. 'And?'

Larry lied. 'And I'm workin' on getting the prick's new name and photo. Soon as I get anything, you'll be the first to know.'

'Thanks,' nodded Cam, already planning how, when and where he would whack Larry. Of course Larry planned on returning the favour.

Now it's not necessary to add *Spoiler Alert* here because it surely must be obvious that the future relationship between the Mobsters is going to get ugly. *Head's up.* Do not expect a happy ending.

Having Vlad's new name was Larry's only lead. He sure wanted to find the guy, kill him, and screw Cam out of half his cocaine. Vlad, now in either Canada or Australia, was officially the prey.

12

COOPER YALE DROVE his truck into the yard of *Melton Sand and Screenings,* keen to knock off. In the office, his boss, Russ Gravel, remained seated. 'How'd y'go?' he asked.

'No worries,' said Cooper, returning the keys. What's on tomorra?'

'Bluestone.' Cooper groaned. 'Bloke building a wall at Darley.' Another groan. 'And he wants a hand shifting the bricks up his drive.'

'*Up* his drive? I get paid to offload the stuff on his nature strip. I don't get paid to push a wheelbarrow up Mount fucking Everest.'

'You'll do as you're told, mate.' Cooper stared at his corpulent boss. 'And if what I heard today is true, shifting bluestone pitchers will be the least of your worries.'

Whack. Cooper blinked. 'What are you talkin' about?'

'Two women came here today.'

Cooper scoffed. 'What are you doing with two women?'

'Two coppers asking about you.'

Cooper felt squeamish. 'Me? What about me?'

'They were Homicide cops investigating a murder.'

'It's nothin' to do with me.'

'So you know about it?'

'I said it's nothin' to do with me.'

'Then why were they here? No smoke without fire, mate. If you're involved, you're out. I won't have no murder suspects workin' f'me.'

Cooper lost it. He added spittle to his fruity denials. 'I ain't the fuckin' suspect. It's someone I know and I know he didn't do it.'

They stared at one another. Gravel was rash and Yale was locked.

'I don't wanna see them cops again. Now sort it or piss off.'

Cooper glared at his boss then slammed the door on his way out.

He arrived at his flat in North Melbourne, fuming from the police invasion, ready to give the tram driver and murderer, Kevin Grande, a serve. *I'm not happy, Kevin.*

Then he remembered his house guest was on the dawn shift so would have his head down. As he moved quietly around the snoring killer, Cooper's phone sounded. He grabbed it and went to his bedroom. Kevin grunted at being disturbed.

Cooper spoke quietly. 'Hello.'

'Kevin, it's your mother.'

This was unusual. The matriarch rarely phoned her son. 'What's wrong?' he asked. No enquiry about her health or how many winners she backed last Saturday.

'We had the police here today.'

Cooper didn't hold back. His mother was familiar with the *f* word and used it at times when one of her horses lost by a short half head.

'Why would homicide detectives be knocking on my door, Kevin?'

'They're trying to scare me.'

'What, into confessing to murder?'

His voice got louder. 'I never killed nobody. I'm just helpin' a mate the cops are trying to fit up. If they turn up again, tell 'em to fuck off.'

Kevin ended the call and turned to see his house guest standing in the doorway.

'Problem?' asked Kevin.

Cooper was livid. He wanted a way out. He couldn't go back on his statement which gave Kevin an alibi because it would land his mate in trouble, and Cooper himself would be charged. One of the cops reckoned he could get 15 years for making a false report to police. But if the cops kept giving him a hard time, he could lose his job. *Ahhh!*

'Let's go the pub,' suggested Kevin wanting to get Cooper back on the crooked and wide way. They left not knowing what to say.

Up north in Sydney, Vlad, a.k.a. James Lawrence Anderson, made rapid progress. Selling real estate suited him. With the gift of the gab, and rugged good looks, women admired him. He moved into a bigger apartment, and found a woman. It wasn't love, but rather convenience and sex; convenient for Sasha the beautician, who seemed to never remove her makeup and who got free board, and convenient for Vlad, who didn't have to sleep alone.

One night they were in a trendy wine bar in gentrified Surry Hills. They'd eaten out, and were drinking with friends. Vlad looked at his phone. People do it at meal times, in conversations, at the football and constantly when walking along busy footpaths. Politicians read texts while parliament is sitting. Vlad did so when copulating.

He faced an early morning meeting. 'Time to split, guys,' he said. 'Come on, babe.'

He led her from the bar where a giant TV screen clung to a wall. Vlad glanced at it and stopped. There was a news item about a massive cocaine bust in LA. He stared. Sasha looked at him.

'What's up?' she asked.

'Nothing,' he said and left. But it wasn't nothing. It was definitely something. He worried, panicked because that could have been him.

In his apartment they prepared for bed. He made coffee and stood on his balcony staring into the night. Sasha called and he called back. 'I'm coming.' He didn't and stayed on the balcony, deep in thought. The drug bust news clip haunted him.

That could have been me. I've messed up big time.

With Sasha asleep, he climbed into bed, lay on his back and relived the massacre in Venezuela, the rescue at sea, the DEA offer, and his decision to leave his wife and son and flee.

Sasha stirred and rolled towards him. She stroked his chest then pulled back in alarm. She frightened him. He sat up.

'Jesus, James, you're all wet.'

He touched his chest. Sasha was right. He was sweating like a pig.

'What's wrong?' She touched his back. 'You're wet all over.'

'Flu,' he said. 'I felt it yesterday. I'll have a shower.'

He stood under the water for ages. Sasha fell asleep with the worried Vlad wide awake. Back on the balcony, he wanted to throw himself off. He'd made one God almighty mistake.

What a fool, what an imbecile I am.

In Australia, he reckoned he'd be safe with a new name, new face, and new passport. And he would have been were it not for two things—the Mob bribed cops, and he went public online.

Oh shit, oh hell, oh fuck.

Once he saw the drug bust on TV, his stupidity screamed at him. His boss would have bribed the DEA to tell all. Actually it was Cam's fellow drug lord, Larry who discovered Vlad's new name and new look but it was still the Mob. And because Vlad put his name and picture online, he as good as said, "Here I am, boys. Come and get me".

In Miami, Larry paid a nerd in cocaine to do IT favours. It took the nerd 13 seconds to find a real estate site in Sydney, Australia. Hi Vlad!

On the site was a photo of the dashing agent with his new name and mobile number. Vlad knew what would happen. The shooter would book a viewing with James (Vlad), and once inside the property, go pop. Every booking was now a potential hit.

I am dead.

He tried to think straight. He needed to escape but quietly, normally. If people thought he'd been kidnapped or killed, the cops would start investigating, the last thing he wanted. So he lied.

His note for Sasha was about his horrendous disease which was back. He didn't want her saddled with a dying man. He knew a clinic in Switzerland where miracles happen. She could stay in the flat and the rent was paid for ages. If he survived, he'd let her know.

The note for his boss was personal. Vlad's sister rang from Canada. "Mother in a coma, must rush home before she dies". He apologised profusely and promised to keep in touch.

Quietly he packed his 80 litre rucksack, dressed for travel, and crept to the door. He stopped when he saw the package Sasha set aside for her sister, Zoe, in Melbourne. He took it and fled.

Back in Victoria, in a North Melbourne pub, Kevin and Cooper nursed their beers. 'Listen, mate,' said Kevin. 'The cops have got nothin', so they pick you as the weak link.' Cooper grunted. 'They stir your boss and your old girl hoping they'll pressure you into rolling over.' Cooper sniffed. 'If we stick together, mate, they can't touch us.'

Cooper swigged. Inside, he spewed. 'How did they know where I work? What if I lose me job? I can't pay the lawyer's bills as it is.'

'Listen to y'self. This is what they want, to push you into panicking. Say nothin' and they've got nothin'. Now, do you want the steak or the parma?'

13

BEFORE SHE TURNED IN, Jo sent a text to DI Elly Rose.

Dear Ma'am. Sad to report my grandmother died tonight. Needless to say, DCI Robertson is shattered. He has asked me to arrange the funeral so I may be a poor team member for the next day or two. Thanks, Jo.

A text arrived within minutes

Deepest condolences, Jo and please pass same to Robbo. Once funeral details are known, please advise. I will expect you at Homicide when I see you. Elly.

Jo was impressed. Unlike her predecessor DI Steel, DI Rose had a heart. She commanded respect but had humanity to spare.

Jo thought about the people who knew Pop and how his loss would hurt. He worked with many colleagues and most, if not all, would know about his lifelong partner.

Jo opened Pop's envelope with details about his and Nan's affairs, including their funerals. Jo made notes, cried quietly then retired.

Sleep was nigh on impossible. Her mind was awash with memories of her childhood and Pop and Nan. She cried the more. She switched channels and replayed her latest conversation with DI Richelieu. At least the elephant in the room had been acknowledged. Their next face to face meeting could go either way.

Next morning, DI Rose informed her fellow detectives about the death of Ida Robertson. Then they discussed Kevin Grande, his mate Cooper Yale and their alibi. If true, Grande could not have murdered his wife. Without a confession from Kevin or a retraction from Cooper, the victim might never see justice. There were no other suspects. It was either charge Kevin or charge no-one. Billy reported on Cooper's boss.

'We told his boss a few home truths, and when we mentioned murder, he went right off. He knows Grande and guessed we were after him. Cooper will have copped it from his boss and probably Kevin.'

'Ditto,' said DS Fletcher. 'Cooper's mother and sister were not happy and he'll cop pressure there too. And his daughter Chloe told the Family Court she'd spend time with Dad if he was nice to Mum.'

'We could use that to pressure Cooper,' added Baldwin.

'Follow it up,' said DI Rose. 'So what else?'

'He needs to be reminded of the perjury laws,' said Billy Hughes.

'True,' argued Fletcher, 'but if he thinks he'll go inside if he buckles, that may force him to clam up.' That point flattened the mood.

'He's between a rock and a hard place,' added DI Blunt. 'Why not strike now while he's under pressure?'

The others looked at Blunt. 'Strike?' asked DI Rose.

Blunt struggled. 'Get him in again and threaten him with charges.'

The new DI was the odd man out at Homicide, and unique in being the first member of the squad to be universally disliked.

Billy Hughes introduced a new possibility. 'Have we considered getting Social Services to offer him a carrot?' Ears pricked.

'How so?' asked Rose.

'Both men hate the Family Court. Both reckon females get special and favoured treatment. Both men have limited visiting rights to their kids. If we tell Cooper we'll have a word with Social Services to maybe get the Family Court to give him a better deal ...'

'We can't do that,' said Rose killing the idea.

'What, not even off the record?' asked Hughes. 'We've got a savage murder here, ma'am. Why can't we bend the rules? Unless Cooper caves in or Grande confesses, we've got nothing.'

'What if Cooper's a part of the murder?' asked Baldwin. That got people thinking. 'We know he's probably lying to give his mate an alibi but is he giving himself an alibi as well?'

Several officers spoke at once. 'One at a time,' called Rose. 'Charlie.'

'He might have been the lookout, the driver, or even involved in the actual killing. If that's true there's no way he'll change his statement. If he won't put his hand up for perjury, he'll never do so for murder.'

Silence. 'Thanks for nothing, Senior,' said his boss. 'We need to go back to Forensics and the pathologist. As it is, we've got nothing to link either man to the scene.'

'And the grandmother and neighbours saw nothing?' asked Fletcher. Rose shook her head. 'A car parked up the street; a dog-walker we missed?' More head shaking; more silence.

'At the risk of getting my head bitten off,' said DI Blunt who drew everyone's attention, 'could someone else be responsible?'

This got short shrift. 'I think you suggested a burglary or druggie who lost it before, Inspector,' said Rose, flattening her colleague.

Blunt persisted. 'Or mistaken identity or a hit because she owed money.'

Hughes lost it. 'Are you saying the victim's a drug dealer?'

Blunt shrugged. Nobody supported him. They knew this was a long and torturous murder. Blunt's anger grew. He hated his colleagues.

'We need Jo Best to help sort this mess,' said Hughes and several murmurs of support were heard. Not from DI Blunt who was growing to despise the missing detective senior constable.

Rose ended the meeting. 'Right, more calls to Forensics and the pathologist. Billy, talk to Social Services about the access rights of both men but just for information purposes. And any neighbours not yet interviewed need to be seen.'

'Ma'am,' said Billy with mutterings from the team.

'And don't forget I want a full roll call at DCI Robertson's wife's funeral. I may be the only current officer to have served under him but remember how he and a couple of other former Homicide officers solved that cold case last month. Don't be late and it's a ties-for-guys day. And clean shoes. None of this beach volleyball gear. Understood?'

'Ma'am,' was spoken by all except Blunt.

Jo felt terrible, washed out, flat—and looked it. She'd spent the last two days meeting with her grandfather, mother and sister and the funeral director. Arranging a funeral is tough at the best of times. When the deceased is a loved one, tough is replaced by bloody awful. Her grandfather left detailed instructions as to coffin, service, speakers and even the flowers. Jo merely painted by numbers but even so ....

It was an 11 am service followed by a cremation, all at Springvale. Jo offered to take her mother but Shirley's chauffeur was her elderly beau, Antonio from Italia. Jo reckoned Shirley wanted to show her former husband, Malcolm X, she could still pull a bloke.

Jo's sister was going with her husband, and Pop's neighbours of 49 years were taking him. *Bloody hell*, thought Jo. *I haven't got a date.*

Her phone rang. 'Hello Dr Chan.'

'Jo, I'm so sorry. Charlie Baldwin rang and I've only just heard about your grandmother. Please accept my condolences.'

'Thank you, Michael and I'm sorry I didn't call you.'

'No problem. So how is the redoubtable Detective Chief Inspector?'

'Bearing up. It's hard to imagine what losing your life's partner feels like even if the signs were there.'

'And how are you?'

'Well in the words of the poet, I've been better.'

'Which poet?'

Jo smiled for the first time in a long time. 'Thanks, Michael, I needed that.'

'And the funeral's tomorrow?'

'Yes, 11 at Springvale.'

'I'd like to come.'

'Fantastic, Michael. You're a star.'

'Can I offer you a lift?'

Jo breathed a sigh of relief. 'Thanks; that would be brilliant.'

'I'm no expert but funerals and driving don't always go well together.'

'Wise and kind.'

'How about 9 for 9.15?'

'Perfect. And thanks again.' The call ended.

She pondered her friend Michael Chan, the man who helped her solve cases and continually demonstrated the meaning of friendship. Sadly, certainly for Michael, their friendship didn't involve romance.

If you reckon yellow is a happy colour, it was a good day for a funeral; overcast with showers. Jo slept badly and was up running at dawn, then, as the family representative, rehearsing her speech for the service. Pop refused point blank to speak and those who knew him understood. If the term, "leader of men" applied to anyone, it did to DCI John Robertson. But now, for him, faced with a tragedy of super proportions, he couldn't bring himself to go public. His love for Ida was all consuming and he knew he wouldn't be able to hold it together.

Jo opted to wear her police uniform. Complete with hat she looked sharp. She knew her grandfather would approve and be proud. He was.

Michael was early and she admired his quality suit.

'Good morning,' she said. 'I don't think I've ever seen you in a suit.'

'Weddings and funerals,' he replied but didn't start the car. She looked at him. 'Have we forgotten anything?'

'I'm not sure about the royal we but thanks and no. I've got my speech and two boxes of tissues.'

He gave his ubiquitous half-smile and they drove to Springvale. Jo wasn't sure which chapel to book but settled for the one with a capacity of about 200. She knew Pop's funeral would attract a huge crowd although perhaps not so for his wife. Jo was wrong. It was packed.

Michael was Mr Understanding. 'I'll be here if you need me and good luck with the service.'

Her feelings for him kept getting stronger. 'Thanks,' she said and kissed his lips gently then wandered off to find the funeral director.

Everything was so-so until she saw Pop. He'd aged in a few days. His elderly neighbours supported him. Jo moved in and his face lit up, and her embrace put some fire in his belly.

'Hello, love. How are you?'

'I'm fine, Pop. But how are you?'

'Not bad for an old bloke.'

He looked frail and Jo felt helpless. Then Don Quixote and Sancho arrived, the other members of WATTI, Robbo's former colleagues. DS Tuck and DSC Colin Melk eased themselves either side of their former boss. They winked at Jo and pushed her to the edge of tears.

The service went well. The celebrant researched Ida and spoke with understanding. Ida's cousin, the family history buff, gave a fascinating account of Ida's life. Jo spoke for the family. When she stood she got her first look at the bumper crowd. There were cops and ex-cops with several of the top brass. She prepared notes on cards and referred to them until blurry eyes made reading tricky, so placed them on the lectern and spoke from the heart. It was a good move.

She remembered the love her grandmother showed to Jo and her sister Caitlyn. The cooking treats, birthday presents and hugs; stories full of love. The tale about chocolate frogs from both grandparents, who weren't aware the other was doing the same thing, got a big laugh.

If the service and attendance were good, the sandwiches and cakes were outstanding. Many people greeted Jo with congratulations and condolences. As people drifted away, she spotted her family. There were many kind words including from her sister, stoic in light of her cancer battle.

Jo was approached by a gathering of police officers, both active and retired. Those who worked with Robbo spoke about him, while her fellow officers stepped forward to offer their sympathy and support.

It was time to move and most of the police drifted away. Jo looked at her family who seemed to be distracted. She turned to see why and there stood a surprise guest, DI Pierre Richelieu.

His colleagues were as surprised as Jo. He stood still, a few metres from Jo and her family. Everyone stared. Everyone sensed this was a significant moment. Why? Some knew, and several put two and two together. Who would move first?

'Bonjour Mademoiselle,' said Pierre, giving the hint of a bow.

Finally Jo spoke. 'Bonjour Monsieur.'

'I am so sorry for your loss.'

'Merci,' said Jo. He held out his hand giving Jo the chance to take it. If this was a scene in a movie, the music would have switched to sweeping and heart-tugging. Jo approached Pierre, took his hand and used it as a steadying influence as she stood on tip-toe and kissed the Frenchman. If ever a short kiss could pack a punch that was it.

Wow. Death and sex make for a powerful mix. Wow again.

14

MOURNERS KNOCKED OFF THE SANGERS, said their goodbyes and drifted away. Homicide cops chatted about DI Richelieu's unexpected return and his interesting "handshake" with a certain Detective Senior Constable.

DI Rose sidled up behind Jo and whispered. 'Congratulations on your eulogy, Senior.' Jo looked at her boss. 'That was an interesting greeting for someone who is just a friend.'

'Ma'am?'

Rose made powerful eye contact. 'See you tomorrow.' She vanished leaving Jo doubly upset.

Michael Chan appeared. 'Brilliant eulogy, Detective. Your grandmother would have been thrilled.' Jo beamed but wanted to cry. 'Can I book you to speak at my funeral?'

His kindness and sincerity tipped her over the edge. Tears crept out. He hugged her and she liked and needed it.

'Enough!' The command separated the couple. But more hugging ensued as Gabrielle Strange cut in, embraced Jo and winked at Michael. He half-smiled. 'Bloody good speech, girlie. I nearly missed it because someone failed to send me an invitation.'

Not many people can get away with being critical at a funeral but the strange medico was just being herself.

'How did you know?' asked Jo.

'DS Hughes kindly gave me a call. I was caressing a cadaver only two hours ago so I won't shake hands. And I'll have you know I broke several traffic laws to make it.'

Jo smiled. 'Thank you, Doctor. I really appreciate you being here.'

She smiled and they hugged again.

Jeremy, Jo's narcissistic brother-in-law hovered. 'Jo, I think we should go.' He spoke in an apologetic voice as the cremation service was due to be held.

'See ya,' said Strange who departed calling. 'Ring me.'

Jo looked at Michael. 'I'll wait,' he said.

'Are you sure, Michael? I can get a lift with someone.'

'It's no problem. When you're ready.' She squeezed his arm and joined her family. Michael would always hang around for Jo Best.

Ida was cremated in a brief, family-only ceremony. Robbo seemed better and looked better because his wife's suffering was no more. Sadness and relief went hand in hand.

Outside in the sunshine, several chauffeurs waited beside or in their vehicles. Shirley's senior beau, Robbo's senior neighbours and Michael Chan opened respective doors. It was farewell to Ida as the various mourners left the Springvale Botanical Cemetery.

'Thanks for waiting, Michael,' said Jo as they drove across town.

He sang a well-known song about friends and made both of them smile. A silence settled until Jo asked about the elephant in the room.

'How would you describe the kiss I gave Pierre?'

'What kiss?'

She ignored his response. 'My boss thinks we're having an affair.'

'You do know my thesis was in IT and not *Sex in the City*.'

Jo's frustration showed. 'I should have confronted him earlier about his wife. I had plenty of chances but blew it. Now he'll think I've forgiven him and will want to pick up where we left off.'

'And do you?'

She shook her head. 'That's the problem, Michael, I don't know.'

He paused before he replied. 'So it's love or career.'

She looked out the window and spoke to herself. 'But can you have both, Joanna?'

In Paris, the English aristocrat entered the bank, took the lift and approached the receptionist. 'The Honourable Antony Heron-Royhay to see Monsieur Droit.' Antony waited on an expensive settee.

Droit appeared with hand extended and the men entered the banker's spacious office with carpet and furniture to sigh for.

'You have news, sir?' asked Florent.

'I do. Your brother-in-law has made a new will. And in addition, has made a gift of his mother's house in Paris to your sister.'

The banker whistled. 'The house in Rue Cremieux? Fine, but she will never live there until he dies.'

'It's not a bequest. He wants an immediate change of ownership.'

Droit was suspicious. He saw trickery in others. 'What? But why?'

'Because Inspector Richelieu wishes to divorce your sister.' Droit blanched. 'I think he plans to marry his colleague, Joanna Best.'

'Does he now? When?'

'As soon as possible.'

'Can he be stopped?'

Antony shook his head. 'Of course not, and I would advise against making a fuss as, apart from the house in Rue Cremieux, he will continue to pay for your sister's medical needs even after they divorce.'

Droit pondered the news. 'Richelieu is bloody wealthy. Can we squeeze a better deal than just the house and the cash?'

Antony was both shocked and impressed. 'Greed is usually the domain of lawyers, Monsieur. Besides, the Parisian house is worth a lot of money.'

Droit thought it over. 'What do you suggest?'

'Say nothing and do nothing. Just take the money and run.'

Droit was wary. 'Will we ever hear from the man again?'

Heron-Royhay smiled. 'Indeed. There is plenty of publicity to come from his suing the authorities for his false arrest and imprisonment. It was a fascinating scandal and one which should generate a lot of money from book, film and television deals.'

'More money for Inspector Richelieu. His estate grows by the day.'

Antony hesitated. 'It does but not everything is his to command.'

'Meaning?'

'Pierre has given me authority to act as his agent in certain matters.'

Florent stared at the scheming lawyer. 'And for which you will be paid a fee.'

The lawyer sniffed. 'The labourer is worthy of his hire, Monsieur.'

Florent too had a scheme of his own but preferred to keep it quiet. He said nothing to the lawyer. The two men were like peas in a pod.

Droit and Heron-Royhay—deux bâtards.

15

HIS BIRTH CERTIFICATE read Wesley but everyone called him Wes. He killed people for a living. His career sort of chose him; bullied at school, bashed by the old man, dysfunctional family, joined gang of thugs, and worked his way up to assassin. He was good, no, perfect. Apart from knowing guns and being fit, he lacked emotion; a robotic psychopath. Wes could kill without feeling. He did not care. Pleas from the victim meant zip. Nothing said, trigger pulled, end of.

Wes was average everything—height, weight, looks and attire. He was invisible in a crowd. His acting skills were top class and if he ever fancied a life upon the wicked stage, he would have been a natural.

He preferred having only one employer because that limited his chances of being knocked after a job—so long as he succeeded.

Wes got a call from his boss, Larry "The Bitch" Connolly. The job appealed. The target was a rat, a stool pigeon, a grass. But he wasn't stateside. Vlad, now James, skedaddled to Australia. Wes once heard the word Australia but thought it was in Europe.

'You ever been Down Under?' asked Larry.

'Nah,' replied Wes knowing the less he said, the less likely his ignorance would jump up and start singing.

'You'll need a local guy to help you.'

'I don't need no-one,' protested Wes.

'Just to drive you round, and get to the kill spot. When you find the mark, only you will do the business.'

More protesting. 'I tell ya, Mr Connolly, I don't need no-one.'

'They drive on the wrong side of the road in Australia, Wes. They have kangaroos, footpaths and bonnets. What's a footpath, Wes?'

The killer surrendered without grace.

He took the Vlad package of photo, name, place of employment, air ticket and the name of his criminal contact Down Under—Desmond Spear. Wes liked his fee.

'You call Des, Mr Spear. He'll supply your driver and piece.'

'I want me own piece,' said the non-stop protesting Wes.

'Oh great,' moaned Larry. 'You don't drive to Australia, Wes, you fly. So how do you get your piece through security? Use y'brain.'

Vlad slept rough. He was terrified of any assassin but more so of his own stupidity. He went to a Sydney park where he once enjoyed a picnic, and hid in some bushes. Sleep was difficult coming in snatches. Any sound woke him. When he finally got to sleep, he overslept. Rush hour sounds jolted him awake. He peed where he'd slept, brushed his wavy locks and headed for Sydney Central railway station.

He reckoned a big city was his best chance of disappearing, and knew Melbourne was about the same size as Sydney. Besides, Sasha's sister, Zoe lived there. He fronted the ticket window.

'A ticket to Melbourne. What time's the next train?

'You've just missed the morning train, sir.'

'What?'

'The next train leaves at 8.42 tonight.'

Vlad swore under his breath. The sooner he was shot of Sydney the better. His assassin could land in Sydney any time. He did. Wes was due to touch down in eight hours. If only Vlad knew.

The employee sold Vlad his economy one-way ticket, and the American went to find the *Gents*. He washed and removed his shaver. He stopped. A beard might help his disguise. Hirsute it was. He paid for a locker, stored his rucksack and devoured breakfast courtesy of Macca. He made sure his sunglasses never left his face, found a mini mart and bought fruit, water, sandwiches and chocolate. His jacket pockets bulged. Survival became his raison d'être.

He wandered into the city and sat in a corner of a coffee shop. Ten hours before his train. What to do? A mobile advertising board went past promoting a new movie. That settled it. He remembered a cinema complex he went to with Sasha, and settled in for the first screening. He saw three movies with pit stops in between. If asked to crit any of the films, he would've failed miserably; his mind being elsewhere.

Wes landed at Sydney airport. He loved his work but hated having a partner. In this case, the partner was a local punk who waited in *Arrivals* to collect the hired gun. Reece "Rabies" Horton thought of an idea, which was rare for him and dangerous. He found a dumped food carton, made it flat then wrote WES in big letters.

Wes approached from an angle, fuming, and snatched the sign.

'Hey,' yelled Rabies making a second blue. He advertised the criminal's arrival and then attracted attention with his vocal reaction.

Wes moved to one side forcing Rabies to follow. 'Listen shit-for-brains, why don't you get the airport to make an announcement?'

Rabies hated being criticised and especially hated sarcasm. 'How else was I gunna find ya?'

'Where's the car?'

This was not a warm handshake and a "did you have a nice flight?" greeting. These men would never be bosom buddies, and war broke out when Rabies hit the remote and Wes headed for the driver's door.

'Oi,' barked Rabies, 'I'm drivin'.'

Wes remembered the bit about driving on the wrong side of the road. He swore and got in the other side.

'Let's get one thing straight, arsehole,' said the visitor, causing Rabies to be tempted to use the piece he was to give to the passenger *on* the passenger. 'You do the driving, I kill the president. Capiche?'

Rabies knew the odd gangster movie and got the drift. He kept chewing but grunted and drove.

'Now where's me piece?'

'What, now? I'm driving.'

Wes growled. 'Where is it?'

Steering with one hand, Rabies undid his jacket. 'Left side.'

Wes leant across and removed the gun, a Beretta M9A3. He bent forward and checked the weapon close to the floor. Satisfied, he looked at Wes. 'Slugs?'

'Right inside pocket.'

Wes took the 10 round magazine and prepared his armoury. Rabies drove to a cheap motel where Wes checked the room.

'What now?' asked Rabies hating the subservient role.

'Take me here.' He showed Rabies the address of the estate agency where Vlad worked as James. They arrived. Wes got out, studied the photos of houses in the window then entered.

'Good afternoon, sir, how may I help?' beamed the receptionist with unnaturally white teeth.

'The house in Cleveland Street; can I take a look.'

'Certainly, sir. When would suit you?'

'Today, this afternoon, as soon as possible. I'm a busy guy.'

'Certainly. May I have your name and number.'

'Yeah it's Hank Greenway.'

'And your mobile please?'

'My what?'

'Your mobile phone number.'

'You mean my cell.' He told her. 'Look a friend of mine bought a house from you recently and she told me the agent she dealt with was a fantastic guy. Could I have him show me the property?'

'I can try. Who was the agent?'

'Ah, ...' He looked at his phone. 'He's an American like me called James Anderson.'

'I'm sorry, sir, James doesn't work here anymore.'

Wes moaned in silence. 'Damn. My friend only dealt with him a coupla weeks ago.'

'Yes, James' mother is ill and he flew home to Canada suddenly.'

Wes played it cool. 'No problem. My friend might have been mistaken. She said he was American.'

'No, Canadian.'

'Never mind. So I meet the agent at the property in say, one hour.'

'No problem, Mr Greenway.'

Wes got in the car grinding his teeth. 'All set?' asked Rabies.

'He's gone.'

'Gone? Gone where?'

'Back to Canada.'

'What, you come all the way out here and the schmuck's in your joint?'

Wes pondered, mumbling to himself. 'Unless that's what he wants us to believe.' He looked at Rabies. 'I need to talk to an agent from that realtor's office.'

Rabies frowned. 'What's a realtor?'

Wes remembered the address of one of the rental properties in the window. 'Where is 24 Bayswater Road?'

'Not far,' replied Rabies. 'You wanna go there?'

'No, I was just testing your geography.' He snapped. 'Drive!'

They drove and Rabies felt his rage festering; it was that damn sarcasm. They found the apartment. Wes read the board and saw the name of a female agent and her number. He stood on the nature strip and called her. She answered. He told her he was outside the apartment right now. She told him she would be there in ten minutes.

Wes approached Rabies and made him lower his window.

'I'm gunna look at an apartment. Drive up the road but be ready when I call.'

Rabies looked at Wes, shook his head, and drove. Wes combed his hair then stood facing the display board. After a few minutes, a car pulled up and the agent, Fiona, hopped out and called.

'Mr Reynolds?'

Wes turned and smiled. 'Hi.'

They walked to the apartment and Wes turned on the charm. He gave some tale about being transferred from the LA office and needing a smart apartment. Inside Fiona led Wes from room to room. They came back to the kitchen and Wes stood in the doorway blocking the only exit.

'I don't want the flat,' he said in a calm but eerie voice. He drew back his jacket revealing his gun. Fiona was instantly afraid.

'Please don't hurt me.'

'Give me your phone.' She did then stepped back, shaking. 'Tell me what I need to know and we both walk away.'

Fiona struggled. 'Okay.'

'James Lawrence Anderson.'

'He's gone. My boss said there was a health issue with his mother back in Canada. That's all I know.'

'Not good enough.'

'Please, if I knew any more I'd tell you.'

'Where did he live? Where did he drink? Where did he hang out? Did he have a girlfriend?' Wes oozed evil. 'Talk to me.'

Fiona went back to shaking. 'He has a girlfriend, Sasha. They share an apartment we found for him.'

'Address?' She told him. 'Tell me about Sasha.' Fiona told him.

'Now, this is how we finish. Give me your car keys.' She hesitated. 'Keys,' he snapped, and she gave them to him.

He held them up. 'These and your phone will be returned to your office within 24 hours, even sooner. But you tell anyone about me or this meeting and you won't need either ever again; understand?' Fiona nodded without hesitation. 'Do you understand?'

All she could do was keep nodding. He left and she burst into tears. Wes dumped Fiona's phone and keys in a rubbish bin, called Rabies who arrived, and they sped off. Sasha and Vlad's apartment was nearby. There was no vehicle in the car space. Again Rabies was sent away. Wes entered the block and rang Sasha's doorbell. No answer. Wes called Rabies and they sat in the car and waited. To avoid attracting attention, they got out and walked, pretending to be real estate salesmen canvassing properties.

It was nearly two hours later and dark when Sasha arrived home and parked in the spot for Apartment 4. 'That'll be her,' said Wes. 'Move the car but be ready when I call.' He climbed the stairs.

Sasha barely got inside when her doorbell rang. She opened the door and faced Wes. He didn't speak but, pointing his gun, pushed his way inside. He had a finger to his lips as in a shush signal. She obeyed. He closed the door and Sasha had a good idea why he was there.

Nearby, Rabies sat in the car, his blood boiling. *This arsehole better be gone quick otherwise* <u>*he's*</u> *gunna be the victim.*

16

'TELL ME WHERE HE IS AND YOU LIVE,' said Wes in a quiet voice. There was no swearing, shouting or spittle. Sasha hadn't thought much about dying in her 32 years to date. Now the thought slapped her face. 'Sit,' he said and she did.

'I don't know where ...'

Wes spoke louder with menace. 'And only tell me what I want to hear. Last chance. Speak or you die.' He moved a step closer and the gun seemed much larger. His aim was perfect.

'He left a note. He told me ...'

'Get it.' Sasha stood. 'Slowly,' hissed Wes, and Sasha stayed in first gear. She collected the note and turned back to him. 'Read it.'

She did. Wes knew it was crap. Vlad fled because he knew he was sprung. Wes now had a much harder task. He worked on Sasha. Killing her would tell him nothing.

'What has he talked about? Who does he know in Australia?' Wes spat. 'Talk to me.'

Sasha spoke for her life. 'He knows the people he works with.'

'Who else?'

'Ah, some of my friends.'

'What have you told him about Australia? Tell me!'

'I told him about Melbourne.'

Wes was calm but his acting skills made Sasha think he was about to lose it and shoot her. 'What about Melbourne?'

'I come from there and he met my sister who lives there when she came to Sydney. She told him it was a great city.'

'Is it big?'

'Yes, about the same as Sydney.'

'Give me your sister's details.'

Sasha hesitated. Wes cocked his gun and the sound and action caused Sasha to cry. 'Please,' she begged.

'I don't want you, lady or your sister. I want Vlad.' She looked confused. 'James, I want James. Now give me the details.' Sasha wrote her sister's address in Flemington near the famous Melbourne Cup racecourse. 'Put your number.' She wrote it and gave him the paper. He punched the number and it rang.

He moved around the flat keeping an eye on its occupant. Clues, he wanted anything to help him find Vlad.

'Where would he live in Melbourne?'

Sasha shook her head. 'Perhaps with my sister.'

'What sort of jobs could he do?'

More head shaking. 'Anything; he is good with his hands.'

'How does he travel?'

'He drove a company car.'

'No, long distance.'

'Probably by plane.'

'Not by plane.'

'He liked trains. He talked about taking the Indian Pacific.'

'Do you love him?'

Sasha paused. 'No. Not after he stole my grandmother's jewellery.'

Wes headed for the door. 'I'm working with seriously tough guys here in Sydney. You tell anyone about me and this visit, anyone, and you'll wanna move to Melbourne—if you can still walk.' He stared.

She shook her head. 'I won't say a thing.'

She dropped her head expecting the worst. Only when the door closed did she look up.

Wes called and Rabies drove up. 'I'm goin' to Melbourne.'

'What?'

'Take me to the railroad station.'

'What's a railroad station?'

'Trains,' growled Wes.

Wes looked at Rabies who wanted to drop Wes in the city or, preferably, drop him permanently. They drove to Sydney Central.

Grabbing his bag, Wes got out. 'I don't need you. Piss off.'

'Hey!' yelled Rabies to no avail. He pulled over and rang his boss who rang Larry in Florida. Wes was not to work alone. Stateside, yes, but in some foreign country, no way.

Wes fronted the ticket window and flashed a fake ID. Using his best normal accent, he performed as if using a Stanislavski routine. 'FBI, ma'am. We're looking for this US citizen.' He held up the latest DEA photo of James Lawrence Anderson. 'Have you seen this man?'

The employee, new to his shift, didn't know Vlad from Adam. A supervisor overheard and approached. 'Show me.' She looked. 'Yeah, I was here this morning and that guy with an American accent bought a ticket to Melbourne.'

'When?'

'This morning about 8.'

'No, when does that train leave?'

The supervisor looked at the clock on the wall. 'One minute.'

Wes fled. He didn't know which platform, there were 25, or which train but his fee for killing Vlad made him a madman. Passengers moved sharpish to avoid the lunatic. No ticket, no luggage, only his Beretta. Run, Wesley, run. He saw a train about to depart and raced.

Puffing, he stopped an official. 'Is this the train to Melbourne,' he gasped. The official shook his head and pointed as, three platforms away, the Sydney-Melbourne train, headed south.

To his credit, Wes kept his cursing to a small tsunami size volume. He headed back to the ticket box. He reached the concourse to be confronted by the grinning Rabies.

'Now, now,' said Rabies, 'who's been a naughty boy?' Wes scowled. 'Your boss in Florida is not a happy bunny.' That stopped Wes. 'You're stuck with me, Sunshine.'

'Take me to the airport. I gotta get to Melbourne.'

'Airport? You said you were goin' by train.'

'He's on that train. We can meet it in Melbourne. C'mon.' He set off but stopped when Rabies called. People looked at the two crims.

'Oi!' Wes glared at Rabies who moved to the American and spoke softly. 'Can you carry guns on domestic flights in America?'

Wes felt doubly bad having made a dumb mistake, and then being mocked by an idiot. He and Rabies headed back to the ticket window.

'Back luck, sir,' said the ticket-seller.

'When's the next train to Melbourne?'

'First thing tomorrow morning, sir.'

Wes removed his wallet. 'One ticket.'

'Two tickets,' said Rabies.

Wes wanted to explode. 'Two tickets.' Having to travel with this moron made Wes contemplate a double murder.

Rabies grinned. 'You can spend the night at my joint—on the floor.'

Wes walked away. Staying a moment longer would see blood spilt. Rabies knew he'd lost control so yelled. 'Don't forget my ticket.'

On the train, Vlad couldn't sleep. Sleeping rough the night before should've made him tired. But worry kept him awake; that and hating himself for making the most stupid of mistakes. Crooks bribe cops and no-one is safe from the long arm of the Mob. Don't leave a trail. Lie low. To stay alive, just follow the damn rules, man.

There was no scenery at night. The clickety-clack of the wheels and the clang of crossing bells kept him company. Other passengers slept.

He planned his immediate future. He would need accommodation and work. Having access to his healthy funds meant work was not necessary but he needed to do something. Work would keep him sane. But working for a company was the best way for any killer to find him. Giving his name and Medicare details to an employer were beacons or flares for any investigator. He would have to work for himself.

Self-employed? Yes. He liked the idea; be his own boss. *But doing what?* Something with travel. Having a base would help any killer on his trail. He would go to the customers. *But who are they and what am I doing for them?*

Dawn broke and Vlad got his first look at the Victorian countryside. He snatched a couple of hours of interrupted sleep, and was prepared to pay a king's ransom for a hot bath. He arrived in Melbourne and found what he called a bathroom. Down Under it was a dunny, loo or the *Gents*. Washing felt good although his prickly unshaved face itched. He shaved then walked out of Southern Cross station as Vlad or James or … (Insert latest name here) to start *another* new life.

At the same time, Wes and Rabies set off from Sydney. Neither man wanted to sit next to the other and for the next 11 hours did just about everything to avoid just that.

Vlad chose an inner-city, low-budget hotel popular with backpackers, and tourists with little money. He booked in, went exploring and bought a new phone. He needed accommodation and work.

He settled in a small café and drank coffee. On his phone he found countless websites offering accommodation and employment. His mind buzzed. Where to start? He was about to explore the city when he saw a community noticeboard. The main clientele in this café were students hence the noticeboard. *Housemate Wanted*. The sign revealed the need for a non-smoker, quiet, and a "tidy person who doesn't nick stuff from the fridge".

Vlad thought about it. Nothing to lose. He rang and a female answered. They arranged a time to visit the nearby Kensington property at 6 pm. With hours to kill and movies verboten, Vlad hopped on a free tourist tram for a grand tour of Melbourne—twice.

After lunch he showered and put his head down. With his worldly possessions in his rucksack, he caught the train to Kensington and, using Google maps, found the house with room for a housemate.

It was love at first sight. The residents were female and attractive with one from Ireland and the other from California. The women were on a working holiday Down Under. Vlad called himself Mike Grosvenor from Canada. They liked him and the feeling was mutual.

He suggested they go out for a meal to celebrate. 'My treat,' he said. *Good looking and generous,* thought the housemates. Mike was a hit.

As Mike and his new housemates dined out, Wes and Rabies arrived in Melbourne. They transported their weapons across the Murray River and into the sporting capital of the world.

'Where are we staying?' asked Rabies.

'We're not if we do the job tonight.'

Rabies was impressed. 'Tonight?'

Wes set off for the nearest hire car place. 'It'll be in your name, and we're heading to Flemington. Google says it's 12 minutes away.'

'In good traffic. I've heard Melbourne's worse than Sydney.'

'Shut up,' said Wes and gave Rabies another reason to go berserk.

The Aussie did the car-hire paperwork and as they drove, Wes switched on Google maps and a woman with a pleasant voice gave directions.

'What do you do, Mike?' asked the Colleen whose name *was* Colleen.

'Good question. Back home I worked in the lumber industry but I can turn my hand to pretty much anything.'

'I've got a stuck window in my room,' said Pam from Fresno.

'No problems,' grinned Mike.

'And the back gate can't be locked,' added Colleen.

'I think I'm gunna need a rent reduction,' he said and they all laughed. But their jokes inspired Vlad. *What about a handyman to females in distress.* He asked his housemates.

'Home Handyman for jobs big and small,' said Pam.

'Sounds grand,' said Colleen. 'I'll make you a flyer.'

'We'll help you in return for fixing our place,' added Pam.

This was going well. Two days ago, Vlad was distraught. He panicked but survived. Now he seemed safe and in a good place. He wondered if the women fancied him. He fancied them.

He found accommodation and possibly perfect employment in a big city. The Mob might struggle to find him now. He removed his wallet to pay, and took out the address of Sasha's sister, Zoe.

'Are we anywhere near this address?'

'Flemington,' said Pam. 'You could walk there in ten minutes.'

'Great. I promised a lady I'd deliver a special package. Can I drop in for coffee on my way back to the hotel?'

The females both uttered an enthusiastic yes. Vlad paid and the women kissed his cheek, thanked him for the meal and walked home.

Using his phone, Vlad headed to Sasha's sister place, the same address to which two armed criminals were currently heading.

Vlad didn't have much of a conscience—he was a drug runner—but knew Zoe desperately wanted her favourite earrings and eternity ring having left them by mistake at Sasha's. The jewellery was bequeathed by the sisters' grandmother and would never be trusted to the post.

He crossed Flemington Road, found Zoe's apartment and knocked on her door.

17

ZOE WAS NOTHING LIKE HER SISTER SASHA. Zoe checked her peep-hole and smiled. She opened the door and opened her arms.

'James, it's great to see you.' They embraced.

'Am I interrupting anything?'

'Of course not; come in, come in. What are doing in Melbourne?'

He gave some baloney about work. Zoe provided wine and nibbles and couldn't stop talking. She did, momentarily, when Vlad handed her the jewellery box. Zoe came alive and gave Vlad an almighty kiss.

He wondered whether he'd shacked up with the wrong sister. Then it was time to talk.

'Zoe, I need you to listen.'

She could see he was serious. 'I hope this isn't bad news.'

Vlad gave her a story about disputed debts in Canada and bad guys chasing him. 'I told them to sue me but they won't because they know I'll win. For them, it's either make me pay or make me suffer.'

Zoe cringed. 'James, you must call the police.'

'And tell them what? It's a civil matter and I've got no evidence they've threatened to hurt me.'

'So what will you do?'

Vlad shrugged. 'Get away. I've heard Perth is a nice city so I plan to,' raising his voice and hand he cried, 'go west, young man!'

His levity flopped. Zoe despaired. 'What does Sasha say?'

'Oh no, I've kept her right out of it. I don't want those debt collectors anywhere near her—or you.' He stood. 'So I'm afraid this is goodbye, Zoe.' He picked up his rucksack and walked to the door. She followed. He took out his phone and put in an Uber request.

'You're welcome to stay here,' she said looking at him with feeling. He cursed his luck, bent and kissed her sweetly. She threw her arms around him. He waited till her hug ran out of steam, kissed her quickly, opened the door and left. At the end of the short path, he turned and waved. She blew him a kiss.

Outside he looked for his Uber driver who came from the southern end of the street. Vlad climbed in and bobbed down to straighten the rucksack between his feet. It was a lucky move because headlights from an oncoming car shone brightly as Rabies and Wes drove in from the northern end. Vlad sat up as the vehicles passed each other.

'Stay here,' snapped Wes hopping out of the hire car. Being a pro, Wes would never kill unless he could be sure of success and his escape. But he would always be ready if the opportunity arose.

He crept quietly, looking and listening. Zoe saw a shadow pass her bedroom window. She was sure it was James coming back for one last kiss or maybe to stay the night or, fingers crossed, forever. She bounded to the door and flung it open.

She and Wes both got a fright. Her smile vanished. He never smiled. 'Oh, sorry,' she said, 'I thought you were someone else.'

'James?' asked Wes as he put his foot in the doorway.

Zoe pushed harder. 'He's gone. He just left. He got an Uber.'

Wes decided to believe the woman. If true, his quarry was close. Wes fled and trembling, Zoe closed and double locked her door.

Rabies saw Wes exit the apartment block at a hundred miles an hour. The hire car was started and rolling as Wes yanked open his door and dived inside.

'Go, go, go,' he snapped. 'That was him.'

Rabies was good with a motor. His three point turn and departure would've won applause from petrol heads. 'The white VW Golf,' spat Rabies loving the chase. They reached a T intersection. 'Which way?'

'Where's downtown?'

'What?'

'The city,' screamed Wes.

Rabies turned left and floored it. It certainly was brilliant driving but with both occupants of the vehicle carrying an unlicensed firearm, such an exhibition could well attract a mobile gendarme. A vehicle search by the cops would be a disaster.

'Easy,' said Wes while still wanting speed.

'There,' cried Rabies spotting the white VW Golf heading in the opposite direction. The lights turned red against the killers. Rabies didn't hesitate. He drove up and over the concrete dividing hump. Scrape. Who's paying for the hire car damage? Car horns blared as Rabies cut off vehicles and chased the target. Wes gave instructions.

'Slow down, keep back. We follow.'

They did and the Uber found its way to Vlad's new home. He went inside. Down the street, with lights out, Wes and Rabies watched.

'Is that his joint?' asked Rabies.

'Wait here,' said Wes and got out.

'Hey,' called Rabies who went quiet when Wes stared at him. 'Prick,' said Rabies under his breath.

Wes walked along the footpath attaching a silencer to his gun. He reached Vlad's house, and looked up and down the street. Nothing, no-one. He was about to enter the property when a car turned the corner, headlights blazing. The gun disappeared and Wes turned his back and walked. Car gone, he headed back to Vlad's place.

At the house, he crept along the drive. Lights shone in a front room. He stood in the shadows and listened. He caught snippets of conversation about Mike's gear and his moving in tomorrow.

So it's Mike now.

A female voice got louder and the front door opened. Wes pushed back into the garden and felt a sharp pain in his left calf.

'Ronnie,' cried the woman, and a cat brushed past and scampered inside. The door closed and Wes left. Removing the silencer, he returned to the car. There would be no assassination tonight.

'Are we good?' asked Rabies. 'Is he dead?'

'Listen, Dickhead, I'm a pro. When I do a job, there ain't no come back, no mess, no cops, nothin'. I have standards. I get work because I'm good. So you stick to driving and keeping outa the way. Capiche?'

Rabies was ready to shoot the smarmy bastard there and then.

'I know where he is. I come back, and I do the business.'

They drove to a motel in Sydney Road and took two rooms. Sharing would mean swearing, glaring and daring. Wes rang Larry back in Florida while Rabies rang his boss up in Sydney. The news was good to excellent with the perfect result expected in the next day or two.

Vlad enjoyed coffee with Colleen and Pam, and fixed the stuck window before he headed back to his hotel. He was looking forward to tomorrow even if it was to be his last on planet Earth.

18

AFTER THE FUNERAL, Michael dropped Jo home. 'Do you want to have dinner tonight?' he asked not expecting her to accept. She didn't.

'Thanks Michael, again. I don't even want my own company tonight. Going back to work tomorrow should appeal but now I've got to work with a man who's got my heart in a mess.'

'You need a cup of tea, a Bex, and a good lie down.'

'A Bex?'

'An aspirin.'

'You might be right, again.'

She kissed his cheek. At her front door, she paused, gave him a smile and a wave and went inside. Driving home, he spoke aloud.

'You ain't the only one with their heart in a mess, Detective.'

Jo checked her phone. There were texts and emails from many people congratulating her on her eulogy, wishing her well and offering their sympathy on her loss. She remembered reading a biography of a famous person where the star was in love but the object of his desire didn't reciprocate. It was the waiting for the phone to ring that hurt the most. The star couldn't bear the waiting. Life oozed misery. Jo knew that feeling although it wasn't only romance putting her in a funk.

The one text which grabbed her attention was written by a child.

Dear Detective Jo. I hope you are good and I am good. Can you take Rags for a walk please? I will be waiting. Harry Carr

Now there was a boyfriend she could love and trust.

But what about his old man giving that blonde a smooch?

She smiled and wished for a boring life. *Not really. Let's face it; girlie, even if your life is tough, there is always someone worse off than you. What to do, Joanna? You could sit here and feel sorry for yourself, text or phone family or friends, try and solve the latest homicide, or go running.* Good idea. She ran.

Usually she kept to the quiet streets with visits to the Darling and Edinburgh Gardens but this time she went over the top throwing routine to the wind. Out of Clifton Hill she ran, into Collingwood, across the Yarra, beside Studley Park and beyond. Run, Jo, run.

Her thoughts of grief, love, career and life in general grew dim as she ran for her mental, emotional and physical wellbeing. Her fitness became her medicine, her release from stress, and it worked.

Back home, sweaty and pumped, she hydrated and then some. A bath would take too long. She stood under a shower for five (or was it ten?) minutes.

She whacked a so-called healthy meal in the microwave and turned on the telly. Oh no. It was a soppy rom-com where unresolved sexual tension lingered until a nanosecond before the end, when true love triumphed. Jo knew the film and now was not the time for a repeat.

She killed the TV and her phone rang. She looked at the number and felt worse. About to send it to voicemail, she changed her mind.

'Good evening, Pierre.'

'Bonsoir ma chérie and 'ow are you after your day of sadness?'

'Recovering and thank you again, Pierre, for coming to the funeral.'

'It was the least I could do. Now, Mademoiselle, I know you must be drained and tired from such a day, but I would be 'appy to take you to a quiet place for dinner or supper, whatever your 'eart desires.'

'Thanks, Pierre, but no thanks. I'm exhausted, mentally and physically.'

'But not emotionally?'

Jo hesitated. At least now he was addressing their relationship and perhaps his failure to tell her he was married.

'That too, Pierre, definitely that too.'

He paused wanting to get his thoughts and words correct. 'I know I 'ave 'urt you, Joanna, but please believe me, it was not deliberate. I would never deceive you, ma chérie but I was uncertain.' He paused. 'Are you still there?'

'Oui.'

'I knew my feelings for you but did not wish to assume you felt the same way towards me.'

'You thought my kisses were insincere?' That was harsh and Jo regretted her words.

'Ah, again I 'ave offended you and again I must apologise.'

'No, Pierre, I think … Look, with your mother's passing and your arrest in Paris, the death of my grandmother, the pressure of working together, and your marriage situation, it might be better if we remain friends but cool our romantic relationship.'

There was a long pause. Was she giving him the flick? She hadn't prepared that speech. She hadn't decided to dump him. It just slipped out. She opened her mouth without engaging her brain.

He sounded flat, in pain. 'Of course I will do as you suggest ma chérie. But you will need to do much more than that to stop me from falling in love with you. Even now, it is probably far too late.'

Silence from Jo. Tears welled then decorated her cheeks. She couldn't speak. He did. 'Sleep well, my favourite detective. Au revoir.'

Jo tried to say au revoir but choked. She dropped on the sofa and had what could best be described as a bloody good cry.

A suburb or three away in Kensington, Vlad was settling in with his new buddies. Pam and Colleen reckoned Mike was Mr Perfect. He was good-looking even if his nose looked a tad unreal, seemed loaded and was generous with it, could fix things, and packed a sizeable dose of sex appeal. What's not to like?

Pam made an A5 flyer under the heading *Captain Fix-It*. He took it to a print shop, and the girls helped him carry out a letter-drop to chunks of Kensington. Soon after, Mike's phone started to ring. Life rolled along nicely.

19

WES WAS A TOP ASSASSIN because he prepared well. He took pride in his work, never rushed a job, and never left a mess. There were unsolved murders in several US states thanks to the brilliance of Wesley Johannsson. Talk about a pro, he was the best in the business.

He worried about his latest assignment for two reasons; he was in a foreign land, and working with a partner, a first-rate knob. Rabies was straight from Looney Tunes land. If ever a hit was likely to fail, killing Vlad was it. Rabies had a tatt which summed up his life—*Psycho*.

With Rabies in charge, the plan would go as follows. Barge into Vlad's abode with all guns blazing. Yes, the hit would succeed but the cops would find the crims in five minutes. With Wes in charge, the hit would go like clockwork with nary a trace of the assassin to be found.

Next morning, Wes wandered the streets where Vlad lived and spotted a young mother with pram. He followed discreetly and saw where she lived, diagonally opposite Vlad's house. Wes reckoned the peeling paint and weeds meant she was renting. She and the boyfriend were. Wes charmed his way into their life by giving his phoney ID routine with a story about catching visa and dole cheats. The woman was naturally wary but knew about the foreign females over the road, and when the cash was flashed, she agreed. The boyfriend too was suspicious but the cash won him over. From their front room, the lounge, Wes sat in his OP (Observation Post) diagonally opposite the target's abode. He only worked the night shift. Killing in the dark has so many advantages—victim doesn't see you, cops can't find you, weapons not seen, etc.

'Where are you goin'?' asked Rabies.

'Planning the hit, but you wouldn't know about that. Stay here and be ready when I call, *if* I call.'

Rabies told his boss in Sydney who told Larry in Florida. 'Leave my man alone,' ordered Larry. 'He's the best. Do exactly what he says.'

So Wes carried on observing and making plans for the faultless hit. Rabies carried on drinking and fuming in his motel room.

Vlad found work. He got a few smallish jobs but then a bigger one. Housemate Pam's friend, Dani, lived in the next suburb, North Melbourne. She was planning to sell her flat and wanted it fixed for the sale. Vlad dropped in for the guided tour.

'Pam reckons you're the best handyman in town.'

Vlad laughed. 'She has to say that, she's my agent.'

Dani liked Mike, and he thought her Rubenesque proportions would be wonderful to paint—with chocolate. Dani wanted taps and tiles replaced, floorboards repaired, and most of the flat painted. Vlad used his clipboard and calculator and came up with a price. 'Cash of course,' he added with a grin.

She smiled. 'Wow, that's cheap. When can you start?'

Vlad opened his arms. 'I'm here, what's wrong with now?'

He measured while Dani made coffee. He found items she didn't know needed fixing, and she was delighted with her knight, the shining charmer. They chatted and Vlad fell in love with Melbourne.

He told Dani how much paint she'd need and agreed to start the next day. 'Can you make it in the afternoon?' she asked. 'I'm a late riser.' He grinned. 'Perfect,' she said, and followed him to the door. There was genuine affection with a tinge of lust as they said goodbye.

Next day, Vlad was on time, Dani had bought the paint, taps and other items, and the flat refurbishment began. He was good, and a lot was done when he called it quits. Over coffee, Dani got serious.

'Mike, I hardly know you but I have a problem and need some help.'

'Sure, what's up?'

'I'll pay you.' His curiosity kicked in. 'I have an ex-boyfriend who doesn't think I'm serious when I told him it's over.'

'How big is he? Does he play footy?' Vlad was pleased he'd learnt the local jargon and asked half in jest.

'No, he's not violent just persistent. He's married and well, it's not going anywhere. If you were here when he arrives, he'll think I've found someone else and hopefully get the message.'

'I knew I was fast but not that fast.' He grinned and she liked him.

'Then you'll do it?'

'Sure, why not?'

'He wants to come round tonight about 9. If you could be here by 8.30 that would be great.'

'Not a problem. Telling my housemates I'm working nights might be interesting though.'

They laughed and he left, his mind bursting with ideas including several of a carnal nature.

That night, Wes arrived at the OP and handed cash to the young mum.

'How long will you be coming here?' she asked, wanting to know how long the extra income would continue. So did the boyfriend.

'Hard to say,' said Wes. 'Could be a day or two, might be longer. Is there a problem?'

'No, not at all. Can I get you a coffee?'

'Thanks, I'm fine.' He looked at her and she got the message.

She told her mother about the arrangement and Mum went right off. 'He could be a rapist or murderer. What's he doing?'

'He says it's government work and he's trying to catch dole cheats and people who've overstayed their visa.'

'You were a dole cheat.'

'Thanks, Mum. See ya.'

Wes considered several plans but hoped Plan A was all he'd need. At 8 pm, he got some action. Vlad opened the front door, called goodbye to his housemates and walked into the street. Wes moved. He left the OP house and slipped down the drive, stopped at the fence and peered around a bush. Vlad was on foot. He wore dark jeans, a dark jacket and a black baseball cap. He could have been a footpad.

Wes followed, calling Rabies en route, telling the Sydney thug to bring the car to Kensington and to be ready; for what he didn't say.

Vlad kept walking. Wes tailed him from the shadows. When they reached Macaulay Road, it was hard to hide. Street lighting flooded the area. Wes hung back and Vlad got ahead. Once he saw Vlad's direction, Wes sprinted across against the lights and copped a few blasts from drivers. He hoped it wouldn't cause Vlad to look back.

No chance. Vlad was on a promise and found his stride quickening, his heart pumping faster and his mind feasting on possibilities.

One more intersection and he turned left and headed to a block of trendy flats. Wes saw the street name, and called Rabies with the address. Rabies spoke to himself. 'What am I, a fuckin' cabbie?'

Rabies crawled along Notting Hill Crescent then stopped when Wes stepped out of the shadows. He got in the car, on the correct side.

'Park there, where it's dark. Our guy's in that apartment block.'

'So what's the plan?' Rabies wanted to do something, anything.

'We wait and watch.'

'Wait and watch? I thought we were supposed to knock the prick.'

Wes was close to losing it. Having a partner was bad enough. Having a moron was too much. Wes spoke with evil in his voice.

'For the last time, pal, there is no we. *I* do the shooting, you do the shitting. Now shut it.' He tipped his seat back and watched. Rabies fumed. Then the rain arrived and got heavy.

'Oh great,' moaned the Aussie. 'How do we wait and watch when the windscreen is a wall of water?'

'We can see if he comes out. If he does, you switch on the wipers.' Wes shouted softly. 'Now shut the fuck up.'

They waited. This would not make a 41 minute TV show about cops and robbers. Nothing happened. Time dawdled. The rain persisted.

'I wanna piss,' said Rabies.

'Get out,' said Wes.

Steam rose from Rabies' ears. He slipped down a lane and peed against a house. He got back in the car and flicked water over Wes. After more sighing and mumbling from Rabies, Wes snapped.

'Get out! Go back to the motel.'

'What?'

'If I need you, I'll call.'

'Are you serious?'

'Get lost. Call a cab. Go.'

Rabies hopped out, jogged to the end of the road and disappeared.

The rain stopped and Wes went for a walk. He checked the car park of the apartment block, the stairs, letterboxes and windows with lights. Back in the car, he checked his armoury. Midnight came and went. He tried sleeping with one eye open. Then he hit on an idea.

It was put out your rubbish bin night. He collected bottles and cans and placed them by the flat entrance. Anyone coming in or out would knock at least one of them. He dozed trying for a catnap. It started raining again.

The sound of the bottles being kicked snapped him awake. It was someone coming home who made the racket. Wes looked at his watch—0350 hours. Plan A was looking shaky. He stretched and felt sore then nearly died. Someone tapped on the driver's window. Wes thought police and shoved his gun under the seat.

'Open up, Yank,' said Rabies who bent down with face against the window. Wes unlocked the doors. Rabies climbed in dripping water. 'My boss said you wasn't allowed out without a friend.'

Wes thought about smashing Rabies in the face but stopped when someone came out of the flats. Wes stared. It was Vlad. 'It's him,' whispered Wes. Rabies panicked. 'The cap, jacket, height, it's him.' Vlad headed towards the killers.

'You sure?' snapped Rabies.

'Yes, it's him.'

Rabies grabbed his gun. Wes stopped him. 'Wait. You stay here.'

Rabies was having none of that. 'No way. Let's do the business,' he hissed. 'It's dark, no-one's here. Come on.'

He quietly got out of the car. Still it rained. Wes wanted to shoot Rabies but scrambled out to control his lunatic minder. Both killers crouched behind the back of the car as Vlad headed their way.

He was on the other side of the road, and for protection, pulled his jacket collar higher. He was 20 yards away and closing. With no sense of danger, he was walking to his death.

The killers froze, waiting. 'It's my kill,' spat Wes. 'Do not fire.'

The men looked at each other. Rabies thought about shooting Wes and then the target. Vlad came closer. Wes took aim. Then panic kicked in as Vlad left the footpath and crossed the road heading straight for the car hiding the killers. The darkness and rain became the perfect cover for the murder. This would be dead easy.

Wes knew the rules of assassination. Rabies couldn't read. The plan was simple. No wild shots in the dark. Use the silencer. Aim for the heart. Get up nice and close, my son.

Look out, here he comes.

20

VLAD CROSSED THE ROAD heading to the footpath beside the assassins' vehicle. He would pass within touching distance of the killers. With everything working perfectly, Wes steadied his stance. This was shooting fish in a barrel time. Goodnight Vlad. Wes held his breath to maintain a rock solid position and started to gently squeeze the trigger. Rabies bobbed up, pointed his gun, and spoke. 'Oi.'

Wes suffered a rage attack. Vlad froze, saw the men and guns, knew what they were there to do, turned and sprinted down the middle of the road. Rabies swore and followed. Incensed, Wes played Chasey. Three men raced, two with guns. Vlad headed for Dani's apartment. He reached the entrance, kicked bottles and cans, made a heck of a row, and in his desperate haste, fell. He didn't get up because Rabies arrived and put two bullets in his back and, for luck, one in his head. Goodnight Vienna.

Wes arrived and again wanted to scream.

'Let's go,' whispered Rabies rapt he'd done what the great American superhero couldn't do.

Wes leant down to feel the neck of the victim. He was dead but Wes felt sick. The baseball cap was dislodged revealing Vlad's face.

'He's dead, come on,' hissed Rabies.

'It's not him,' spat Wes.

The look on the face of Sydney's finest moron was difficult to describe. Rabies was confused, angry, scared and nervous all at the same time. 'You said it was him,' he gasped.

Wes didn't hang around and raced back to the car. Rabies followed. More Chasey. They climbed in. Rabies didn't need to be told to get moving. They drove with Rabies cursing and blaming Wes who said one word. 'Airport.'

'Airport?' shrieked Rabies.

Wes roared. 'Take me to the airport.'

'Why?' asked Rabies who now started to seriously worry.

Wes cracked. He pulled out his gun and shoved it into the ribs of the driver. Wes could not believe the mess he'd left behind. His unblemished copy book now sported big black blotches, and worse, far worse, his target was still alive. To compound his fury, Wes knew no-one in this town or this country and needed to get out—now. This was failure with a capital F.

'Listen, arsehole, unless you get me to the airport I'll shoot you and drive meself. Now drive.'

Rabies felt fear nibbling on his ears. He believed the Yank, and drove but en route tried to talk the assassin down.

'Where will you go? You'll need your passport and money.'

'Drive,' growled Wes. Of course he carried cash and passport. He was a pro. Getting rid of the gun might be tricky but first things first.

They drove and the tension in the hire car kept rising. Both men breathed with difficulty. They sweated, Rabies big time. That's how he got his nickname, often looking like a mad dog. Wes stared at Rabies who every now and then would glance at the assassin.

'Watch the road,' snarled the American and pressed the gun harder against the driver's ribs.

The airport signs became bigger. They were close to the airport car parks. Rabies tried to think of a way to survive. 'Where do you want me to drop you, national or international?'

'Here.'

'What?'

Wes screamed. 'Pull over here, now.'

The car stopped beside land near the airport entrance. 'This is not the drop off. It's too far to walk,' pleaded Rabies.

'Give me your gun,' ordered Wes. The look in the assassin's eyes told Rabies to do it. 'Slowly.' Rabies handed his gun, handle first and only then noticed Wes was wearing flesh-coloured gloves. Rabies felt sick. 'Drop the window.' A gun against his ribs helped Rabies obey. 'Now get out.'

'Come on, man. How can I get back to town?'

'Move,' shouted Wes, and aimed his gun at the head of the driver. Rabies couldn't believe he was about to die.

'Okay, don't shoot.' He got out but there was no way he would turn his back.

'Move away,' spat Wes who, with difficulty, climbed into the driver's seat still pointing his gun at Rabies. It was decision time.

Do I shoot the moron?

Then Wes struck trouble. Back home in Florida, his boss, Larry, told him about Oz. 'They drive on the wrong side of the road in Australia.'

For Wes, right now the steering wheel was on the wrong side of the car. The gear shift in the middle was okay but you needed to use your left not your right hand to move it. Confused, Wes moved his eyes from Rabies to the controls. In that instant, Rabies bent and pulled a pistol from his ankle holster.

Wes looked up and saw Rabies performing his "I'm fighting back, scumbag routine". It was raining and dark but the silver pistol made a statement. "Hi!" it yelled. Wes tried to do two things at once—shoot Rabies, and put the car into D for Drive. By succeeding with the second, he failed with the first. The vehicle lurched forward in a perfect kangaroo hop, appropriate for the locale, and Wes fired and missed. Rabies ran after the car, fired, hit the assassin of the century, and the car veered left and smashed into a wire safety fence. Having failed to obtain his Australian driving licence, Wes fell forward on the steering wheel, and died alone, unloved and on foreign soil.

Rabies leant in, grabbed the two guns, and panicked. *Should I drive the car? What do I do with the Yank? Am I up a certain creek sans paddle?* Rabies didn't know any Latin but he knew what Shit Creek looked like. He grabbed the keys and the motor died.

Thinking clearly was not his forte. Clutching a small arsenal, he started running along the side of the road heading back to Melbourne. After about a hundred metres, he stopped and heaved the two guns and keys into the dense scrub. He thought about his pistol then reluctantly undid his ankle holster, with pistol inside, and gave it the heave-ho too. He boarded Shanks's pony and headed to town.

What a night.

As Rabies staggered along the side of the road in the pre-dawn light, in the rain, he rang his boss in Sydney. What else could he do?

Desmond Spear, arguably Sydney's Mr Big in crime, lost it. 'Why are you ringing me at this time?'

'Sorry boss. I thought you'd wanna know the job is done.'

'What? Good. Now get your arse back here.'

'Ah, there's been a slight problem, boss.'

'What problem?'

'The other guy didn't make it.'

Des was only half awake and being told the top Mafia hitman, all the way from the US of A was dead, meant it took time for the concept to introduce itself to his brain cells.

'I hope I heard that wrong.'

'I had to, boss, he hit the wrong target.'

Des was climbing the wall. 'You had to? *You* had to?'

'He blew it boss then blamed me. He called me a useless dog.'

Des was close to a seizure. The veins in his temples throbbed in stereo. 'You knocked him?'

'No choice, boss.'

'Are you fucking insane?' Rabies didn't like his boss scolding him. 'Get back here now so I can congratulate you m'self!'

Rabies knew *congratulate* was crim speak for testicle removal without anaesthetic. He couldn't spell *depression* but the condition grabbed him in a bear hug. Not one, but a pack of black dogs leapt at him with ferocious barking. He felt he was in the world's deepest cesspit. He was also unlucky, or not, depending on your point of view.

Tramping along in the rain, his worry beads retired from exhaustion. His career prospects vanished. He muttered, cursed and even wept although with the rain splashing against his face you couldn't see his tears. He threw up, put his hands to his head, lost his sense of direction, and stumbled backwards towards the road. An airport worker, running late and driving too fast in the wet conditions, only saw the shape a split second before the hit. Whack! Rabies flew into the air and the airport worker braked, swerved, corrected, thought about his life then accelerated. It was a fatal hit and run.

The body count kept rising as the fallout from the drug heist in Venezuela hit a new low. Or was that a new high?

21

JO WOKE EARLY. How could she sleep? Her grandmother's funeral, the break-up with Pierre, and her concern about its impact on her Homicide career, all bounced around inside her head. Her chest pain was new.

It wasn't as if Pierre was madly in love with his wife and only used Jo as his bit on the side. He was a gentle man, a gentleman with a velvet voice and the sexiest lips this side of the Eiffel Tower.

But did I have to dump him? Did I dump him?

Having to work with him, and knowing her colleagues knew there was something between the DI and the Senior Constable, ramped up the pressure on Jo.

Should I leave Homicide? Should I move in with Pierre?

She felt a sliver of relief when her phone rang. It was pre-dawn. *This must be work.* It was.

'Morning, Sarge,' said the bleary-eyed and weepy senior constable.

'Rise and shine, my girl; shooting in North Melbourne, and it's good and bad news.'

'Sarge?'

'I'll tell you when I pick you up in fifteen.'

'Shit,' said Jo to a dead phone. Springing out of bed hurt. All that running last night made her muscles scream for a massage. Forget breakfast. DS Billy Hughes was Ms Punctuality.

Suited and booted, Jo closed her front door as her colleague pulled into the street. There were no journalists hiding in bushes. Jo was back in town and back in the body business—the *dead* body business.

Jo sat beside the DS who drove. 'Nice to have you back, Senior,' said Billy. 'Are we sleeping alone these days?'

Jo's spirits crashed. If her favourite colleague was having a dig, what would she cop from the others?

'Thanks for nothing, Sarge.'

'Just preparing you for what's to come. Shagging in-house always leads to tears, and rank and gender always win. He's the senior officer and male so it's forty love and balls to him.'

Jo decided to fight. 'For your information, Sarge, I *am* sleeping alone, and DI Richelieu and I are not having an affair. I consider him a friend just as I consider you a friend. So can we please give it a rest?' Wow. Pause. Silence. 'Of course, if you're not happy with my work.'

Hughes looked at Jo who turned and looked at the DS. 'Good for you,' said Billy, 'and it's even better to have you back on board.' Jo wanted to cry. 'Now for the good and bad news. We've solved one homicide and gained another.'

'You've lost me,' said Jo feeling a teensy bit better.

'For Christine Grande, our young mother brutally murdered in Frankston, we have only one suspect.'

'The estranged husband, Kevin Grande.'

'Correct, only he's no longer much use as a suspect, he's dead.'

'Murdered?'

'Well suicides don't usually shoot themselves three times including the back of the head.'

'Ouch.'

'So the good news is we can close the Frankston homicide but the bad news is ...'

Jo finished the sentence. 'We need to find the killer's killer.'

'Or killers. So, any thoughts?'

'The obvious one is his mate, Cooper Yale.'

'Because?'

'Cooper was Kevin's alibi and they fell out.'

'Or Cooper was lying and knew if we cracked the case, he'd go down for perverting the course of justice. Best way to stop the investigation is to stop the suspect.'

'What happened?'

'Kevin was found outside that block of flats we visited.'

'Where Cooper lives?'

'Where Cooper lives.'

Billy and Jo were not the first to arrive. Police, press and people filled the street. It was still dark and flashing lights dominated. Uniformed officers stopped the detectives who showed their ID.

'Jo?' said a constable who recognised her from their working days together at Flemington when Jo was last in uniform.

'Matt,' smiled Jo. 'I'll catch you up, Sarge.' Hughes gave Jo a stern look which, in spoken form said, "Two minutes, Senior".

Jo and Matt exchanged news. He raved about her success which was known to the universe. Jo asked about life on the beat and felt a flicker of nostalgia for those days working on a booze bus or in properties trying to sort domestic violence issues. Back then there was no French senior officer whispering sweet nothings in her shell-like. Mind you, her yearning for days of yore didn't last.

She caught up with Billy and the team. DI Rose fumed and her anger influenced the other detectives. DI Richelieu stared at Jo and she caught his eye. Her heart monitor pinged and she returned his half smile. How could she not?

Rose addressed them. 'We know the victim and his situation re the death of his wife. But we treat this homicide like any other. Do not allow his presumed guilt stop us from finding his killer or killers. Understood?' The word *ma'am* was heard. She gave instructions and Jo joined Charlie Baldwin on door-knocking duties. As they headed off, they heard the raucous sound of a certain pathologist who quietly bellowed. 'What time do you call this then?'

Jo smiled. It was good to be back in harness.

Baldwin and Jo disturbed residents with most mightily pissed to have anyone, even if they were the cops, knocking on their door so early.

Almost all saw or heard nothing. Those who did mentioned cans and bottles but on rubbish bin night, such sounds were not unusual.

After their fruitless search, Jo and Charlie headed back to the murder scene. DI Rose looked at them and both shook their head. Dr Strange looked up and saw Jo.

'Well, well, if it isn't the international sleuth. Good morning, Detective, and how are you at this ridiculous hour?'

Jo warmed to her old life when people like Gabrielle Strange treated her as she did. But danger lurked as DI Richelieu came out of the flats and spotted Jo. He approached and Jo held her breath.

'Bonjour, Mademoiselle, 'ow are you?'

'Bonjour Monsieur, thank you, I am well. And you?'

He nodded. Others observed, and Jo felt pressure building and fast. People were watching them but the lovers were forgotten when DI Rose swore, and called the detectives together.

'It never rains,' she said, standing in the rain. 'There's a shooting near Melbourne Airport, definite homicide.' She looked at DI Richelieu and DI Blunt and hesitated. The Frenchman was newly returned from a harrowing experience in Paris, and the new DI's last investigation saw him shot at thanks to his stupidity. She didn't want to appoint either but to not do so would look wrong. She bit the bullet.

'OIC here will be DI Blunt with DS Hughes, and for the murder near the airport, DI Richelieu will run the show with DS Fletcher. Questions?' Silence. 'Right, gentlemen, start your engines.'

Jo dreaded having to work with Pierre. Time may heal her wounds but for now, as little contact as possible seemed a good idea. Billy did the selecting for Blunt and snared Jo. Blunt was not happy and called Billy aside. He mentioned Jo's troubles. Billy gave him short shrift.

'Do you want to solve this homicide, sir?' Blunt didn't answer. 'Then you need Detective Best.' A Blunt grunt ended the discussion.

DI Richelieu departed for the airport with DS Fletcher and Senior Constables Baldwin and Payne. DI Rose hung around. She didn't trust DI Callum Blunt and he hated being OIC while wearing L plates.

As Richelieu and his team approached the crime scene, flashing lights and temporary speed restrictions caused them to slow. They were down to one lane and crawling. Fletcher dropped his window and showed his ID to the cop on traffic duty.

'Problem officer?' he asked.

'G'day sir. Hit and run, fatality I'm afraid.'

'Do you know who?'

'Sorry, no sir.'

Fletcher raised his window and they continued to crawl to the body of Wes, the now former top assassin for the Mob in America.

22

AN HOUR EARLIER, Vlad, a.k.a. Mike, slept peacefully in the arms of Morpheus, a.k.a. the Rubenesque Dani. She was Dani by name and canny by nature. Her no-longer-required boyfriend did arrive, and got the "get lost" message thanks to lover-in-waiting, Mike. By way of thanks, the handyman was offered a bed for the night with a voluptuous body thrown in gratis. He reclined as much on Dani as he did the mattress.

It was a bit of all right for Mike but ridiculously sensational if you consider the alternative. If Kevin had slept in or Vlad had sneaked out early, Mike could and should be dead in his bed, well, in the street.

Wes and Rabies were outside ready to ambush and destroy the drug-runner who almost got stiffed in Venezuela. Wes and Rabies got the wrong man. Same body size and outfit plus a dark night and rain, not to mention an idiot with a gun, meant Kevin Grande copped three free bullets while Vlad copped a free shag; well two actually with "anyone for seconds?" being answered in the affirmative.

Once the ruckus with the police and every man and his dog kicked off, Dani went outside then returned to report the news.

Vlad was dressed and ready for the off in a flash. He knew he was the intended target. 'Listen, babe,' he said sounding innocent and oppressed at the same time. 'I had trouble with debt-collectors back in Canada. I don't want to meet your friendly police officers right now. Is there a back entrance?'

'I thought you found that last night.'

She smiled and he groaned. 'You're fabulous but if you ever wanna see me again, babe, I need your help.'

She gave him directions, kissed him and held his hand until he begged. Down the back stairs he went, hid outside in the washing, and when the coast was clear, slipped along the easement leading to the street in the next block. He was rapt to be free but knew the guy out front who was seriously dead, should have been him. It meant one thing—his cover was blown—again.

He jogged back to his housemates and slipped into bed. A few hours later when he heard them pottering, he packed his rucksack ready for a departure, and wandered into the kitchen yawning.

'And what happened to you, last night?' asked Pam. She and Colleen were busting to know.

'Boring, I'm afraid,' smiled Vlad.

'I'll tell her you said that,' threatened Colleen.

Vlad was keen to change the subject. 'Listen, girls, I'm in a bit of a quandary.' They were all ears. 'Mate of mine has offered me a job, a real job, good money.'

'Lucky you,' said Pam unable to hide her disappointment.

'You're leaving,' said Colleen, who knew when a man was doing the soft soap routine before the male equivalent of the "Dear John" letter.

Vlad sighed and put on his sad face. 'The job's in Perth.'

DI Rose gave Billy Hughes strict instructions. 'Do not let DI Blunt make any loopy decisions.'

'I want extra money, ma'am.' Rose looked at her. 'I'm a DS, not a nursemaid. And how come he got the job in the first place?'

Rose maintained her demand. 'Call me the moment there's a problem,' then softened, 'please.' Billy nodded and the boss left. Blunt was talking to the pathologist; listening more like.

'Bullet removal works better in the lab, Inspector. Besides, it rarely rains indoors. Pop in this arvo if you're not too busy. Toodle pip.'

Blunt now hated Strange as much as he hated Jo Best. Billy and Jo joined Blunt, and Billy guided him towards making a decision.

'Senior Constable Best has already formally interviewed the deceased's housemate, Cooper Yale, and she and I chatted to residents in this block trying to break the alibi Yale gave for his now dead mate.'

'Right,' said Blunt scrambling for an idea. Billy helped him out.

'If you're happy, sir, we could re-interview those same people, then report to you as co-ordinator of the two homicides.'

'Co-ordinator?' Blunt's mouth opened and stayed open.

'Didn't DI Rose tell you, sir?'

'Yes, of course. Right, carry on and report to me later.'

He turned and left. The women looked at one another.

'You just made that up,' said Jo.

'You're in no position to criticize, Senior.' Billy winked and Jo shook her head. 'Let's get a few folk out of bed, especially Mr Yale.'

When DI Richelieu and his team finally got to the murder scene, uniformed police and forensic officers were there and busy. The detectives approached the vehicle and peered inside. The driver was shot in the head—a lucky shot by Rabies whose luck ran out 200 metres up the road.

Fletcher, Baldwin and Payne awaited orders.

'Not a lot of witnesses, sir,' said DS Fletcher, looking at the surrounding building-free land. They were close to the airport and this bush land would remain free of development forever.

'We need Dirty Harry, sir,' said Baldwin who was a fan of music theatre. The others didn't have a clue. 'Clint Eastwood had a hit with *I Talk to the Trees*.' Fletcher grinned.

Payne thought aloud. 'Pity the hit and run victim died. He might have seen the killer.'

Richelieu topped that. 'Or per'aps 'e was killed because 'e saw the killer or even was the killer.' If only they knew.

The new pathologist, Dr Petr "Rowdy" Laudi arrived, dressed for action. Did he sleep in his gear? The time and cause of death seemed straightforward. Forensic officers collected and bagged certain items some of which were shown to Richelieu.

'American,' said the French speaker. 'Tourist visa, and 'e arrived this week.'

'Was he heading back to the airport at the end of his trip?' asked Fletcher.

'Per'aps,' replied Richelieu, 'but 'e landed in Sydney.'

'Not wanting to upset DI Rose, sir,' said Baldwin, 'but surely the murder in Flemington requires more bodies than out here with few if any witnesses.'

'Unless,' said DS Fletcher, nodding, causing his colleagues to turn and see DI Blunt striding towards them.

'Gentlemen,' boasted Blunt, 'DI Rose has asked me to co-ordinate the two murders.' His colleagues, with darting eyes, all thought the same thing. *She what?*

'What do we know, Inspector?' Blunt asked his colleague.

Richelieu explained then added, 'And we may 'ave too many officers 'ere, Inspector. Per'aps some could return to the other 'omicide.'

Blunt found decision making tricky, and besides, it wasn't his idea.

Fletcher tried to help. 'Is there a connection with the fatality up the road, sir?'

'We're Homicide, Sergeant. Let Traffic do their job.' He looked at them. 'Carry on,' he said, turned and left. His colleagues exchanged looks with the word *tosser* forming on their lips.

Billy Hughes and Jo knocked on Cooper's door. They heard him grumbling before he appeared. When he saw them, his mood nosedived.

'What now? You drag me to the cop shop, wind up me boss and me mother, and now kick me door down in the middle of the night.'

'Good morning, Cooper,' smiled Hughes. 'May we come in?'

He didn't reply, just walked inside, so they followed.

'I'm not changin' me statement. Kevin was with me the night his bitch of a wife got bashed.'

'When did you last see Kevin?'

He stopped. 'Kevin? Why?'

'Answer the question.'

The detectives stared at Cooper. He was either a damn good actor or didn't know.

'Last night. He's driving the first tram out of Preston.' Cooper pointed to the sofa covered with crumpled blankets. 'He was asleep there when I turned in.'

Billy kept probing. 'Did you hear any strange noises during the night?'

'Nothin'. I sleep like a log.'

Billy made a face at Jo as if to say, "He doesn't know" then said it. 'Kevin's dead, Cooper.' She paused and they watched his reaction. Again he was either a natural at acting or ignorant.

'What?'

'Kevin's dead.'

He slumped on a chair. 'Dead? How? When?'

They questioned him under caution but both Hughes and Jo felt Cooper was not involved with Kevin's murder. Was it a relative or friend of Kevin's dead wife seeking revenge? Was Kevin involved in crime and did he rip off someone?

'Don't leave town, Cooper,' said Hughes. 'We'll need to talk some more.' He didn't follow them, being genuinely stunned. They stood on the landing.

'What about the woman with the missing boyfriend?' asked Jo. 'She or he may have seen or heard something.' Hughes nodded.

'You lead,' she said as they knocked on the curvaceous sheila's door.

'Not you again,' she said drawing her voluminous outer garment across her voluminous body.

'Sorry to call so early, Dani,' chirped Jo, 'but we're talking to all the residents after an incident this morning. May we come in?'

'What's it got to do with me? I didn't kill him.'

Alarm bells clanged. 'Ah, well as you know about the incident, we have to talk to you which can either be here or down at the station. Which would you prefer?' A third option was not offered.

Billy glowed watching Jo's technique as Dani surrendered, the trio sat inside and the interview began.

'Tell us what you know, Dani?' There it was again. A question, short, straight to the point and giving the interviewee lots of rope with which to hang herself.

'I was asleep, heard a racket, went outside and the cops and stickybeaks were everywhere.'

'You said, "I didn't kill him". Who told you someone was killed?'

She paused. 'Dunno. Everyone. People were talking.'

'And what about your boyfriend? Did he go outside?'

Dani flushed. 'What boyfriend? You asked me that question last time. I haven't got a boyfriend.'

'Dani, look at me. This is murder. If your boyfriend was here last night then he's a potential witness.'

She snapped. 'He didn't go outside.' She froze and hated herself. Jo slowed the pace and Hughes revelled in her colleague's style.

'Is he here now?'

'No.'

'When did he leave?'

'Hours ago.'

'Which way did he leave?'

'Out the back.'

'Why out the back?'

Dani was short of believable answers and needed think music.

I can help Mike. I know he didn't kill anyone. If he's in danger from those debt collectors, the cops can help him. I'll tell them.

'Dani?'

'If I tell you, you have to promise to give him protection.'

'Why does he need protection?'

She babbled. 'Some Canadians want to get money out of him.' She spoke quickly. 'Money he doesn't owe them.'

Dani was in deep now. There was no turning back. She made no mention of their personal relationship being a whole 10 hours old. She told them his name—Mike Grosvenor—that he was Canadian and lived with two women at 29 Darling Street, Kensington.

'Thanks Dani,' said Jo and meant it.

Dani was curious. 'The guy who was killed, was he the one you came to talk to me about?'

The detectives stood and Hughes took over. 'We can't say, Dani, but we can ask you to make sure your flat is secure at all times. Can you do that?' She nodded. 'Thanks again.'

'And if you want to help your boyfriend,' added Jo, 'don't tell him we're on our way to have a chat.'

Dani nodded again, and the cops discussed the new information en route to their car.

'Okay, Senior, who is Mike Grosvenor, and has he got anything to do with Kevin's murder?' They drove to Kensington. 'Is he the hitman paid to knock off the murderous Kevin?'

'It's too hard for me, Sarge. I was taught to follow the evidence.'

'Smartarse.'

As they drove, Billy asked about Robbo. 'How is the old boy?'

Jo felt lousy not having been in touch since the funeral. 'Fine,' she guessed and vowed to ring him as soon the day got cracking.

23

RICHELIEU'S TEAM HEADED BACK TO TOWN. As they reached the scene of the road fatality, they stopped and spoke with the officers who identified the deceased, one Reece Horton. The name Rabies didn't appear on his driving licence. DS Fletcher spotted the link.

'The hire car form, sir, in the vehicle with the body; it was in the name of Reece Horton. There's your link.'

'Merci, Detective Sergeant.' Pierre turned to the Traffic officer. 'Where was the victim taken, s'il vous plaît?'

'To the morgue, sir.'

'Merci, and I think it's called the mortuary today, officer.'

The homicide team drove to town and Pierre gave an order. 'Call DI Blunt, our new co-ordinator, and inform him of our news, s'il vous plaît.' Fletcher looked at the DI. All three officers thought the same thing—*Our new co-ordinator?* Nobody laughed but all wanted to.

Billy Hughes and Jo parked near the Kensington address. The day's quota of sunshine was at last being distributed. 'Slip round the back,' said Billy and Jo departed. Hughes knocked on the door and held up her ID. Pam invited the detective inside.

The back door opened and Vlad appeared complete with rucksack. Jo smiled holding up her ID. Where the lino stopped, he halted. 'Good morning, Mr Grosvenor. I'm not a Canadian debt collector.'

Vlad entered the kitchen followed by Jo and joined his housemates and DS Hughes.

'You okay, Mike?' asked Colleen, genuinely concerned.

'Fine, just a little misunderstanding,' he grinned.

Jo liked the look of him and thought his nose unusual. The smell of burning toast prompted a change of conversation before Billy got things back on track.

'We're homicide detectives, Mr Grosvenor, investigating an incident in North Melbourne near where you were staying last night.'

Vlad looked calm and spoke with ease. 'I was visiting not staying, and I'm sorry, officers, I saw nothing and know nothing.'

'Are you a visitor to this country, sir?' asked Billy, assuming the bleeding obvious as Vlad spoke using his pseudo-Canadian accent with a hint of Eastern European.

'I am indeed, officer, and loving my stay here, especially with such fine Aussies as my beautiful housemates.'

He overdid the fake sincerity.

'Idiot,' said Pam. 'I'm American and she's Irish.' Colleen smiled.

'May we see some identification, sir?' asked Billy extending a hand.

And so ended Vlad's bravado. He wasn't Mike but James. Actually he was Vlad. He'd been sprung, and went all meek and mild. 'Officers, can we continue this somewhere safe.' He should have said "private".

His housemates went right off their new pal. Somewhere safe!

Billy took no chances. As she spoke, Jo produced handcuffs and Vlad went from DEA stool pigeon to Victoria Police murder suspect. The runaway was nabbed. No wonder he didn't protest. The killers couldn't get him now.

They couldn't anyway being, as you say, brown bread.

'Michael Grosvenor, I'm arresting you on suspicion of murder.' The housemates gasped as the handcuffs snapped. 'You don't have to say anything ...'

'All understood officers,' smiled Vlad and he left complete with his worldly possessions. Pam and Colleen looked at one another.

'Murder? But that means no more free pizza,' said Pam.

'Shite,' said Colleen.

DI Richelieu and his colleagues arrived to visit the pathologists. Dr Strange was conducting a post mortem on Kevin Grande, the tram-driver cum wife beater who some might say got his comeuppance.

'Gentlemen, I believe the buck's night is next door,' jibed Strange.

'Bonjour Madame,' oozed Pierre. 'It is a night to remember, n'est-ce pas?'

'I'm told the latest score is three, Monsieur Inspector. Please don't tell me another wicket has fallen.'

'We 'ave two 'omicides with per'aps a third at present listed as an 'it and run. What, pray tell, 'ave you discovered with the victim in North Melbourne?'

'Three bullets, all sitting over there; the first two in his back while lying on the ground probably killed him. If not, the one to the back of his skull was, as you Francophiles might say, the coo dee grass.'

'And do you 'ave a time of death, Doctuer?'

'Not long before I got there. You know the traffic is so light in the wee small hours. I got from Fitzroy North to North Melbourne in six minutes. Can you believe that? Six minutes.' Richelieu humoured her.

As they conversed, the failed, dead criminals arrived in separate ambulances with Rowdy Laudi in tow. Strange introduced him.

'Bonjour Monsieur Doctuer,' greeted Richelieu. This threw the new boy who, for a moment, wondered if Peter Sellers was still alive and Inspector Clouseau now worked for Victoria Police.

Strange inspected the new corpses and indicated where they were to be placed. Rowdy acquiesced without a murmur. Strange addressed Richelieu.

'No use hanging around Inspector. You'll be sent the PM reports when they're ready and whatever needs to go to Forensics likewise.' She slipped into an American accent. 'Now y'all have a nice day.'

The detectives headed back to HQ.

Billy Hughes and Jo were already there having escorted Mike, James and Vlad to an interview room. The formalities were explained and he declined access to a solicitor.

'So Mr Grosvenor,' began Billy, 'let's start with your real name and some genuine ID.'

Vlad relaxed, glad to be in a police station where he and his rucksack were searched. He was innocent of the North Melbourne murder. He was the target but no way was he the perpetrator.

'Officers,' he said, handing them a plastic folder from his rucksack, 'please, be my guest.' Jo extracted a passport, opened it and passed it to Billy who was keen to solve the callous murder of Kevin Grande.

'So Mr Anderson, you've declined a lawyer and you understand we are investigating a murder.'

'I do, officer, and I know nothing about the homicide.'

'So what were your movements from say 8 last night to when we arrested you in Kensington this morning?'

He gave a detailed answer mentioning the three women currently in his life. Jo got the nod from Billy.

'Why are you in Australia, Mr Anderson?'

'Call me, James, please.' He smiled and Jo thought he was cute. *Isn't that what North Americans say?*

Billy laid down the law. 'Answer the question.'

Vlad stood corrected. 'Sorry. I have dual citizenship with Canada and Australia.'

'Why did your female friends call you Mike?'

'Ah, that's a little delicate.'

Billy was losing patience. 'There's nothing delicate about murder, Mr Anderson. Let's lose the bullshit.'

Vlad got the message. 'I ran into debt collectors back home in Canada and am using a different name in case they come calling here.'

Jo jumped in. 'Where in Canada are you from?'

Vlad hesitated for a nanosecond. 'Toronto.'

Jo didn't hesitate. 'My sister went to Simon Fraser University and reckoned Toronto is the best city in the world.'

'And she'd be right,' added Vlad.

'Except that university is not in Toronto let alone Ontario.'

The women stared at him. Billy again purred at the skill displayed by her colleague.

Billy turned up the heat. 'So you're using a false name and your knowledge of your home town is suspect. We know you're a liar Mr Anderson or Smith or whatever, so let's have the truth about your movements.'

'Bowel?' asked Vlad without a trace of a smile. Billy thought it was funny and Jo half smiled. Billy kept questioning.

'Where were you last night from 8 until we met this morning?'

Vlad clung to his relaxed persona. 'Ate a meal with my housemates then went to Dani's apartment to help her get rid of an unwanted boyfriend then went home and got some shuteye.'

'What time did you leave Dani's apartment?'

He made a face. 'Can't be sure; sometime after midnight.'

'Dani said otherwise.'

Vlad trod water. 'Look officers, do I look like a killer?'

Jo attacked. 'I get the impression, Jimmy, you're glad to be inside a police station because your debt collectors can't serve you in here.'

Vlad smiled. 'I like a smart cop and even more when she's so cute.'

'Assuming you *are* in debt,' fired back Jo.

Billy was fed up with the bullshit. 'Tell us about your debts.'

Vlad shrugged. 'A debt's a debt. I gambled and lost.'

The interview slowed. Vlad was laid back and nothing seemed to faze him. Jo studied his face then got under his skin.

'James,' she mused, 'have you had a nose job?'

Bullseye. The smooth-talking American drug-runner blinked.

'What?' he tried to scoff.

'You have,' teased Billy.

Jo went for the kill. 'If you've changed your appearance, and your name, and swapped countries, and are still lying, chances are you owe more than money. How about the killers outside Dani's apartment this morning, James? Were they your debt collectors? Sounds like heavy duty debt collectors, Mike. Were they after your money or you?'

'You've lost me,' he replied not sounding confident. Billy grinned.

'They got the wrong man,' she said leaning forward and pointing. 'You were the target, James, you, the pretend Canadian with the nose job and the trace of a Russian accent.' They had him.

He shut up shop and went for the indignant response. 'I'm not Russian, and I want my lawyer.'

The women smiled and congratulated one another with their eyes. Vlad settled in a cell.

24

DESMOND SPEAR MIGHT HAVE BEEN the Crime King of King's Cross in Sydney, but even he turned nervous when told the news. The Mafia assassin is dead. No! Rabies is dead. Okay, fair enough. But how the hell do I tell The Bitch in Florida his prized possession is cactus?

Everything was fine when Vlad lived in Sydney. Des could control Rabies. But when Vlad fled to Melbourne, Wes and Rabies gave chase. Out of Sydney, Des couldn't control his boy, and look what happened.

Rabies shot the wrong target then crowned his incompetence by killing the Mob hitman. Why? Because the Yank belittled Rabies. Rule #24 in the *Criminals' Handbook*—never rile a dim crim.

The only silver lining, more like lead lining, was that Rabies would never make another mistake having been smashed in a hit run. At least Des could use Rabies' death as some form of mitigation. Des thought about an unknown assailant. Both our guys got whacked.

Now Larry "The Bitch" Connolly hated failure. His hitman, Wesley, was the best, and for him to fail was not on. For Wes to be bumped off by his so-called partner, oh my lordy lord; that meant Mt Vesuvius was primed and ready to blow in uptown Miami.

Of course all Mafioso know their phones are tapped and so give nothing away, but when Des from Down Under rang with momentous news, Larry didn't give a rat's about who might be listening.

Des though was in strife. He gulped. Before he made the call, he went for a third pee. He made notes. He knew his chances of ever scoring another drug delivery from Larry were shot. But it was *getting* shot that had him worried. Larry was Mr Loose Cannon. He could snap his fingers in Florida and have Des drilled in Darlinghurst.

Des dialled the 0011 overseas code then 1 for the US of A. He sounded matey. 'Larry, maaaate, how's it goin' buddy?'

Larry could detect bullshit from outer space. 'Is it done?'

Des needed the loo. 'I've got good and bad news, mate.'

Larry would have made a good investigative journalist. 'Is it done?'

'No,' said Des in as soft a voice as he could muster.

'And?'

'Your man has decided to quit.'

Larry didn't do cryptic. 'Quit? Waddya mean, quit?'

'Yeah, he don't wanna work for you no more.'

Larry didn't speak but the sound of his breathing scared the waste products out of Des.

'Put him on,' snapped Larry, not caring about the risk of being associated with a multiple murderer.

'Sorry, buddy, he ain't here.'

This next sentence sounded like an ultimatum of war. 'Put him on.'

Des lost it. 'Oh for fuck's sake, Larry, he's swimmin' with next Friday's flake and chips.

'What?'

'He's chatting with St Peter.'

'Who?'

'He's dead.'

'Peter's dead? Who's Peter?'

It took a while but eventually Larry got the facts. The target still lives. The hired gun is no longer for hire, and of course, explaining how Wes expired required a delicate choice of words.

'He what?' exploded Larry.

'The deputy whacked the sheriff and then topped himself.'

Understandably Des was desperate to avoid the wrath of Larry arriving in the Harbour City. If Larry ever pondered the fact that Rabies, handpicked by Des, rubbed out the man with the golden gun, well Des would soon be doing a Mussolini on the Coat hanger.

But Des was lucky because Larry was far more worried about his deal with Cam. Larry could forget Cam's cocaine because he, Larry, monumentally failed to complete his part of the deal. Not only did Larry's man *not* kill Cam's Satan-like snitch, the snitch was alive and presumably still spending Cam's cash. Try explaining that to Cam.

So Larry was outraged about the loss of his prized asset, and his ruined deal, and Cam was about to be outraged about Vlad's continued good health and happiness.

Spoiler Alert. This is not going to end well.

Larry was in a pickle. Admitting his man failed spectacularly, and Vlad was alive and well, would bring dishonour to Larry. And we all know how dishonour is anathema to every indecent, law-deriding Mafioso.

Larry needed a plan. He could say the manhunt was ongoing, but for how long? No way could he admit the truth. He planned another solution—kill Cam. So both Mafioso refused to honour their respective part of the deal, and to get out of same, each planned to kill the other.

Larry's people called Cam's people and a meeting was agreed between the drug lords in a fabulous condo owned by a politician who happily took money from both mobsters.

'The place is yours,' said the politician. 'The housekeeper lives in the cottage. She'll let you in.'

It was like a scene from a gangster movie with men in swish suits, hiding hardware under garments. With each Mafioso bringing three goons, it was too dangerous for one side to produce their weapons and start firing. That way equals bloodbath. It was the nuclear deterrent.

Larry's team arrived early and cased the joint. No CCTV inside so they munched on nuts while waiting for the other party.

Cam arrived as a loser. He lost his cash and coke in the jungle, and agreed to give Larry half his future stash in return for fixing Vlad. So when leaving this meeting, Cam was determined to lose the loser tag. His party arrived and all six heavies were ready to rumble.

The two Mafioso sat outside catching the breeze. The goons relaxed inside not interested in discussing climate change. Cam wanted news about Vlad. Larry, having thought of various answers, decided to come straight out with it. He opted for the truth at least for the first part.

'I've got good and bad news.'

'I hate bad news,' said Cam. 'What happened?'

'You owe me zip, none of your coke shipments. The deal's off.'

Cam worried. 'And this is because of the bad news.'

Larry looked grim. 'My man got topped.'

Cam was expecting lies, bullshit and threats. What he got threw him, big time. 'Your man is dead? The hit man got hit?'

Larry nodded. 'My loss, your gain—you keep your coke.'

'How come, and don't tell me that rat Vlad did it?'

'Not sure what happened but your man's not involved.'

'And he's still alive?'

More nodding. 'So I make no claim on your future shipments.'

Cam sniffed and asked. 'You got another guy?'

Larry switched to head shaking. 'Yeah but not in the same league.'

The gentle breeze flicked the curtains. The goons kept their guns under wraps. The tension rose in tippy-toe fashion.

Cam whispered. 'I gotta kill that rat, Vlad.'

There was now a beat or two between each speech.

'You sure he's guilty?' Larry wished he'd never said that.

Boy did that grab Cam's attention. The one thing he never doubted was Vlad's guilt. 'Waddya mean?' he snapped. The goons twitched.

Larry pushed it. 'I heard something.'

'What?' Cam was champing at the bit. Heavies felt for their pieces.

'You shot y'self in the foot, pal.'

Cam was on his feet. His men copied him. Larry's men copied them. Larry did nothing. Cam seethed. 'Tell me.'

Mr Calm replied, matter of fact like. 'You upset one of your team, they wanted revenge, and they screwed you.' Cam emitted steam.

This was hell. Cam's life was devoted to the annihilation of Vlad. Now comes the news that Vlad survived the assassination, but worse, horrifically worse; Vlad may not be the guilty party. Cam demanded specifics. He sat as his mood bristled. The heavies stepped back from the brink. Larry milked the moment than gave Cam both barrels. He told him about the young worker bee and his grandfather, a resident in one of Cam's nursing homes. Larry called Kris, Joe—fake names to protect the innocent. Protect Larry more like.

'You stiffed the old guy to get his bed.' Cam couldn't speak. It was oh so true. He designed and approved the policy. 'His grandson, one of your team, heard about it and stitched you up.'

The pain for Cam was intense. His ulcers could not control their glee. He struggled to speak. When he did, the US official with the starting gun for World War 3 shouted, "On your mark!"

'Who told you this?' demanded Cam. Larry stalled. 'Come on, how come you know this?' Cam screamed. 'Tell me!'

Larry tried to change the subject. 'Vlad survived the killing and my man got wasted. But Vlad had nothin' to do with the raid.'

Larry didn't think Cam would join the dots. He did. He twigged. *Larry knows about this because Larry's involved. Larry did it!*

Steam or smoke or both arose from Cam's body. The goons smelt blood. Armageddon was no longer a prophecy.

Cam screamed again. 'Who told you about the grandson?'

'I heard,' said Larry as a throwaway line.

Cam dropped his volume. 'You heard? Who told you?'

Larry shrugged. 'Word got out, people talk.'

'Well how come I never heard?' Larry shrugged. Cam twigged. 'You heard because the grandson, my guy, told you.'

'Bullshit,' replied Larry thinking dark thoughts.

The penny dropped. Cam pointed. 'It was you!'

'Bullshit,' snapped Larry, now desperate to escape conviction.

Cam lost it. He didn't whistle for his team. They knew what he knew. Larry screwed Cam.

He hit the loud button. 'You whacked me. It wasn't Vlad in the jungle, it was you.' Cam went to withdraw his weapon. 'You ...'

He was unable to finish the sentence because one of Larry's team shot him—short, sharp and straight, three times. Cam's white shirt and suit turned red, and he auditioned for the Olympic diving team using a self-choreographed, windmill-in-a-storm dive with the splash of a drunken whale. Degree of difficulty was at least 4 with pike.

The gunfight was brief but intense. It's not the sort of activity you can plan. Being armed and able to shoot is essential. But the problem is not the timing because the time to shoot is yesterday. The *who* you shoot is obviously relevant as the participants were not planning on having a beer together after the game. Shoot first, ask questions later.

Both drug lords and five of the six goons were dead. One of Cam's goons survived. He copped two slugs which both missed vital organs. This survivor was the only living person, apart from Kris, who knew how Cam was ripped off by Larry. Mind you sharing those secrets could get a guy in deep trouble. Say nuttin', buddy.

The cops sat by the surviving goon's bed, and chatted in vain. The medical staff added a new condition in the patient's file—amnesia.

25

DI ROSE CALLED THE SQUAD to order. This was their first meeting since the slaying of Kevin Grande and the death of an American near Melbourne Airport.

'One at a time,' said the boss. 'North Melbourne and Kevin Grande, what do we know?

Before anyone could speak, DI Blunt jumped in. 'As co-ordinator of the two homicides, ma'am, I believe they're related.' Rose looked puzzled. Billy Hughes wished she'd spoken to DI Rose about the "new" co-ordinator position, and Jo worried for Billy. Blunt was unaware he'd delivered a statement of the bleeding obvious.

'Thank you, Inspector,' said Rose and turned to Billy. 'DS Hughes?'

Blunt looked miffed as Billy explained. 'Our only suspect for the Frankston homicide was shot and killed outside the flats where he was staying, in a flat rented by his mate, Cooper Yale. Cooper seemed genuinely shocked to hear about Kevin's slaying.'

'Cooper had a motive to kill his mate,' said Rose.

'True ma'am, but we've arrested a Canadian who was in another of the flats when the murder took place.'

'What's he got to do with it?'

'Not sure at this stage,' continued Billy, 'but he's using a false name, knows bugger all about Canada, and has had plastic surgery. When we got heavy with him, he clammed up and asked for a lawyer.'

The DI wanted more. 'But how does having Botox and failing Canadian geography make him a murder suspect?'

'Not so much a suspect, ma'am, more a target.'

'A target for whom?'

'For debt collectors who may be assassins and who both died near the airport about an hour after Kevin was gunned down in North Melbourne.'

A buzz raced around the room. Blunt ground his teeth. He'd missed most, no, all of that. It was a lot to digest and if even half were true, it made for a ripping yarn. DI Rose spoke for several detectives.

'I'm confused.' She turned to DI Richelieu. 'Can you enlighten us, Inspector?'

'Oui, Madame.' He stood and explained his findings. Jo watched him with an inner yearning. 'The man shot in the car near the airport is an American who landed in Sydney this week. We 'ave contacted the US authorities and await their input. The vehicle in which 'e died was 'ired only day before by a man who was killed in an 'it and run 200 metres from the murdered driver.'

'Whoa, hold it,' said Rose raising her hands. 'The two dead males by the airport are possibly connected because of the same hire car?'

'Absolument. One hired the vehicle and the other died in it.'

'And Billy, you've got a Canadian who may not be Canadian, in disguise, and who is supposedly fleeing from irate debt collectors?'

'Spot on, ma'am.'

'Bloody hell. So is there a connection between all three deaths, and if so, what is it?'

DI Blunt saw an opportunity to re-join the human race. 'If I may, ma'am, the two murders are ...'

'Three,' said a voice from the rear.

Blunt was thrown. 'Three?' he asked, fuming. Rose smiled.

Richelieu took over. 'We 'ave not finished dealing with Traffic re the death of the 'it and run victim, ma'am. If 'e was deliberately killed, then indeed we do 'ave three 'omicides.'

Rose felt pressure. There were unknowns, even known unknowns. 'Right, we need answers. Did anyone want to kill Kevin Grande because of what he did to his wife? Who are the dead men near the airport? Were they murdered? Who is the confused Canadian, is he connected to the three deceased victims, and if so, how? Questions?'

'Are we still looking for the weapons, ma'am,' asked Jo.

'Good point, Senior. Find out.' Jo nodded. 'Right, share your findings via ... DI Blunt.' He beamed. 'DS Hughes, a word.'

As the detectives broke, Richelieu manoeuvred to cross paths with his favourite senior constable. 'Bonjour, Mademoiselle.'

'Sir,' replied Jo, being glad to see him up close yet keen to escape.

'Several 'omicides at once is always a challenge, n'est-ce pas?'

'Oui.'

'And 'ow is your grandfather? Well, I 'ope?'

'Thank you, he's making the best of a sad situation.'

'Of course. Please remember me to 'im, s'il vous plaît.'

Jo began to move. 'Of course, merci, I will.'

A few of her colleagues observed the behaviour of the DI and the young senior constable.

In the corridor, Jo bumped into DS Hughes who kept walking. 'With me,' she said, and Jo tagged along. 'I've just explained to DI Rose about the new co-ordinator of the two homicides.'

'And?' asked Jo.

'She laughed. She called him a Clayton's Co-ordinator and suggested it becomes a permanent position. Now this way, Senior, our Canadian mystery man awaits.'

Vlad was dragged out for another interview. For the last two hours, reclining on his cell bed, he wondered what to do. *Damn those female cops; they cut through my baloney with ease. How did they pick my nose?* He thought that could have been expressed better.

'How are you, James?' asked Billy.

'I wanna come clean.'

'No, I asked how you were.'

He turned angry. 'Can we stop with the bullshit? I wanna come clean.'

The detectives looked at one another.

'Sure,' said Billy. 'Let's start with your real name.'

He sniffed. He knew they'd find out sooner or later. Better to control the situation. 'It's **Vladyslav Davydenko** but everyone calls me Vlad. I'm an American citizen and was given a new name and identity thanks to the Victim Witness Assistance Program better known as VWAP, which is part of the DEA.'

Bang. His words packed a punch. The detectives absorbed the details, and both were inclined to believe him.

'What's the DEA?' asked Billy, already knowing the answer.

'It's a federal US body known as the Drug Enforcement Agency.'

Billy reckoned it was crunch time. 'So what did you do to get into Witness Assistance?'

Vlad blew air, his cheeks puffed. 'Ask them.'

'Now Vlad, it was you who asked if we could stop with the bullshit. If you want to get out of here, you need to tell us *everything*.'

The females locked eyes with the male. He blinked. 'Okay, here goes.' He took another deep breath. 'I was running coke for the Mob from Colombia to Florida via Venezuela. A shipment got hijacked and I was blamed. It didn't matter that I was not involved. I became a dead man walking, but got lucky when rescued by the DEA. For singing like a canary about my boss, I got a ticket to DEA-VWAP.' The detectives struggled to keep up. 'Part of the deal involved a new ID with this crappy nose job, some bucks and a plane ticket to anywhere this side of Mars.' He opened his arms and sang. 'Da da!'

Jo liked him. He was good looking with a sense of humour or, as Vlad the American would write, a sense of humor.

'Thanks for the story, Vlad,' said Billy.

'It's all true,' he fired back, miffed. 'Just ask the DEA. And because I've helped you guys, I'd like a little mutual back scratching, if you please.'

'We don't necessarily do *please* here at Victoria Police, Vlad.'

He was angry and a tad worried. He'd spilled his guts and expected a little reciprocity. He knew cops all over the world could lie like the best crims, but he'd never dealt with only female cops before. They were smart and hard to pick. But despite his situation, he pressed the angry button.

'Hey? How about we get the US consulate in here?'

'How about we chill and get something down in writing?' Vlad pulled back. 'We start with a written statement, which we then verify.'

'And how long will all this take?'

'Vlad,' said Billy trying to help. 'We're homicide detectives with three stiffs to sort, and you're up to your neck in one, two or possibly all three of them.'

'I never killed nobody.'

'Anybody,' corrected Jo, surprising the others and even herself. 'Sorry, that was my Pop speaking.'

'And how is the DCI?' asked Billy turning to her colleague.

'Okay, I think. I've been neglecting him since the funeral.'

'Give him my best,' added Billy and Vlad lost it.

'Oh come on, what is this, old home week?'

'Sorry,' smiled Billy, and Vlad sucked on angry pills. 'Right, I'm going to ask Senior Constable Best to take a detailed statement from you, and then we'll see what sort of support you get from your colleagues stateside.'

'Brilliant,' spat Vlad sarcastically, thinking the police showed him little respect.

'But I must add you're still under arrest on suspicion of murder so there are several balls in the air, so to speak.'

'Including mine,' said Vlad who was returned to his cell.

Hughes gave Jo an order. 'Grab someone and take the Yank's statement. Remember we're investigating at least two homicides. Vlad's criminal past with drugs may be irrelevant. What is relevant is who killed Kevin Grande and the guy in the car by the airport. Copy?'

'Yes, Sarge,' said Jo and went looking. She found Charlie Baldwin and gave him the background on Vlad.

Baldwin was curious. 'So is he connected to any of the three bodies?'

'No idea, Charlie. Let's get his statement and find out.'

Vlad was keen to get on with things, and pleased to see at least one of the cops not wearing a bra. Jo led the interview.

'You talk, Vlad, and if necessary, Detective Senior Constable Baldwin and I will ask questions. We'll make notes and from those type up a statement. If you're happy, you sign it.'

'And then?' asked Vlad.

Jo looked at him and shrugged, 'One step at a time.'

He sighed and spoke. The detectives didn't ask questions because Vlad was a good storyteller; was he ever? He revealed the South American jungle massacre, the theft of cash and cocaine, snakes and spiders, his ocean escapade, chance rescue and rolling over, telling the DEA about his boss, about how he, Vlad got a new name, nose, notes and ID, about arriving Down Under, and then fleeing Sydney when he realised his cover was blown. Wow. It sounded like a movie script.

Jo scribbled then asked her first question. 'Who was the dead man outside Dani's flat in North Melbourne?'

'No idea.'

'Who was your boss, the drug importer in Florida?'

'Camilo Gonzales.'

'How would he try to kill you?'

'Slowly.'

Jo reprimanded him. 'You know what I mean.'

'He would send a top killer from the States.'

'An American?'

Vlad nodded. 'Probably, I doubt he'd use a local guy here.'

Jo and Baldwin exchanged glances. The guy in the rental car with the bullet in his head owned an American passport. Jo asked Charlie if he wished to ask any questions. He addressed Vlad.

'Just one question, sir, if I may.' Vlad liked the respect. 'How much did you pay for your nose job?' Vlad sucked in air and Jo wished Charlie hadn't asked such a ridiculous question.

Then Vlad expelled air. 'It was free, part of a DEA package but it was still too damn much,' he said and laughed in a self-deprecatory way. 'Never go cheap on plastic surgery, officers. You get what you pay for.'

Everyone paused before Vlad laughed again. His reaction surprised the detectives who caught his laughter. Charlie pushed his luck.

'So you took the economy model?'

Vlad froze thinking he was being ridiculed. Then he chose to go with the flow. 'I did. I ordered Kim Kardashian but got Miss Piggy.'

That set the room alight. Baldwin roared and even Jo shrieked with laughter. It was genuinely funny. Then Jo worried. She knew she was taking a statement from a man arrested on suspicion of murder and here she was cracking gags. She pulled herself together. 'Okay, Mr Davydenko, Detective Senior Constable Baldwin will escort you back to your cell, and I'll have your statement typed.'

They stood, laughed a bit more, and Jo opened the door for all three to exit. They stopped because DI Richelieu stood there staring at Jo. 'A word, Detective, s'il vous plaît.'

Not making eye contact with the DI, Baldwin escorted Vlad to his cell, and Richelieu closed in on his would-be lover.

'Sir?' she asked with a touch of trepidation.

'I could not 'elp but over'ear the sounds coming from your interview, Detective Senior Constable.'

'It was nothing ...'

'Do not interrupt.' Wow. This sure wasn't the silver-tongued paramour from Paris. 'Any 'omicide suspect must be interviewed in a professional manner. From what I 'eard, you were anything but.'

'I apologise, sir.'

Richelieu ignored her contrition. 'You will not remain in the Squad if you cannot up'old the standards required. Do I make myself clear?'

Jo experienced a memory rush. When she rejected Antony Heron-Royhay in his family pile in Northamptonshire, he turned nasty. Likewise, when she cracked a case showing up her more experienced colleagues, her former boss, DI Steele, once turned super nasty.

Is Pierre doing the same thing? Bloody men. Reject or outsmart them and you ignite their fury. Hell hath no fury like a fella flicked.

'Sir.'

Baldwin returned from escorting Vlad and stood at the end of the corridor, observing.

'I 'ope I do not 'ave to report this to DI Rose.' Jo was struck dumb. *Who is this threatening bully?* He stared at her and she saw a vision of her former boss, DI Steel. 'Dismissed.'

Jo looked into Richelieu's eyes, searching for a reason, paused then departed. The DI glared at Baldwin before walking away.

'Bloody hell,' said Charlie to himself. 'Was that a lovers' tiff?'

26

THE MIAMI COPS were overwhelmed. The white interior of the politician's condo was splashed with gorgeous bright-red blotches and swatches of blood, courtesy of seven bullet-ridden stiffs. Larry died screaming. The body of Camilo Gonzales floated in the pool.

The FBI and DEA were involved, and when a female Homicide cop from Melbourne, Australia jumped on the blower, life turned hectic.

DI Rose sent a photo of Wes with his eyes closed, and another of Vlad with his nose in profile. The Americans confirmed the identities of both men. Rabies was identified by NSW police who knew him as Reece Horton, an "associate" of Desmond Spear who in turn was linked to crime figures in Florida. The jigsaw pieces slipped into place.

The DEA told DI Rose that Vlad's former boss, Camilo Gonzales, was no more, and it looked like *Case Closed* all round.

Rose addressed the squad. 'We have news, ladies and gentlemen.' She told them the facts from Florida and Sydney. Detectives buzzed. 'So, have we got resolution of any, some or all of our three cases?'

'At least two, ma'am,' said DS Fletcher. 'But if the hit and run is an accident, the victim copped his just desserts and the case belongs to Traffic.' DI Blunt wished he'd said that.

Billy Hughes said her piece. 'The North Melbourne shooting is rough justice, ma'am. Kevin murdered his wife, and only his mate's lies kept him from being charged. We couldn't break down Cooper's alibi, and Dr Karma stepped in and helped us out.'

'So we reckon Kevin was killed by mistake?' asked DI Rose.

Billy explained. 'It has to be. He and the American drug runner are the same size, wore similar clothes, and it was a dark and stormy night, perfect for mistaken identity. Vlad's in the same block of flats as Kevin.

He sets off for work in the wee small hours, and the two killers shoot who they think is Vlad.'

Rose surveyed the room. 'What's wrong with that?'

Nothing; the detectives supported the theory.

'What's happened with the firearms, Jo?' asked Rose.

'All three firearms were found and sent to Forensics, ma'am, and we've got confirmation the bullet in the American in the car came from the pistol found near the hit and run scene, and the bullets in the North Melbourne murder were from one of the other handguns.'

'Excellent,' said Rose. 'Those dead guys near the airport hit the wrong target. We know they're crims. The Yank landed in Sydney then came to Melbourne because Vlad left Sydney for Melbourne. Rough justice is right and Christine's mum can sleep easier now her daughter's killer is no more.' The room agreed.

'Moving on,' said Rose. 'The guy in the car who was shot in the head is an American assassin working for the Mob in the States. Vlad we know is an American cocaine drug runner working for a guy called Camilo Gonzales, based in Florida. As of two days ago, Mr Gonzales is no longer with us.'

'Mistaken identity, ma'am?' asked Baldwin with a straight face, creating a few laughs, but Rose's story made good listening.

'We all saw it on TV. Mob bosses in gangland massacre.' Nods and murmurs as most knew of the bloodbath.

'Does Vlad know about his boss's demise?' asked Billy Hughes.

'Good question. Has he been told?'

Jo said nothing. She was still smarting from the session outside the headmaster's office following her last interview with Vlad.

'No ma'am,' said Billy. 'And what do we do with him?'

'The Americans say it's up to us. If he wants to go home, it's his call. Tell him about the Mob shootout, Billy.' Hughes nodded. 'Now about the criminals near the airport; what else do we know?'

Richelieu began. 'It would appear one shot the other and the survivor was then killed in an accident.'

'Was it an accident?' asked Hughes. 'And has the vehicle which hit the dead man been found?'

'Anyone?' asked Rose. 'Who's dealing with Traffic?'

Baldwin replied. 'I am, ma'am. It was wet and dark and the officers involved said finding data was difficult if not impossible. No skid marks and the vehicle didn't leave the bitumen. They're still investigating but reckon the driver stood no chance to avoid the victim who in dark clothing apparently stepped onto the road.'

'Suicide?'

Baldwin shrugged. 'We can't rule it out, ma'am.'

'So we close two cases, and wait for the Coroner on the hit run. Yes?' Rose looked at her officers.

General agreement and the meeting began to wind up when Jo spoke without thinking. It was a habit she found hard to break.

'Could it be the RTA victim knew he was in trouble from the underworld because he killed an international assassin? Rather than be hunted and killed by crims, he took the easy way out?'

'Interesting; thanks Jo,' said Rose. Blunt hated the teacher's pet.

'The driver's no doubt shit-scared and doing whatever he or she can to repair their vehicle on the quiet,' added Fletcher.

Jo kept going. 'Being from Sydney, can the police up there tell us anything about the victim's character or history?'

Rose was about to thank Jo again when Richelieu jumped in.

'We 'ave it under control, ma'am. I 'ave spoken with senior officers in New South Wales. It might 'elp us 'elp Traffic, and the Coroner, if we stick to working on the cases you 'ave allocated.'

Wow. What brought that on? A stillness and a silence gripped the meeting. Jo felt sick. She thought everyone was looking at her. Rose grabbed the initiative.

'Thank you, Inspector. Right, crack on.' The officers broke up and Rose stopped beside Richelieu and whispered. 'My office, Inspector.'

He arrived and she beckoned him in. 'Close the door, Pierre.' He did and sat. He said nothing. She thought of how she would approach the subject and decided to keep it simple.

'How are you, Pierre?'

'Merci, I am fine, ma'am.'

'We haven't discussed your Parisian adventure in detail.'

'Nothing more to discuss, ma'am. All's well that ends well.'

'And is it true that Jo Best and Michael Chan were the main reason you got yourself out of a nasty situation?'

'Oui, without their 'elp, I might still be in jail in Paree.'

'And Jo Best; how is life with you two?'

136

'Fine, merci, ma'am.'

'You were critical of her work at the end of the meeting.'

'Not critical, ma'am, just wanting to make our job easier.'

'Have you been critical of Senior Constable Best in recent times?'

Baldwin told Hughes about the dressing down in the corridor. She told DI Rose. Richelieu suspected that. Gossip within a police station does occasionally occur—as in about every five minutes.

'Oui. I 'eard the officer laughing with a suspect during an interview.'

'Why was she laughing?'

'I didn't ask but it sounded unprofessional and I told her so.'

Rose decided to leave it there. As a woman, she felt relaxed asking a junior female officer if she was sleeping with another member of her squad. She didn't feel relaxed asking the same question of a male officer with the same rank as her.

'Thank you, Inspector. That'll be all.'

He nodded and left. Rose sighed. 'Bloody office romances,' she said, 'they come back to bite everyone.' She was not to know how that comment would come true.

A shattered Jo stayed out of everyone's way, especially DI Richelieu, and asked DS Hughes if she could visit Beryl, the woman whose daughter Christine was brutally murdered by her estranged husband, Kevin Grande, himself now murdered thanks to the bumbling, and also now dead thug, Rabies.

'A face to face explaining what happened might be good, Sarge,' said Jo.

'Good idea. Do you want company?'

'Ah, no. I mean, definitely no.'

'Did I not tell you an office romance means the woman ends up getting screwed both ways?'

'You did.'

'Well?'

'The problem, Sarge, is your screwing assumption is wrong.'

The women looked at one another. 'I'm sorry,' said Hughes.

'I'll be off then.'

She left, drove to Frankston and shared a cuppa with Beryl who was keeping super busy raising her two grandchildren. For this victim of crime, there was little solace in the murder by mistaken identity of her erstwhile son-in-law. He being dead did nothing for Beryl's slain daughter or her grandkids.

Driving home, the 70 odd kilometres from Frankston to Clifton Hill, gave Jo time to think. She whacked on her favourite Gershwin CD and pondered life. Career? Okay. Love life? Rotten. Family? Ha.

She remembered reading a quote by Chekov, or was it Tolstoy?

"Happy families are all alike; every unhappy family is unhappy in its own way."

Mine are indeed unique. We have death, disease and divorce with snobbery, stupidity and selfishness for afters. Oh, apart from Pop of course, and the kids. But me?

She was glad of her sunnies as her eyes filled with tears, boosted by the haunting harmonies of the Jewish genius from the Big Apple.

Her phone rang and she spoke hands-free. 'Pop, how lovely to hear from you. How are you? I'm so sorry I haven't been to see you. I've been a bit busy with three homicides and ...'

'Hey, have you stopped to take a breath?'

Jo laughed. 'Come on, how are you?'

'Three homicides? Do you want a hand?'

'Stop changing the subject. I want to know exactly how you are.'

'I'm fine, Senior. Got a lot of time on my hands now I'm not visiting your Nan every day.' Jo didn't know what to say. 'But it's good to have some company at last.'

Jo wondered if he was going the way of his wife. 'Sorry?'

'I've got your Nan's ashes here on the mantelpiece.'

'Oh.'

'And this is the first time we've shared a meaningful conversation without her interrupting me.'

Jo wanted to laugh and cry. 'Are you up for a cuppa this week?'

'Now let me check my diary. I think I can just squeeze you in every day this century, 24/7.'

Jo laughed loud and long. 'I'll call you, Pop. Bye.'

'Bye, love.'

She hit *End* and cried like a baby.

Being miserable was bad for the sole because her runners copped a pounding. She donned the leotard, shorts and shoes and ran.

After the hydration and shower, she ate sparsely. If bingeing on food was one way to exorcise pain, Jo found the opposite true. Her worries were treated with exercise, and her weight, already in the svelte category, dropped towards the anorexic.

She knew about depression but believed her response to Pierre's recent behaviour was a mix of shock and sadness. Mentally she was fine but reckoned a cry on a good shoulder might be just what the doctor ordered. And in this case, the doctor was the doctor.

Jo drove to Gabrielle Strange's home in North Fitzroy. The pair met on Jo's first day as a detective in the Homicide Squad. And what a meeting. Gabrielle introduced herself as the "pathetic pathologist" to which Jo replied that she was the "deranged detective". They became soul-sisters there and then, although not sole-sisters as Gabrielle was as wide as Jo was thin.

She used the knocker, and grumbling accompanied the heavy footsteps. The door opened and the smile began.

'Good evening, Detective. Have you brought the drugs?' Jo held up the box of dark chocolates. 'Excellent. Walk this way.' Strange set off trying to imitate a Monty Python Ministry of Silly Walks walk, although with her body shape, a normal walk was almost a silly walk.

They sat in her squeaky clean kitchen. You could perform an autopsy on her table. Jo was pleased to see no sign of alcohol. They drank exceptional coffee and devoured a number of chocolates. Jo asked about Strange's sadness with her biological father.

'Moved on I have. Life's too short, girlie. There ain't no life after life so I say get stuck in while you're here.' She looked at the description of the chocolates on the inside of the lid. 'Hmmm, haven't tried one of those.' She fixed that quick smart.

Jo wondered how to broach the subject of her current misery. The one person she could trust and was willing to invite into her sadness was the pathetic pathologist. But before Jo spoke, the lady of the house beat her to it.

'So the Prince of Paris has given you the old heave-ho.'

Jo stopped chewing. *How did she know that?* 'How do you know that?' she asked.

Strange feigned shock. 'You mean you don't know I'm a perceptive female with a deep understanding of the male psyche?' Jo shook her head at the wit of her friend who leant forward and spoke intimately.

'But I'm offering no advice unless you provide a dingle-dangle description of the what-might-have-been jiggery-pokey.'

Jo looked at her. 'We've been through all this.'

Strange thought Jo misunderstood so threw in an explanation. 'Oh come on, the possible hanky-panky, the bam-bam in the wigwam, and the bringing an al dente noodle to the spaghetti house.'

Jo smiled as the euphemisms flowed. Soon she laughed aloud, and such was her glee, felt her spirits soar. She didn't need any advice.

Strange, despite her crude and over-the-top behaviour, was a caring and sensitive woman. Jo explained her latest Richelieu encounters and Gabrielle offered sound advice. It more or less consisted of a mix of "don't let the bastards grind you down" and "there are plenty more fish in the sea". Jo was glad she called.

They hugged and Jo promised to keep her friend "in the loop". Driving home, she made a rash decision and headed to Northcote. The last time she arrived unannounced at Michael Chan's home, she caught him *in flagrante* with one of Jo's then fellow officers. Does lightning strike the same place twice?

Michael opened his door lit by the lamp from *The 39 Steps*. 'Well, well, who is this I see before me?'

'Good evening, sir. Could I see your licence please?'

He laughed, as opposed to his usual half smile, and waved her inside. He made the tea and as usual, wondered what spectacular crime or international incident she wished to discuss. In fact it was merely a lovers' tiff but to Michael, that tiff soared above murder and worldwide corruption. Yet he, a brilliant and clever man, misread the signs.

Jo called to ask his advice because she counted him as a friend, and because Michael was involved in the recent overseas venture to save Pierre Richelieu and knew both parties in the romance.

The tea was drunk and the conversation continued. 'I should have confronted him about his wife as soon as I heard,' said Jo.

Michael understood. 'But you were in shock and about to fly home.'

His words gave comfort. She wanted advice. He wanted her.

It took a while before Jo twigged. She told Michael before she wanted friendship not romance. She was clear. He got the message. *Surely he doesn't think I've dumped Pierre because I fancy him or, because I've dumped Pierre, Michael is next in line. Oh no.*

But that's exactly what he did think. She decided to leave.

'You don't have to go,' he said giving her a serious look.

She wanted to scream. *What is it with men?* She moved Alan from her lap to her chair and headed for the door. *Keep talking, Jo.* 'I always appreciate your friendship, Michael. I know if I'm ever in a jam, you're the one person I can trust and rely on.'

She waited for him to open the door. It was embarrassing for both. She came for advice not sex. He got his wires crossed. The sooner she escaped the better for both of them.

He opened the door and stood back. She almost hurried to step forward and kiss his cheek. In that instant they were siblings. He was dancing with his sister. She left, he closed the door, and slapped himself hard.

27

THE PERSON WAS UPSET, SCREAMING, their voice muffled. 'He's killed her, he's stabbed her. She's not moving. She's dead.'

'Calm down, where are you?' asked the Triple O operator.

'Get an ambulance. Get the cops. Help! Help me!'

Another calm response came from the operator. 'Where are you?'

'What?'

'What is your address?'

'Oh shit, he's coming back. Hurry.'

The operator felt a touch of panic. 'Please tell me your address.'

'I'm in the gardens. Come quickly.'

'Which gardens? What is their name?'

The terrified woman spoke to someone else. 'Where are we?'

Another muffled voice was heard this time in the background. 'Fitzroy Gardens near the Pullman. Come on, let's go.'

'The Fitzroy Gardens,' screamed the distressed woman, 'near the Pullman,' and the line went dead.

The experienced operator roused the emergency services. Police and ambulance officers headed to the 26 hectare East Melbourne site.

A senior police officer looked at a screen. 'Is that a homicide?'

'She said the woman was stabbed and dead,' replied a colleague.

'Better give Homicide a heads up. I'll do it.' He rang the number.

'DS Hughes, Homicide.'

'Senior Constable Gooch from HQ, ma'am. There's a Triple O call about a possible homicide in the Fitzroy Gardens.'

'And?'

'Unconfirmed but we have officers en route. Just giving you a heads up, ma'am.'

'Thanks, Senior, I'll send someone.'

Billy scratched her head. It was a long drive from her Doncaster home but DI Richelieu lived near the murder scene. She rang him.

A drowsy DI answered. 'Bonjour Detective Sergeant. I was of the belief *you* are the officer on duty.'

'Sorry, sir, but there's a report of a homicide in the Fitzroy Gardens and I thought ...'

'Oh oui, I am next door. I can be there in 'ow you say, "two shakes of a lamb's tail"?'

'You're a star, sir, my favourite DI.'

'Mon dieu, flattery in the wee small 'ours.' Billy laughed. 'I will let you know. Au revoir.'

He pulled a track suit over his silk pyjamas, slipped on his upmarket slip-ons, grabbed his clutch bag with keys and ID, and left his apartment. He jogged along Hotham Street. It was dark, dead quiet with the gardens at peace. The whole suburb was at peace. The murder may have happened in such a tranquil setting, but the usual lights, action and camera hubbub was yet to begin. He slowed to a brisk walk. Fifty yards to go. Thirty. The gardens loomed large.

He approached the laneway, Trinity Place, at the back of the church, when a car's engine roared, tyres squealed and Richelieu looked to his left. No headlights.

It happened in a flash. When people say an accident happens in slow motion, presumably they can see events unfold. Richelieu didn't have time to ponder the possibilities. He was smashed, run over and the vehicle was gone before any neighbour even got out of bed.

It was not much later when Assistant Commissioner John Crowley's phone rang. Crime was his portfolio and it needed to be more than a stolen bicycle or a scuffle outside a nightclub to wake the senior cop.

'Crowley,' he said trying not to wake his wife.

'Senior Sergeant Paul McIntyre, Traffic, sir. Apologies for the time but we've been called to an RTA which you may wish to know about.'

'Go on.'

'Hit and run with the person taken to St Vincent's in a critical condition, sir. The victim is a member of Homicide.'

'Who?' demanded Crowley now wide awake and out of bed.

'Detective Inspector Pierre Richelieu,' said the senior sergeant.

'Where did it happen?'

Ah, corner of Hotham and Clarendon Streets, sir, in East Melbourne, close to his home address.'

'Who else have you told?'

'You're the first, sir.'

'Thank you. I'll contact Homicide. You find the driver.'

'Yes sir.'

'And how critical is critical?'

'It looked pretty bad, sir.'

'Okay. Thanks. Goodnight.'

Nothing stirs a police officer like hearing about a colleague being injured or killed. It might not be the same as with members of the military in a war zone but if not, then pretty darn close.

Crowley went to his study and rang DI Elly Rose. Upon hearing the news, she felt a sharp pain in her chest. When she spoke, the AC felt pleased. She remained calm while acting decisively. Nevertheless, she asked for his advice, and that pleased him too.

'What do you recommend, sir?'

'Well it's not a case for Homicide, at least not now. I would tell your team, then get someone to the scene and to the hospital. Offer counselling if necessary. Is anyone close to the DI?' Rose hesitated. One name sprung to mind. 'Apart from Senior Constable Best, of course.'

'Leave it with me, sir, and I'll keep you abreast of any news.'

'Thank you, Elly, but make it good news.'

Rose felt sick. Her last interaction with DI Richelieu was to call him to her office and quiz him, or did she reprimand him, on his behaviour? She knew the dangers and possible consequences when work colleagues developed an intimate relationship. Now one half of the so-called "loving couple" was fighting for his life and all the "hidden" romance details would come out in any investigation. As worried for Richelieu as she was, the thought of her career being damaged, even ruined, haunted her.

Lacking any religious faith, despite a Presbyterian girls' school education, she thought of a prayer for the injured officer then began phoning.

'Ma'am,' said Billy Hughes wondering why her boss was ringing. 'I was about to call you.'

'You've heard?'

'About twenty minutes ago. Because DI Richelieu lives so close, I asked him to look and report.'

'Look at what?'

'Possible homicide in the Fitzroy Gardens, ma'am.'

'Forget it. DI Richelieu's been hit by a car and taken to St Vincent's in a critical condition.'

The silence lingered. Hughes was in shock. 'When?'

'Just now. AC Cowley rang me. He was rung by Traffic. The car and driver disappeared.'

'Jesus,' whispered Billy. 'I sent him there and wondered why he didn't call me.'

'Tell all squad members. Not Jo Best, I'll tell her. You go and talk to Traffic. Send Justin and Charlie Baldwin to the hospital. Everyone else to HQ as soon as possible.'

'Ma'am,' said Hughes, and as she hit *End*, she noticed her hands were shaking.

Jo struggled to sleep. Bad dreams and bad thoughts kept her restless. She grabbed snatches of sleep but even one of those was interrupted when DI Rose called.

'Ma'am?' said a croaky Senior Constable.

'I've bad news, Jo. Are you okay?'

'Yes, ma'am. What's happened?'

'Di Richelieu was in a hit and run and has been taken to St V's in a critical condition.' Jo froze. 'Jo? Are you there?'

'Yes ma'am.'

'Of course I want you to know but I don't want you involved.'

Jo was a mix of panic and anger. 'Ma'am?'

'I know you and the DI are close and I can't have you running around wearing your heart on your sleeve. Stay home and I'll call you as soon as we have any news. Understood?'

Jo was struggling to compute the facts. 'Ah, yes ma'am. Did you say he was critical?'

'Yes.'

'A hit and run? What was he doing at that time?'

'Checking a reported homicide in the Fitzroy Gardens.'

'Which hospital is he in?'

'St V's but I don't want you going there. Understood?'

'Ma'am.'

'I'll call you as soon as I know any more. Okay?'

Jo seemed vague. 'Yes ma'am.'

'And Jo, that's an order.'

The call ended and Jo fell back on her bed and felt the same emotions as when she heard about her grandmother. Grief, sadness, despair, with a pain in her chest. She wanted to scream but couldn't. Her mind buzzed with horrible thoughts. She couldn't remember everything DI Rose told her.

Why was Pierre investigating a murder alone at 3.30 am? Why wasn't I called? Was it anything to do with me dumping him? Did I cause him to have this accident? Was it an accident?

Her flat was pitch black except for her fit-bit and clock radio. But in the darkness she could see Pierre. He was smiling, his eyes were laughing and worse, his voice was as clear as a bell.

'But you will need to do much more than that to stop me from falling in love with you. Even now, it is probably far too late.'

Jo needed to swallow but couldn't. The lump in her throat kept growing. Tears appeared without being asked. She heard Pierre speak again. *'Sleep well, my favourite detective. Au revoir.'*

Then she tried to speak but could only bawl. She wanted to say sorry and ask why. Nobody listened. Nobody replied.

Her misery lasted for about ten minutes before she sprang out of bed, got dressed, washed her face, tied her hair and headed to her car. She knew the order from her boss. *Stay home.* She knew it was wrong to get involved but couldn't wait around and do nothing.

I have to get to the accident scene and the hospital. I have to try and help Pierre.

28

IF YOU WORK IN A HOSPITAL'S Emergency department, you get to see horrible sights. Motor vehicles are brilliant for transporting people but horrible when harming them. The results can be devastating.

DI Richelieu had no chance to avoid the accelerating vehicle. Within a few metres, it got up a head of steam, hit his left thigh, knocked him forward, and then ran over him as it continued to accelerate. This was no accident.

Several good East Melbourne burghers, roused from their slumber, did what they could for the moaning detective before help arrived. The ambos were old hands at RTAs. They treated DI Richelieu as he lay on the footpath in an unnatural position.

If the Anglican Archbishop of Melbourne had been home, he could have walked across the road and given succour to the wounded French Catholic.

The trip from the accident scene to the hospital took all of 140 seconds and while the closeness of the hospital was a bonus, the real issue involved the number and extent of Pierre's many injuries. His ruptured spleen was life-threatening. The car smashed his left femur, and when he fell and was run over, his spleen copped the equivalent of repeated heavy blows from a heavyweight boxing champion.

Straight to theatre went the inspector with various professionals assessing his condition while others worked to keep him alive and reduce his pain and suffering.

A CT scan was deemed too time consuming and as Pierre's blood pressure plummeted, surgeons decide to remove the spleen. This was potentially a life-saving operation but with no guarantee of success.

Homicide squad members willingly headed into work, not to work but to see what could be done to help their colleague. All the conversation was about Pierre.

Rose arrived and was bombarded with questions. She held up her hands, told them what she knew which prompted more questions. Billy Hughes arrived and gave the squad the background.

'I was told about an unconfirmed homicide in the Fitzroy Gardens. Because DI Richelieu lives a block away, I rang him and he offered to check it out and let me know.'

A murmur sounded. 'Not good,' said someone.

'Yes, I know,' said Rose,' it sounds like a set-up.'

'It *is* a set-up, ma'am,' said Billy. 'No sign of any body in the Gardens—it was a hoax call.' The murmur grew louder.

Fletcher and Baldwin arrived and everyone turned to them. The DS addressed the group. 'It's not good. Multiple fractures, concussion and he's in surgery to remove a ruptured spleen.' This time the murmur became a groan. 'Recovery from that alone is up to six months.'

The mood was bleak. Silence took over.

'What do we know about the incident?' asked Baldwin.

Billy Hughes reported on her meeting with Traffic. 'No witnesses. The vehicle was in a small lane facing Hotham Street just east of Clarendon. The DI was on foot heading to the Gardens when the car flew out of the lane and hit him.'

'Joyrider or crims fleeing a break-in?' asked Stephen Payne. 'Was he in the wrong place at the wrong time?'

Billy shook her head. 'Traffic reckons the vehicle was stationary and only travelled about ten metres before hitting the DI. The impact they reckon was on the driver's side as he would have been halfway across the lane when hit.'

'And the vehicle?' asked Justin Fletcher.

More head shakes from Billy. 'No witnesses, no skid marks, and so far no paint or vehicle parts. They're hoping to get the DI's clothes to Forensics.'

The mood dropped further. DI Rose made decisions. 'This is not our case.' Immediately people protested. Rose held up her hands. 'I know; it's an attempt on the life of one of our colleagues.' They settled. 'It's an attempt murder and if it becomes a homicide, you know the situation about police investigating their own.'

'Bugger the situation,' said Baldwin. Others agreed. But the mood changed dramatically when DI Callum Blunt asked a question.

'Where is Detective Senior Constable Best?'

At that moment she was defying her boss, driving to East Melbourne. Jo knew the area well and had parked in Hotham and surrounding streets when visiting her friend, the now hospitalized DI Richelieu. Here they kissed in what a novelist of bodice-ripping sagas would describe as a maelstrom of lips and tongues. Now alone, Jo ached.

In Paris, she and Pierre strolled at night near the Eiffel Tower, kissed, and were minutes from consummating their love. The media invasion killed the moment and now, having discovered Pierre was married, Jo sort of dumped him, felt bad, but never imagined their relationship would end because Pierre would be killed in a tragic way.

She dared not ring the hospital. She did not want to hear the news—his injuries were likely fatal. She drove as an automaton, and parked illegally, close to the police van in Clarendon Street.

In the dark and quiet Fitzroy Gardens, possums carried on as if nothing happened across the road. Nothing homicidal did happen in the gardens. Jo approached the police van. The sticky-beaks were gone. Jo looked at the vacant crime scene—no vehicle, no body, no ambulance.

Senior Sergeant Paul McIntyre headed to the van. 'Excuse me,' said Jo. He stopped. She held up her ID. 'Detective Senior Constable Best, Homicide,' she said. He moved closer.

'Sorry. I guess he was your colleague.'

Jo nodded. 'Have you heard how he is?'

He shook his head. 'Sorry again. He was in a bad way and taken to St Vincent's.'

'And there was no sign of the car?'

'It was long gone when we got here. We can estimate size, and hopefully forensics will give us colour, even make and model.'

Jo pointed across the road. 'And it happened over there?' he nodded. 'May I take a look?'

'Sure but you know about the tapes.'

She muttered her thanks and walked to the crime scene. There was nothing to see and the street lighting gave no help for a detailed search. She imagined Pierre being smashed by the car and then lying on the bitumen, barely alive. Her chest pain hurt; her throat ached.

She looked east along Hotham Street and could make out Pierre's home. She knew his lounge-room intimately; the carpet, furniture and furnishings. She wished she could go there now, knock on his door and once more enjoy his company, coffee and kisses. She hated the thought of him dying.

Why did this happen?

There was nothing she could do and nothing to heal her pain. She headed to Pierre's place then stopped knowing how futile it would be once there. She headed back to her car, unlocked it in a daze, and hopped in. A friend would have stopped her from driving. She was in no fit state to be behind the wheel.

Revving her engine too much because of stress, she pulled out but slammed on the brakes as Senior Sergeant McIntyre strode towards her holding up his hand. She lowered her window.

'Switch off your engine.' Jo struggled to understand why he said those words. He raised his voice. 'Switch off your engine, now.'

Jo killed the engine and got out. The officer stood in front of her car. She joined him. 'Is there a problem?' she asked.

He shone his torch on her front driver's side headlight. 'What's this?' Jo looked, surprised. Her car was damaged. Not in a major way but certainly enough to notice.

'I've no idea,' said Jo. 'I've not been in an accident.'

'Who else drives this vehicle?'

'No one.' Jo felt worse which was saying something. On top of all her pain of late, now she discovered her car was damaged, something she knew nothing about. The Traffic officer played it by the book.

'You need to be breathalysed,' he said taking out the device.

'But I haven't been drinking.' Jo spoke without thinking. It was as if she was on automatic pilot.

'Are you refusing to take the test?' The officer couldn't believe a fellow cop would refuse. She must know refusal is a serious offence.

'No,' said Jo shaking her head. She blew into the device. The pressure was building.

The officer looked at the result. 'Clear,' he said and Jo exhaled. Then she slumped back against her vehicle.

'I'm sorry,' said McIntyre, 'I can't let you drive.' Jo looked at him adding confusion to her distress. 'You're not in a fit state and we need to examine your vehicle.'

'My car? But why?' pleaded Jo.

'Why are you unfit to drive or why is your vehicle to be examined?'

It was worse than a bad dream; it was real. Just the news of Pierre's accident caused her serious grief. Now the latest incident compounded her suffering.

Why is my car damaged? How did it happen? When? And how am I going to get home?

Then she nearly died. Her boss gave her a specific order. "Stay home and I'll call you as soon as we have any news. Understood?"

If DI Rose finds out where I am, and my car's been impounded, she will go nuts. I could be suspended or worse.

She knew one person she could trust to say nothing and who would help in an instant. She rang Michael Chan. Unknown to Jo, Michael had dragged himself into the modern era by purchasing a phone with caller ID. His claim about liking surprises when people rang proved silly as his life dealing with criminals took off, thanks to Jo Best.

It was after 4 am when Michael's phone rang. Alan refused to move from his master's legs and the human needed to twist to see his phone. He recognised Jo's number. She would never ring unless something important was on the go, and seeing it was pre-dawn, that only made her call all the more interesting.

But he froze. He hadn't forgotten their last meeting. He misread the signals—again. He thought she came to cry about her broken romance and see if good old Michael was willing to apply for the boyfriend vacancy position. To cry, yes; to seek a new boyfriend, no.

Jo never thought about Michael as her lover. He goofed then and could have kicked himself. But his self-pity, with a touch of bitterness kicked in, and Michael Chan allowed his phone to go to Voicemail.

In the crisp morning East Melbourne air, the desperate Jo Best could not believe her friend was not available. When invited to leave a message, she hesitated then ended the call. She knew Michael would know she'd called at a crazy time. Far worse, she knew her boss would learn about what happened at the crime scene. She walked away from her car and cried, and without thinking, began walking home.

29

'FUCK!' The word was shouted with ferocity and rage. Today, this so-called magic word is spoken with gay abandon, even regularly on the telly. When the suffix *ing* or rather *in'* is added, the word has won *Most Used Word of the Year* every year since the birth of rock 'n roll. Cops live with the word on a daily, hourly basis. In fact if a cop got a dollar every time they heard *fuck* or a variation thereof, they'd be rich.

The speaker on this occasion was the Homicide boss, DI Elly Rose. She swore infrequently but always when the situation demanded it. She flushed with anger and grabbed the squad's attention. What happened? It could not have been DI Richelieu's death. That surely would have caused a groan or a cry of anguish. No, this was pure rage.

'The stupid, fucking bitch,' said Rose. The entire squad was hooked. Billy Hughes spoke for the others.

'Ma'am? What's up?'

'I gave Jo Best a direct order, stay home, and do not get involved. So what's she done? Only rocked up at the crime scene acting like she's drunk, with her car damaged, and can't explain the car or herself.'

The atmosphere turned electric. DI Blunt felt excitement akin to sexual pleasure. Billy Hughes groaned internally. Charlie Baldwin could not believe his colleague would ever do anything *that* stupid.

Officers spoke at once. They wanted details. Rose explained how an officer from Traffic spotted Jo at the crime scene, thought she was intoxicated, breathalysed her and noted her car was damaged in the place where the hit run vehicle was suspected of being damaged.

The more Rose explained, the louder the silence from squad members. But the inference was insane; no way could it be true. Oh sure, homicide detectives have a history of hissy fits, arguments, metaphorical backstabbing, and even the odd spot of fisticuffs but never had one cop killed or tried to kill another. Well, maybe once. *Incredible* was appropriate in the original meaning of the word.

'I'll kill her,' snorted Rose. No-one doubted she meant it. It wasn't about Jo Best being responsible for the crime but how she defied a direct order. Mind you the senior constable often followed her own rules although this incident seemed way beyond the pale.

Hughes tried to calm Rose. 'Will I contact her, ma'am?'

Rose worked on her deep breathing. 'Arrest her more like.'

'We don't know the facts, ma'am. It's understandable she'd want to help. She's clearly upset having just saved DI Richelieu's career, possibly his life, on the other side of the world.'

Silence. DI Blunt couldn't help himself. 'The unexplained damage to her car, ma'am, needs to be checked.'

Rose snapped at him. 'Inspector, the vehicle's been impounded.'

Blunt didn't reply but rejoiced in silence. The mood in the room went from gloomy to disbelief.

Billy persisted. 'We have a duty of care to a fellow officer, ma'am.' Rose looked at the DS and knew she spoke the truth.

'Call her,' she said. Billy walked from the room. 'The rest of you ...' She didn't know what to say or do.

'Could the attack on DI Richelieu be revenge from someone the DI put away, ma'am?' asked DS Fletcher.

Rose was glad to hear something relevant. 'Could be. Charlie, you're on hospital watch. Get back to St V's and let me know the moment there's any development.'

'Ma'am,' said Baldwin and left.

'The rest of you, go over DI Richelieu's cases looking for anyone who threatened him. What else is on the books?'

'Nothing,' said DI Blunt, 'if we reckon the North Melbourne and two Melbourne Airport deaths are sorted.'

Rose nodded. 'Right, get to it.' She stormed off to her office passing Billy Hughes in the corridor. Rose stopped and looked at Hughes who put her hand over her phone.

'Nothing,' she whispered and Rose walked away.

'Well where are you?' asked Billy.

'I'm walking home, Sarge.'

'Walking?'

'They wouldn't let me drive and they've impounded my car.'

'Well call a cab, call Uber. Are the trams and trains running yet?'

'I'm fine, Sarge.'

'Where are you?'

'I'm heading north on Smith Street racing a rubbish truck.'

'What's your next intersection?'

'I'm good, Sarge. I know the DI will kill me but ...'

Hughes snapped. 'What's your next intersection?'

'I've just crossed Johnston.'

'Stay there.'

'What?'

'For once in your life obey an order from a superior officer. I'll be there in five.' Her voice carried a threat. 'Stay there.'

Jo wandered back and forth. The rubbish truck overtook her. The odd car drove by at this pre-dawn hour. A black SUV with tinted windows drove past, slowed then reversed. It stopped beside her.

Great, thought Jo. *My perfect night. I'm now on the game in fashionable Collingwood.*

The front passenger window dropped and a hoon made his opening pitch. 'Can we give you a lift, babe? No charge.'

Jo went for the polite approach.

'No thanks, my lift is coming.'

'Go on,' oozed Mr Sleaze. 'We'll give you the ride of your life.'

Jo lost her politeness. 'Piss off.'

Now that was a red rag to the bullshit bull. He was out and heading towards Jo. If she wouldn't come willingly, there were other ways.

'I'm a cop,' said Jo causing the hoon to smirk.

'Yeah and I'm fuckin' Santa Claus. Now come here,' he yelled and went to grab her hair.

His behaviour could best be described as unwise. He was, he thought, doing the right thing. There she stood, a woman alone on the street, pre-dawn, and obviously available. Everything was perfect except the woman's response.

The would-be rapist coped a jab to the eye—that smarts and is scary—followed by a knee to the genitals—and that more than smarts. It happened so quickly. He swore and staggered, struggling to remain on his feet. The driver, together with another "gentleman" in the back seat, leapt from the car making for the bitch. She was definitely not playing according to Hoyle.

As two aggressive hoons approached Jo, a car screeched to a halt, and a woman exited the vehicle pointing a handgun. Billy Hughes and her megaphone voice took control.

'Police. Freeze. Move and I shoot.'

The hoons were in oops territory. Oops, we shouldn't be here, and oops, we're in the shit.

Jo moved clear of the trio, one of whom continued to groan.

'Call it in,' snapped Billy to Jo who was delighted to see her colleague but worried about what the Detective Sergeant would say once the cops were alone.

The arrested trio sat on the footpath, until a paddy wagon arrived, and all were given a free ride to the nearest cop shop. Parking the SUV was a thrill for one of the uniformed officers who made sure the vehicle was left in a position where a parking officer couldn't miss said vehicle.

Jo climbed into Billy's car and dreaded what was to come.

Hughes went easy on the drive to Clifton Hill, the next suburb. She didn't ask to come inside Jo's flat, she just did. They stood in the kitchen while Jo, without offering or being asked, switched on the kettle. Hughes showed her experience, understood and admired by Jo, by saying nothing, forcing the "suspect" to make the running.

'Should I resign?' asked Jo.

'As opposed to what?' replied Hughes; 'suicide, pleading guilty, or joining a nunnery?'

Jo struggled. 'I know I shouldn't have gone to East Melbourne but Pierre is not just a colleague. We've been through a few scary experiences together.'

'Are we talking about your sex life?'

Jo didn't respond. She'd told DI Rose and Billy the truth about her intimate relationship with Pierre—well parts of it. If they wouldn't accept her word, then so be it. If they believed she was lying, then repeating her claim was a waste of time.

'I can't bear having to face DI Rose. I know I defied her which, apart from being dumb, was a slap in her face. She'll never trust me again.'

'She may not have to.'

Jo started to pour the now boiled water. 'Surely I won't be sacked for ignoring such a relatively minor order.'

'Attempt murder is slightly more serious.'

In shock, Jo's pouring went astray. Boiling water bounced off the sink and scalded her. She yelped in pain and sucked her hand. Hughes stepped to the sink, turned on the cold tap and hustled Jo to the water. It brought some relief. Jo found skin cream which helped even more.

Hughes sent her to the sofa and brought two mugs of tea.

'You okay?' asked Hughes thinking more about Jo's mental health, quietly worried she might do something silly. Jo's world seemed to be trending downwards and fast.

Jo nodded. 'Fine.' They sipped in silence. Jo reminisced. 'You were the first Homicide officer who spoke to me when I joined the squad.'

'I'll bet it was a pearl of wisdom.'

'I hope you won't be the last officer I speak to.'

'What did I say?'

Jo imitated her DS. 'Are you the new detective?'

'Wow, penetrating question and brilliant piece of deduction.'

'And as I chased you down the corridor, you gave your first order, or was it a warning?'

'Waste of time if it was an order.'

Jo imitated Billy again. 'And don't ever call me, ma'am. It's Sarge or Billy.'

Finally, they half smiled; nothing spacious or warming but a nice contrast to the grim expressions on show for the last two hours.

'So tell me about the damage to your car,' said Billy.

'Why?' said Jo. 'When I told you I wasn't sleeping with the DI, you didn't believe me. Why would you believe me now?'

Good question. Hughes tried another tack.

'Fair enough, so when did you notice the damage?'

'An hour ago, when the cop from Traffic asked me about it.'

'Leaving several possibilities.' Jo looked at Hughes who listed the facts. 'Someone drove into you when you weren't in the car, accidentally or deliberately. Someone deliberately damaged your car. Someone used your car to attack DI Richelieu.'

Jo jumped in. 'Or *I* used my car to attack DI Richelieu.'

Both women hesitated. Hughes broke the silence. 'Well if it's the latter, you're pretty good at hiding your stupidity.'

'But Sarge,' begged Jo, 'why would I murder him? I loved him.'

She sounded loud. Hughes wanted to say, "So it was a crime of passion" but remained silent. Their conversation died.

As daylight arrived, DI Richelieu's condition remained critical. He came out of surgery to be placed in Intensive Care. At the hospital, Charlie Baldwin kept DI Rose up to date until she told him not to call unless there was any change. If so, contact her immediately.

The Homicide detectives split into teams studying cases handled by their injured DI, trying to find someone with the motive to do him harm. This was no easy task. Richelieu joined Homicide years ago and most of his current colleagues only arrived in recent times. DI Rose left Homicide before Richelieu joined but had now re-joined the squad.

Billy Hughes was around when the Frenchman joined but she was currently on a mix of baby-sitting and suicide watch. When Jo went to the loo, Hughes stepped outside and rang DI Rose.

'She's under major stress, ma'am.'

'Has she confessed? Did she attack him?'

'No confession and I've no idea what she did or didn't do.'

'There's no change with Pierre. Can you get back in here? Your knowledge of his previous cases will help.'

'I could but I'm still not certain how safe it is to leave her.'

Billy shocked Rose. 'Not safe? You mean she's suicidal?'

'More like super depressed. They were more than colleagues.'

'I knew it. She swore otherwise. She lied to me and defied me.'

Hughes tried to calm her boss. 'Not so fast, ma'am.'

Rose was in a rage and on a roll. 'That alone will finish her and if she's involved in Pierre's attack, God help her.'

Hughes was in a spin. 'So what do you want me to do, ma'am?'

Rose couldn't bring herself to cut Jo loose. Her voice dropped. 'Keep an eye on her. Ring me in an hour.'

Hughes heard Jo moving inside and joined her.

'Tell the DI what she wanted to hear?' asked Jo flopping on her sofa.

Hughes didn't rise to the bait. 'Latest news is DI Richelieu is out of surgery but in Intensive Care.'

The look on Jo's face told Hughes all she wanted to know. Both of them thought this could end badly.

30

THERE WAS NO NEED FOR JO to tell her family and friends about DI Richelieu's accident. The media did it for her. True, a hit and run would always be newsworthy but when the victim's a police officer abandoned in a critical condition, the item hit the headlines. And because Jo helped (read rescued) the injured man in France, her friends and family knew she'd be devastated. It really was big news.

When a journalist with a nose for a story got wind of a cop being breathalysed near the crime scene, the hunt was on.

The scoop came from a freelancer desperate for news. She sniffed around the crime scene, spoke to residents, pestered Traffic police, and scoured the Net for any tweets, and Instagram and FB posts. Her imagination exploded. Her blog released the hounds.

Police impound officer's vehicle found at hit and run crime scene.

It raised questions. Did it ever? But how did she know? Is it true? Who owned the vehicle? How could it be a hit and run if the vehicle involved didn't run? One sensational claim opened Pandora's box.

Hughes remained on duty in Jo's flat, in part wanting to know if Jo was involved, but mainly to ensure she didn't do herself a mischief. Jo's phone rang. She saw the caller ID.

'Good morning, Dr Chan. I gather you've heard the news?'

'I'm so sorry, Jo. Forgive me for not taking your call earlier.'

It took Jo a few moments to understand his apology. So much happened last night. Then she twigged. 'No problem, Michael.'

'How are you and how is DI Richelieu?'

'He's in IC at St V's and the prognosis is not good.'

'God I'm so sorry. And you?'

She was touched by his genuine concern. 'I'm fine, Michael. DS Hughes is with me here in my flat hoping I might drop my guard and confess to the attack on Pierre.'

'What?' Michael was aghast and Hughes angry. She glared at Jo who remained calm, surprising herself. Michael was intrigued. 'What do you mean, confess to attacking Pierre? I heard it was a hit and run.'

'It was and my car's been damaged and impounded for forensic examination. How's that for a tabloid exclusive?'

Michael was gobsmacked. '*Your* car?'

Hughes was unhappy. 'That's enough.'

Michael sounded desperate. 'My God, Jo, how can I help?'

She softened, dropped the sarcasm as tears took their marks. 'Just like you've done so many time before, Michael. Solve the case and get me out of this bloody mess.' She wept, silently. Hughes observed.

'I'm on my way,' he said and ended the call. Jo dumped her phone.

'What did he say?' asked Hughes.

She mimicked him. 'I'm on my way.' She looked at her senior officer. 'At least he's one person who knows I was not involved in the attack on Pierre, even if, unbeliveably, my colleagues think otherwise.'

Hughes stood looking out the window and spoke with her back to Jo. 'If only you'd stayed at home. If only you'd followed orders.' She turned to face the resident. 'If your grandfather had given that order, would you have disobeyed him?' That hurt. Jo didn't answer.

Hughes picked up her bag. 'I'm off to work. I know giving you an order is useless but here's a bit of advice. Do not move from your flat, at all. I'll let you know if there is any change in the DI's condition. Do not contact the hospital or me.' They looked at one another and Hughes softened a smidgeon. 'Take care,' she said and left.

Michael knocked on Jo's door. She opened it and shocked him. Her eyes were red and swollen. She never wore much make-up because of her natural beauty but now she looked tired, untidy and distraught. He stepped forward, careful of her recent rebuff. Everything changed. She opened her arms and hugged him burying her face in his chest. They made it inside and sat on her popular sofa. He spoke.

'I struggle to believe Pierre was attacked in a hit and run. But I have no mental capacity to even consider you were involved.'

She felt strange. To have someone give her their complete trust kickstarted her heart and again her tears.

'Thank you, Michael,' she whispered.

'So, officer,' he said, 'give me chapter and verse and we'll have this sorted in a jiffy.'

'You and your jiffys,' she said blowing her nose. She told him everything.

Billy arrived at Homicide with DI Rose in her office in conference with AC Crowley. The mood was sombre with officers busy. Justin Fletcher brought Billy up to speed. They were going through DI Richelieu's old cases looking for anyone dangerous he put away. Even relatives of crims can rage at the jailing of their mate or loved one, and seek revenge.

Officers fell silent when DI Rose and AC Crowley entered the room. She spoke. 'Thank you, please give your attention to AC Crowley.' She stood back and he addressed the gathering.

'It's a bloody awful business and not knowing how it will end for DI Richelieu makes it worse. At present it's not a homicide and if it becomes one, none of you will be involved.' People murmured. 'We've all seen reports on social media about an unnamed police officer's car being impounded. Understand me. You are not to discuss the situation with anyone outside this room. No-one.' He paused. 'Is that clear?'

'Sir,' was the unanimous reply.

'Online chat is already busy with gossip about who might be involved.' He spoke slowly with emphasis. 'Do not feed the gossip. Say nothing.' He looked at them. 'Let's get to the bottom of this and keep our fingers crossed DI Richelieu pulls through. Understood?'

Heads nodded and the word "sir" ran around the room. Crowley and Rose left and the murmuring began. DI Blunt was the senior officer but Billy Hughes slipped into the role of leader. After all, she knew Pierre's history better than anyone, and Blunt was a dick.

Billy looked at the list of possible attackers from Richelieu's former cases. Two stood out. Three years ago Pierre arrested Duncan Bright, the younger brother of a vicious murderer, Andrew "Big Al" Bright. Big Brother evaded conviction until Richelieu outsmarted the youthful crim. Baby Brother blabbed resulting in Big Al going down. Apart from wanting to kill his sibling, Big Al swore vengeance against the "Frog".

Andrew's mates could carry out his wishes. Framing a cop to kill a cop was well within Andrew's pay grade.

The second case was more recent and involved Jo Best. It happened in a townhouse in Port Melbourne where hired gun, Gary Black, was sent to frighten the older brother of a high-flying businessman. Unluckily for the crim, Jo and Richelieu arrived to interview the homeowner as a background witness to a murder committed by Black, not knowing the armed murderer was inside.

Unusually for the experienced crim, Black panicked and fired at the front door winging the expensive suit of the DI. Jo got inside and, with the help of the occupier's little dog, Chester, arrested the shooter. He hated being knicked by a woman.

Even with an expensive defence lawyer, Black went down for murder and attempted murder. Gary hated the dog, its owner and the cops who busted him in the townhouse—the smarmy French git and the bird. Black knew a small tribe of criminal mates. They could easily arrange a sting for a cop to kill a cop; two birds with one stone.

Billy knocked on Rose's door and interrupted the DI and AC.

'Sergeant, what have you got?' asked her boss.

Billy explained the two possible cases of revenge against Richelieu. The top brass mused over them.

Crowley was interested in someone else. 'Tell me about Jo Best, but leave out the good character witnesses, Detective.'

Billy gave a full briefing. Crowley's admiration for Jo meant he struggled to believe she was involved. 'It can't be her.'

'But sir, she disobeyed a direct order,' added Rose.

Crowley thought aloud. 'We all know she's the smartest detective in th squad; impetuous even stupid but smart. How could she make such a dumb decision to use her own car to kill anyone, let alone a fellow officer she clearly liked.'

Billy chipped in. 'She clearly loved, sir.'

Crowley looked at Billy, then Rose who felt sick. He stood. 'What a mess. I want to hear immediately you have news about DI Richelieu, and equally, anything about Jo Best's involvement.'

A few yards away in the *Gents*, DI Callum Blunt, spoke quietly on his phone. 'It's all true. The silly bitch was dumped by French lover boy so she lost it and ran him over in her own car.'

'You're kidding?' said the listener, DI Grant Steele, former head of Homicide and Jo Best's first boss and nemesis. He and Blunt went back many years and made a good pair. They shared delight in the downfall of the woman who displayed more nous and detection skills than the two of them combined.

'Call me when the silly bitch gets smashed,' said Steele. He made no enquiry as to the health of the seriously injured DI.

Michael Chan spent a good ten minutes quizzing Jo on the events of the last 24 hours. She bared her soul. He would have preferred she bared her body. Michael asked Jo for phone numbers and company names. He made notes. His computer-like mind consumed, sorted and spat out results. He sat in a corner of Jo's lounge and worked.

She made breakfast, entered carrying a tray, and saw he was on the phone with a Notebook on his lap.

'When did this happen?' asked Michael to his listener. 'Okay, thank you so much.' The other person spoke. 'No, she's fine and yes, I'll pass on your message. Goodbye.'

'Breakfast?' she said. 'Sorry, I'm fresh out of croissants.'

He didn't rise to her quip but maintained a serious expression. 'I have news,' he said in a voice which made Jo's stomach drop. 'That was our friend, the Honourable Hooray Henry.'

'Antony? In Paris?'

'Oui.'

'What news?'

'He sends you his kind regards.'

Jo felt anger in her voice. 'Michael?'

'About a week before Pierre came back to Oz, he changed his will.' Michael would have made a good TV Quiz host. The pauses built suspense. 'It's a codicil to his existing will.'

'And?'

Michael began mansplaining. 'It's an addition to ...'

The pressure kept building and Jo snapped. 'Michael, I've got a law degree. I know what a bloody codicil is. Just tell me.'

'Sorry.' He took a deep breath. 'Pierre's left you his apartment in East Melbourne.'

31

THE WHEELS OF JUSTICE and forensic science grind slowly. Jo's car was examined as the possible vehicle used in the attack on DI Richelieu. She couldn't explain the damage to the driver's side headlight. The forensic officer extracted small amounts of material including what looked like hair and blood, no, *were* hair and blood.

Senior Sergeant McIntyre was the lead investigator and took a call from the scientist. 'We found small amounts of blood and hair.'

'Would you expect that?'

'Yes and no. If the victim was hit in the head, sure, but I understand the car hit his thigh and then ran over him.'

'We reckon that's what happened. Was there anything on the tyres?'

'Still looking. Does the vehicle belong to a serving police officer?'

'Yes, a senior constable from Homicide. And did you receive the material we collected from the victim's home?'

'Yes and we're working on the victim's DNA.'

'And if the DNA from the blood or hair on the vehicle matches the DNA from the apartment, we could be in business.'

'Possibly but as always it won't happen in five minutes.'

'I know that but if we've got a cop killing a cop, we need to know as soon as, please. Imagine the public outcry if we delay.'

'No promises; I'll see what I can do.'

From outside the hospital, Charlie Baldwin rang DS Hughes. 'No change, Sarge. I was going to ask if I could come back to work. I'm twiddling my thumbs here. I gave the nurses' station my details and they've promised to call with any news.'

'Okay. See you soon.'

'What's happened at your end, Sarge?'

She hesitated. 'Your colleague is still in the frame.'

Baldwin was adamant. 'I don't believe that. She's a maverick, even a loose cannon at times but Jo Best trying to murder anyone, let alone a fellow officer, let alone a man she seriously fancies, is just not on.'

'Your loyalty is commendable, Detective.' Hughes got an idea. 'Listen, how about you drop in on her and see what you can pick up?'

Baldwin objected. 'You want me to spy on her?'

'Make it a trip to prove she's *not* involved in the DI's accident.'

Baldwin preferred that suggestion. 'Okay, I'll give a go.'

Jo could not get her head around the news from Paris. She is a major beneficiary in Pierre's revised will, drawn up about a week ago. Now he's in Intensive Care close to death. If he dies, she inherits a multi-million dollar apartment, spitting distance from the CBD. Her flat, on which she has a mortgage, is worth a tenth of Richelieu's pad, if that.

Michael was just as shocked. 'And he told you nothing about this?'

'No, nothing.'

'Not even a hint?'

Jo lost it. 'Oh Michael, please. Pierre leaves me his apartment so to say thanks, I kill him. Am I super cruel, incredibly stupid or both?'

'Sorry.'

Exasperation took hold. 'Pierre and I became close in Paris, and yes, our feelings got carried away because of the life and death situation.'

'Life and death?'

Jo bristled. 'Will you please stop nit picking? When Pierre was set free, he was jubilant. You saw him kiss me at the prison. He meant it.'

Michael spoke quietly. 'I saw you kiss him and *you* meant it.'

They both felt flat. 'I'm sorry, Michael.' She returned to Pierre's will. 'But leaving me his apartment is mind blowing.'

'And, as you detectives would say, a motive for murder.'

Smack! Jo felt her face being slapped hard. She gets a massive gift from her favourite DI who is lined up to be murdered—with her car! She despaired and wanted to shout at Michael but couldn't because she knew he was on her side and always would be.

She wanted more details. 'So what else did you find out?'

'Not much. I got the feeling Hooray Henry either doesn't know the full story or is playing silly buggers. What I do know is that Pierre's brother-in-law, his wife's brother, has control of his sister's finances and Pierre continues to pay into some fund for her benefit.'

Jo struggled. 'So, how is that relevant?'

'I'm guessing but if Pierre's wife is the main benefactor and Pierre dies, she will become extremely wealthy and her brother, with power of attorney, will have control of some serious funds.'

'And where do I fit in?"

'If whoever's behind the attack can frame you for Pierre's death, his entire estate, including your East Melbourne share, may go to his wife.'

Jo struggled to take it all in. Her questions were stopped when someone knocked. Was it a journalist listening to their raised voices, or a cop come to arrest her? A voice was heard.

'Jo, it's Charlie Baldwin. Are you there?'

She hurried to the door and Baldwin entered. He and Michael exchanged greetings.

Jo was anxious. 'How's the DI, Charlie? Any change?'

Baldwin shook his head. 'Sadly, no, but they'll call if there's news.'

Jo slipped into sarcasm. 'So, have you come to arrest me?'

He scoffed with a touch of anger. 'Don't be stupid.'

'DS Hughes has me down for attempt murder.'

'Don't be a smartarse, Jo. I've come to see how you are.'

She studied him. 'You never were a good liar, Charlie.' He looked guilty. 'I bet DI Rose sent you to spy on me.' She paused. 'Well?'

He knew she was smarter than him and their colleagues. 'You're wrong.' Jo scoffed. He confessed. 'It was DS Hughes.'

That made the situation worse. 'Great,' said Jo.

Michael butted in. 'Can I make a suggestion?' The others looked at him. 'We know there was a hit and run which looks planned.'

'It *was* planned,' said Baldwin.

'And we know DI Richelieu is critical and may not make it.'

'Please tell us something we don't know, Michael,' said Jo.

'There are only two possibilities here. Jo did or didn't drive the car that hit Pierre. Rather than try and prove she didn't, let's find who did. That'll clear Jo and uncover the killer.'

'The DI's still alive,' said Baldwin, unhappy about everything.

'Thank you, Michael,' said Jo. 'Spot on as usual.'

'So how does this work?' asked Charlie.

The geek explained. 'The hit run was deliberate. The driver waited for Pierre who was lured to the spot using a false homicide report. Those facts point to multiple offenders and detailed planning.'

'I agree,' said Jo.

'So we're looking for at least two perps,' said an interested Baldwin.

Michael continued. 'But why kill the DI? Was it a crim seeking revenge? Is it related to Paris where Pierre upset crims and crooked cops? Who stands to gain from DI Richelieu's death?'

'I do,' said Jo without thinking.

Baldwin stared at her. 'What?'

'Pierre's changed his will and left me his East Melbourne hideaway.'

'Bloody hell,' gasped Baldwin. 'That's worth a mint.' Jo immediately wished she'd kept her mouth shut. She looked at Baldwin begging him to say nothing. 'How long have you known?'

'About ten minutes; we've just found out.'

Michael continued. 'But why frame Jo? This wasn't a "let's kill a cop" but rather a "let's kill a cop to frame a cop". So, who has it in for our favourite Senior Constable?'

Jo wasn't convinced. 'Sorry Michael, but why wouldn't my enemies just kill me? Why go to all the trouble of setting up a detailed sting?'

'Money.'

'But I haven't got any money.'

'Pierre has. With him dead, you own expensive real estate. With you found guilty, you lose that real estate.'

'So whoever attacked Pierre has to know about his will.'

'Bingo,' said Michael. 'They know the will, they want Pierre dead and you ruined. If they succeed, all of Pierre's wealth is theirs.'

Silence settled. Jo asked. 'So who knows about the will?'

'Tricky,' said Michael in his deadpan way. 'Potentially anyone working in the legal firm in Paris could know. Even the secretary who typed up the new will.' They looked at one another.

'So what do we do?' asked Jo.

Baldwin's phone rang. Everyone stopped. He answered, listened, nodded and grimaced. He wasn't able to help the caller. Jo and Michael found it hard to breathe. 'Okay, thanks. Goodbye.'

Jo sounded desperate. 'Come on Charlie, please.'

'The hospital is placing DI Richelieu in an induced coma. They asked me again about his family members.'

Jo whispered. 'His mother's dead and his wife's in an asylum.'

'Asking for family doesn't sound good,' said Michael.

'I'll get back to work and explain Michael's thinking,' said Baldwin.

'It could be Homicide's thinking too,' said Michael.

'And you'd better tell them about me and Pierre's will,' added Jo. 'They'll find out soon enough.'

Charlie took it all on board, nodded and Jo followed him to the door. He left, Jo closed the door and looked at Michael.

'Okay partner, what now?'

'I thought you were the Sherlockian expert.' She twigged and they spoke together. 'We eliminate the impossible.'

Baldwin rang DS Hughes to pass on the latest report from the hospital. 'So what about Jo?' asked Billy. 'Did she tell you anything important?'

'She's working on proving her innocence.'

'That's not what I asked.'

'Michael Chan is with her and has some interesting ideas.'

'Tell me,' ordered the increasingly frantic DS.

'It's complicated, Sarge. I'll be there soon.'

'Well feel free to speed.' Hughes found DI Rose and relayed Baldwin's news. The women discussed the possible revenge attacks while waiting for their "spy" to arrive.

'I don't want Baldwin talking to the squad until we know his news,' said Rose. 'This is way too sensitive to have gossip floating around.'

Billy saw Baldwin in the corridor and signalled. He entered Rose's office and was told to close the door. He opened with the bombshell explaining Richelieu's new will.

'He's left Jo his apartment?' gasped Rose. Hughes couldn't believe it. Baldwin explained. 'Jo was as shocked as anyone. She didn't know.'

'Who told her?' asked Rose. 'Did Pierre tell her last week?'

'She's only just found out. Michael Chan was there. We know he's brilliant at cracking web sites so I guess he discovered it and told her.'

'Or he simply asked someone, like Pierre's solicitor,' said Billy.

'Keep the will detail under wraps. Tell no-one,' ordered a worried Rose. *What is happening to my squad?* 'What else?' she asked.

'Chan's thinking sounded logical to me.'

'Explain,' said Rose, angry one of her officers was a serious suspect in a major crime, and its investigation was being led by a civilian.

Baldwin explained Michael's thinking about the likely culprit being someone with knowledge of Richelieu's will. 'It *is* logical,' said Hughes.

Rose decided. 'You two follow it up. I'll work with the others but no-one hears about the will yet. Yes?' They nodded. This was now a crisis.

'Dad?' asked 6 year-old Harry Carr, son of the Mont Albert GP, and brother of older sister Grace, recovering from an acquired brain injury.

'Yes mate?' replied his widowed father, trying to read the paper.

'When is Detective Jo coming to our house?'

Jack sighed quietly. 'Well Harry, you know she's a busy lady and has to work in the day time *and* the night time.'

'But I miss her, and so does Rags.'

The dog looked up at the mention of his name. "I agree," he barked.

'Could you talk to her on your phone, Dad? Please?'

Jack was torn. He didn't like using his children as an excuse to contact the woman for whom he felt a real soft spot.

And besides, it's possible she doesn't feel the same way about me.

Harry persisted. 'It's my birthday and I'd like Detective Jo to come.'

Jack wanted to smile at the trickery of his son. 'You're fibbing, Harry Carr. Your birthday is a long way away and you know what happens to boys who tell fibs?'

His eyes twinkled. 'They get an ice-cream?'

Jack smiled. His son inherited his mother's cheeky nature and the little boy's jokes reminded Jack of his late wife. He missed her. To lose his wife to cancer at any age was tragic but in her thirties—no. Then to have their daughter suffer a serious brain injury was a double whammy although Grace's slow but steady recovery was encouraging.

'Okay, well you can invite her to Rags' birthday.'

Harry bubbled. 'Is it Rags' birthday? Is it?'

Jack nodded. 'I think so. I asked him and he barked.' Right on cue, Rags barked. Harry beamed.

'Detective Jo loves Rags. She'll want to come to his party.'

'And I hope she does.'

'I like Detective Jo and so does Rags. Do you like her, Dad?'

'Yes, I do.' He didn't want to tell anyone how he felt about the policewoman other than her but feared how she felt about him.

'Can you help me ask her to Rags' party, Dad, please?'

Dad nodded and smiled inside. *Is my son a matchmaker?*

Jo and Michael worked on possible attackers of DI Richelieu and drew up a list. 'This isn't a big list,' said Michael. 'They need to know the will, want to damage you and kill Pierre. Come on, who is it?'

'The French.'

'Agreed, but which one? The bent cop in Paris who Pierre put away years ago is back inside. His criminal boss is dead, blown up by his baby brother, and the corrupt senior gendarme we exposed was jailed.'

'But they have friends and fellow crims who could work for them.'

'True but we're missing the obvious,' said Michael.

'You mean Pierre's wife's family?'

'Yes.'

'They would have to hate Pierre to try and kill him. And they're in Paris, not here,' said Jo.

'Are they? Do we know that? And do they have access to Pierre's will? Is there someone in Pierre's legal firm leaking information?'

They spoke as one. 'Hooray Henry.'

Jo despaired. 'But how do we know he's working against Pierre?'

'Tricky,' said Michael.

'If there's a conspiracy in France, there could be someone Down Under taking orders.'

Michael nodded. 'All possible but whoever is behind this is way ahead of us. They've damaged your car then attacked Pierre. They're waiting for him to die and you to be arrested.'

'Fantastic,' said Jo sarcastically and feeling bilious.

'But the plan fails if Pierre doesn't die or if you aren't charged. They need Pierre dead and you in jail.'

'And if I'm not charged, killing me doesn't help the killers because Pierre's apartment will go to my heirs, not to the killers.'

Michael wasn't trying to be funny when he mimicked Oliver Hardy. 'Well, here's another nice mess you've gotten me into.'

32

WHEN DI ROSE'S PHONE RANG, she expected the worst. It could be the news that DI Richelieu was dead. Worse, he could be dead having been killed by his colleague. Rose answered.

'It's Senior Sergeant McIntyre from Traffic, ma'am. We obtained permission to examine the victim's apartment and gained entry using his keys. We found a handwritten note addressed to your Senior Constable Joanna Best.' Rose said nothing dreading what was to come. 'Are you still there, ma'am?'

'Yes, go on.'

'We found some legal documents and it appears DI Richelieu has made Senior Constable Best a beneficiary in his will.'

'Yes Sergeant, we know he's left her his East Melbourne flat.'

'I'm not sure I'd call it a flat. Have you been there, ma'am?'

'No, and can we please get on?'

'Did you know the apartment is not all DI Richelieu has bequeathed to Senior Constable Best?'

Rose gulped. 'What?'

'He plans to add his share portfolio and Australian savings accounts as bequests to the young lady.'

Rose was stunned. 'How do you know this?'

'We found an unposted letter from DI Richelieu to Senior Constable Best explaining everything, and an email he sent to his solicitor in Paris confirming the new bequests.'

'Jesus wept,' whispered the DI. *Can this get any worse?*

'Now while in the DI's apartment, ma'am, we took some hairs from a comb in the bathroom. A forensic officer found blood and hairs on Senior Constable Best's car, and we are testing both for a possible DNA match.'

Rose felt sick. 'Say that again.' He did. The prospect of it being true was terrifying. 'Have you clearance for all this, Sergeant?'

'Do you mean have we clearance for finding who was responsible for the cowardly and possibly murderous attack on one of your officers, with the possibility the person who owned and drove the vehicle with possibly the victim's blood and hair thereon is a member of your squad?'

There was a long pause. Rose went quiet before adding, 'I hope there's nothing more, Sergeant.'

'No ma'am and I'll contact you with any results.'

Rose called Billy to her office and explained the latest news. Both despaired.

Back at Jo's, Michael was edgy. 'I need to go home, Detective,' he said.

'Of course,' said Jo feeling guilty. 'Thanks heaps, Michael. Yet again you've cracked the case and saved my bacon.'

He looked at her. 'That's nonsense and you know it.' She did. 'But we've made a start. I'll work at home and give you a call.'

She followed him to the door. 'This has to end well, Michael. How else can Holmes and Watson keep on keeping on?'

He half smiled. 'I think you mean Laurel and Hardy.'

She leant in and kissed his cheek with a kick to it. He left and she called. 'I'll let you know if the bad guys turn up.'

She went inside feeling flat and worried. She couldn't forget the link between dumping Pierre, his phenomenal bequest, and the horrific hit and run. Her phone pinged as a text arrived. She read it and smiled— the first time for ages.

Hello Detective Jo. Rags wants you to come to his birthday on Saturday. He misses you and so do I. Love from Harry.

She enjoyed a serious crush on Harry, and Rags was adorable. The whole Carr family welcomed her like one of their own. There were times she rather fancied Harry's old man, and right now she was in need of friends.

Going to work was not an option, and nor was talking to her boss or favourite DS. But sitting at home waiting for bad news was the pits. Not having a car didn't help. The thought of it being forensically examined in an attempted murder investigation made her sick.

She rang her unusual buddy, Dr Gabrielle Strange, and asked if she might drop in. The pathetic pathologist ordered her to do so. Walking to the next suburb meant Jo was soon at Gabrielle's front door.

She knew about Richelieu's situation but nothing more than the basic details. Jo told her everything and the tough, experienced medico was lost for words. Now there's a first.

'He's left you that fabulous apartment?' Jo nodded. 'And you've given him the flick?' More nodding. 'What are you going to do?'

'What can I do? Go home and wait. They've taken my car and told me not to go to work.'

'Ridiculous,' said Strange, who fetched her car keys and tossed them on the table. Jo's eyes grew large. 'Take my car. I don't need it.'

'No, I can't.'

'Go on, take it.'

'But it's your pride and joy.'

'Oh for crying out loud, woman, you're in a jam. Some bastard's out to get you and my money's on those creeps you work with or used to. DI Steele would be first in line. Do what you're good at. Investigate.'

Jo couldn't think straight. *Is Gabrielle right? Can I take her car? It's a hundred years old. Has a cop set me up? Is it DI Steele?*

Ten minutes later she carefully steered the 1960s Humber Super Snipe to the end of Gabrielle's street. She felt like a tank driver at the Battle of El Alamein. She pulled over, rang her grandfather and gave an excuse about being in the area. He ordered her to drop in. 'The kettle's primed.'

She set off for Glen Iris, delaying her reply to young Harry Carr but not knowing why. Her hesitation puzzled her.

Despite being a brilliant detective, she failed to notice a car following her. Why would she? Her depression dominated and the challenge of driving this strange Strange car occupied her mind. The two occupants of the car behind her had been watching Jo's flat for some time. They followed her to Fitzroy North and now tagged along behind the Humber.

This was not the first time Jo was followed. Previous spies were criminal thugs who broke into her flat, and attacked the detective in a terrifying assault. Who saved her then? Why, the one and only Pierre Richelieu, who, tragically, was currently unavailable.

The current spies were not interested in sexual assault and although they were just as evil, they were different; they were female.

Jo made it across town to Glen Iris, approached Robbo's front door and heard laughter. *That's not Pop.* She knocked and heard rapid footsteps. *No way is that Pop.* The door was opened by retired Homicide Detective Senior Constable Colin Melk. Somewhere beneath his forest of facial hair was a grin. 'G'day Detective,' he beamed.

'We're in here,' called Pop, and Jo entered the lounge to find the full complement of WATTI (We Are The Three Idiots) in attendance.

Retired DS Raymond "Tucky" Tuck and "young" Melk dropped in on their old boss; the first time they'd done so since Robbo's late wife's funeral. Jo could see how much the visit meant to her grandfather. Tea and biscuits were under attack.

After the greetings and small talk, the subject of DI Richelieu's hit and run "accident" was raised. Being front page news, it cried out to be discussed, and Jo's brief happiness in the presence of three friendly former coppers disappeared. She slipped back into sadness. The men could see she was upset and assumed it was caused by the suffering of a special colleague. They knew about Jo's recent international heroics with DI Richelieu, but nothing of the romance between the two.

Robbo innocently enquired about the hit and run. 'Do you have any leads on the ratbag who did it?'

Jo paused and her face scrunched into sadness. 'They think it's me.'

The shock was instant and powerful. Three experienced ex-coppers could not comprehend Jo's statement. Her emotions startled them and the questions flowed.

'They what?' gasped Robbo.

'Who's they?' demanded Tuck.

Melk handed Jo a crumpled handkerchief. His washing and ironing skills remained undeveloped but such was Jo's broken spirit, she accepted it and dabbed her eyes.

'Brandy, Ray,' said Robbo and the former DS fetched a drink.

Jo told them the events about her damaged car and how she couldn't explain it. She sipped the brandy. More gentle questions followed. She thought about explaining Richelieu's new will but didn't.

'What can we do, lass?' asked her grandfather.

'Yes, come on, Jo,' added Melk. 'You've got three brilliant detectives here. Say the word and we'll nail the bastards who set you up.'

She looked at their expectant faces. They wanted to help. They knew the police got this horribly wrong and were sure they could prove it. She breathed deeply and shook her head.

'Thank you, all of you, but I know my Homicide colleagues are doing everything to help, and eventually Traffic will find who did it.'

'How is DI Richelieu?' asked Tuck and immediately regretted it.

Jo's face crumpled again and Melk's less-than-pristine hanky got another workout. Jo explained about the DI's life-saving surgery and induced coma, fought back tears, and Robbo looked at Tuck and Melk. They got the message. Handshakes and kisses followed then exits, and Jo was alone with her grandfather.

'I'm sorry, Pop. I should be helping you not scaring your pals.'

'Do you want to tell me the whole story?' She looked at him. 'There's no cop like an old cop.' His eyebrows bounced.

With lips closed, she smiled then told him everything. He then told her a few sensible things. He was never surprised at his granddaughter and her achievements until, at his front door, he waved as she drove away in a Humber Super Snipe. Pop's eyes popped.

The next day, things stood still. DI Richelieu remained critical and nothing new turned up to help solve the crime. That was until DI Rose took a call from Senior Sergeant McIntyre from Traffic.

'Yes Sergeant?'

'It's not good news ma'am. We explained to Forensics about a possible renegade cop and they've rushed through a DNA comparison.'

'Rushed. Since when has DNA testing ever been rushed?'

'I'm sure you don't want a cop killer out there, ma'am.'

'Nobody's dead yet, Sergeant.'

'I was there, ma'am, and believe me, it wasn't for want of trying.'

Rose went quiet. 'Go on.'

'The blood samples were damaged.'

'Damaged? How is blood damaged?'

'They say it appears to have been handled rather than the result of the accident.'

'You mean it was placed on the vehicle before the accident?'

'That's one interpretation, ma'am.'

'That's the only explanation.'

'But the hairs found were good for analysis.'

'And had they been handled as well?'

'They didn't say, ma'am, and we're awaiting results. The possibility is the hair on Senior Constable Best's damaged vehicle is a match for the hair found in DI Richelieu's apartment.' Rose froze. 'Did you hear that, ma'am?'

'Yes.' She paused. 'Does that mean what I think it means?'

'DNA doesn't lie.'

'Who will investigate this?'

'HQ Command will decide but it sure won't be me or you.'

'What can I tell my team?'

'Are you asking me how to do your job, ma'am?'

'Sorry.'

'It's your call, and rather you than me. All I can do is present the evidence.'

The call ended and Rose desperately wanted a way to prove the forensics wrong. She called Billy Hughes to her office.

'Shut the door,' said Rose, and Billy worried even more.

'Is it DI Richelieu, ma'am?'

Rose shook her head. 'He's hanging on. No, Traffic say Forensics reckon small samples of hair on Jo's damaged car are possibly a match for Pierre.'

'Possibly? What does that mean? If we're talking DNA, you can't be a little bit pregnant.'

'These things take time.'

'Are you making this up?'

'I wish,' said the DI.

'Could the hairs have got there by some unnatural means?'

'I thought so too, particularly because the blood they found was ruled out because it's been damaged.'

'Meaning?'

'Not sure; handled many times perhaps.'

'Or planted.'

'Or planted.'

Billy couldn't believe the news. 'It's unbelievable. It can't be true.'

'The boffins at Forensics might beg to differ,' said Rose.

Billy was stunned. 'She's been framed. It has to be a stitch up.'

'If it is, it's a bloody good one.'

'A bloody *bad* one if the blood is obviously a plant. Hughes exhaled. This was a nightmare. 'So what do we do?'

'No idea,' said Rose. 'Pierre naming Jo in his will doesn't help. It's bizarre. No-one who knows Jo will believe she drove that car.'

'A jury won't know her. They'll study the evidence.'

Rose thought her head would explode. 'This is insane. He changes his will to massively favour Jo Best who then murders him. It's crazy.'

Rose looked depressed. Her career as Homicide boss would be forever blighted. Was it already over with or without Pierre's death?

Billy pushed her boss. 'Will you tell the team about the DNA?'

'Not yet. I'll speak to AC Crowley then I want everyone in the Incident Room in fifteen.'

The women looked at one another. Both respected and liked Jo Best. Both felt intense sadness DI Richelieu was clinging to life apparently, due to the criminal behaviour of one of their colleagues, the one both believed was the least likely to even think about such a thing. What a mess. Was it about to become a tragedy?

Callum Blunt was spending a lot of time in the *Gents* of late. He would check the cubicles before telling the person calling him it was okay to speak. As DI Rose contacted AC Crowley, DI Steele contacted his mate, DI Callum Blunt in Homicide.

'You're not going to believe it,' sneered Steele.

'What?'

'Forensics nailed the bitch. I know a scientist who told me the latest. The Frog's DNA is on her car, the one she used to run over the poor bastard.'

'You're kidding? Forensics got her?'

'Little Miss Goody Two-Shoes has pulled her last stroke.'

'Serves the bitch right.'

'I bet Rose hasn't told the squad. She'll be shit scared to tell anyone. Fancy being head of Homicide when one of your team murders another. That's her career down the pan as well.'

Blunt thought of an idea—a rare event. 'I could save her the trouble and tell the squad, m'self.' Steele laughed. He loved the suggestion.

'Do it,' he said and Blunt joined in on his mate's laughter.

33

VLADYSLAV "VLAD" DAVYDENKO alias James alias Mike was keen on his new life Down Under. He once lived in Melbourne, Florida and now Melbourne, Australia suited him very nicely, thank you.

Since the Florida drug lords self-combusted, Vlad slept a lot easier. The DEA lost interest in Vlad, and Victoria Police waved him goodbye. He was a free man, was Mike Grosvenor.

He patched up things with housemates, Colleen and Pam. His drug dealing was a distant memory although the cash from his handyman business was a pittance alongside his former cocaine "wages".

But he wanted to be sure the threat from the US was dead and buried. He remembered two female cops, Billy and Jo, who arrested him over the homicide in North Melbourne. He trusted them. They would tell him the truth. But he didn't fancy fronting the police station.

Dani dealt with them. She might know their full names, and, even if she didn't, a visit to Ms Rubenesque might have side (and front and rear) benefits. *If memory serves, she made a cracking cup of tea.*

Clutching red roses, he knocked on Dani's door. She was told he ran off to Perth to escape crazy debt collectors from Canada, and Vlad asked Colleen and Pam to maintain that tale.

'Mike,' she cried and gave him the greeting every sailor craves when home on shore leave. They got chummy and Vlad eased his way to the topic of the female cops who arrested him.

'They told me you helped them catch a killer, a guy living right here in these flats,' said Vlad.

'You were lucky, darls. Who knows, they could've killed you.'

'I need to tell the cops stuff about those Canadian debt collectors.'

'You're okay aren't you?' asked a worried Dani.

He boasted. 'No problems, babe. But hey, you wouldn't know how I can contact those cops by any chance?'

Dani went looking. 'Both of them gave me a card. Not sure I kept them.' She called. 'No, here's one of them.'

She returned and handed Mike a card which read *Detective Senior Constable Joanna Best, Homicide.*

He pocketed it. 'You're a star. Listen, how's the flat sale going? It looks great.'

'I got an agent in and he reckons I need to upgrade the bathroom.'

'But you have. What about those new taps and tiles I put in?'

'He said the bathroom can make or break the deal.' She gave him a certain look. 'I don't suppose you could do a few more things for me, pretty please?' She smiled. He liked the offer. 'I can pay you double.'

So Dani got a new bathroom, and Vlad got his end away, and the name of a police officer he needed to question about his future safety.

Callum Blunt entered the Incident Room. With no active homicide to investigate, officers were busy checking old cases involving criminals who might have or did make threats against DI Richelieu. It was slow going. They needed inspiration and leadership from DI Rose, and good news from the hospital where their colleague clung to life. Nothing.

'Hey guys,' said Blunt, looking sad but feeling chipper. 'The word doing the rounds is that Senior Constable Best is in a spot of bother.'

Everyone listened.

'Meaning?' asked DS Fletcher, demanding an answer.

Blunt shrugged. 'Ask the DI.'

'We're asking you, *sir*,' said Charlie Baldwin.

Blunt went all innocent. 'Hey, don't shoot the messenger. I'm just reporting what I heard.'

'What did you hear?' asked DI Rose leading Hughes into the room.

Blunt was sprung and backpedalled, fast. 'Ah, it's nothing, ma'am.'

'No, go on, please. I'm sure we all want to hear your news.'

'You know what gossip's like, ma'am. It's the old Chinese Whispers.'

Rose made it an order which sounded like a threat. 'DI Blunt, tell me the gossip you heard.'

He was trapped and every detective stared at him. He tried to make it as official as possible.

'I heard Forensics found some of DI Richelieu's DNA on Senior Constable Best's damaged car.'

People gasped, and murmurs of disbelief and animosity towards Blunt began humming. He'd been riding for a fall and DI Rose was in the mood to give anyone, and especially him, a bollocking. She let fly.

'I would have thought, DI Blunt, an officer of your rank and experience would know spreading gossip can be dangerous, and especially for the one doing the spreading.' What could Callum say? He wanted the floor to open up and swallow him. 'If you have any solid information, I'll thank you to inform your senior officer first.' She looked at him with what could only be described as ball-busting intent. 'Do I make myself clear, Inspector?'

It was not a multi-choice question, and Callum chose the only option. 'Yes ma'am,' he said in a soft voice.

Rose ramped up his humiliation by tilting her head towards him. 'I'm sorry?'

He spoke louder. 'Yes ma'am,' and hated her more than Jo Best.

But it wasn't over for Callum. 'I won't ask for the source of your information, Inspector, but if he or she's the best you've got, I'd be asking your snout for a refund.'

Oh dear. The current boss of Homicide dumped a bucket on her predecessor. Blunt glowered as Rose addressed the others.

'I regret to say there's no change in DI Richelieu's condition which remains critical. If the case moves from attempt murder to murder, we will not be involved in the investigation. Now, questions?'

'What do we do with these former cases, ma'am?' asked Fletcher.

'Thanks Justin, we do nothing for the moment. We're waiting to hear from Traffic and Forensics on DI Richelieu's case. Anyone else?'

'What's the latest with Jo Best, ma'am?' asked Billy Hughes wanting detectives to hear from the boss rather than the likes of Callum Blunt.

Rose hesitated. 'There's a lot of gossip about Detective Senior Constable Best. I'm not sure what, if any of it, is true. There are some who reckon she's involved in the DI Richelieu attack.' A buzz began and Rose raised a hand. 'I prefer to take the word of a colleague, and until I'm convinced otherwise, Jo Best is a trusted member of this squad. Now, as you've been here for days, which feels more like years, I suggest you all piss off for a very long lunch.'

They did although DI Blunt ate alone.

Driving Gabrielle Strange's bulky 4-speed manual Humber Super Snipe forced Jo to think more about steering than her current predicament. She decided to return the car via Mont Albert. She needed to respond to little Harry Carr's invitation to the birthday bash for Rags. Popping into the Carr residence would allow her to accept the party invitation in person. Being a working day, Dr Jack Carr would most likely be at work tending to the sick.

She turned the corner, concentrating on her driving, still unaware of the two women continuing to tail her, although now in two different cars. As Jo approached the Carr house, she spotted Jack's mother Peg in the street pushing her granddaughter Grace, sitting in a wheelchair.

Jo pulled over, switched off and lowered her window. It was tricky. She called. 'Hello Peg. Hello Grace.'

The wheelchair stopped. The females knew the voice but not the car. 'It's Detective Jo,' said Peg and Grace smiled and waved.

Jo hopped out and crossed the road. 'Hello Jo,' said Peg and then nearly died. Her granddaughter pushed herself up and out of the wheelchair and walked across the nature strip to greet the detective.

Both women were stunned and more so when Grace opened her arms and embraced the startled cop. Peg was in tears and moved to the others making it a group hug.

The adults looked at one another. Peg whispered. 'I'll have to start calling you Jesus.'

Jo helped Grace back into her wheelchair and the trio made their way inside with Grace talking slowly but non-stop. Peg spoke surreptitiously whenever she could. 'She's never got out by herself and never walked like that. The boys will be over the moon.'

The females chatted and laughed making Jo feel better. She explained she was in the area and dropped in to accept Harry's invitation. She left with Grace bubbling and Peg hiding her tears.

En route to North Fitzroy, she rang Dr Strange who was unable to take the call because, at the time, her hands were caressing a cadaver. Her new associate, Dr Petr Laudi, answered her phone. He relayed Jo's message although Jo could hear Gabrielle shouting.

'You keep the old girl. Bring her round tonight.' Jo thanked her via Rowdy. 'And don't forget the drugs.' Rowdy gulped. He didn't know they came from Belgium via cocoa beans from Ghana.

DI Elly Rose remembered her first visit to AC Crowley's office. He pushed for her to become the new head of Homicide. He trusted her. He still did but as of now the times were difficult. He and she were in unchartered waters with Jo Best a suspect in a serious crime.

'Come in, Inspector,' said Crowley. Rose worried as he would usually call her Elly. 'Anything new from the hospital?' Rose shook her head. 'Or Traffic and Forensics?'

'Only what I told you, sir.'

'How did the DNA result come through so quickly?'

'It's not through yet. The blood was useless but there's hope of a result with the hair. I thought someone from here might have pushed it, sir.'

Neither knew that the scientist, Alastair Dean, was the driving force behind the rapid DNA examination. He once lost his heart to Jo Best but, having been rejected by the detective, turned nasty. He still harboured a grudge and hell hath no fury like a scientist stiffed. When Alastair discovered there was new material involving Senior Constable Best, he bent over backwards to investigate and gave a "preliminary" report to Traffic. If nothing else, he wanted to start a rumour. If the DNA evidence failed, a damaged reputation was almost as good. Alastair had contacted a former Homicide detective, one DI Steele, with the inside goss. Ah yes, it takes all sorts.

Crowley let Rose's comments pass. 'I spoke with the Commissioner and, like me, he's keen for the matter to be tackled by the book.'

'Of course, sir.'

'Professional Standards got the file this morning, and I reckon the seriousness of the crime will mean they handball it straight to IBAC.'

Rose expelled air. 'Shit,' she said under her breath. 'So what should I do? Solving a potential homicide within Homicide is new to me.'

'To all of us, Inspector,' said the AC.

'What will happen to Jo Best?'

'She'll be suspended on full pay until she's committed for trial.'

'*If* she's committed, sir,' Rose corrected him.

He nodded. 'I still can't believe she's involved. And is it true Richelieu left her a small fortune?'

Rose felt a lump grow large in her throat. 'It's a big small fortune.'

'Well I'd tell her to stay well away from Homicide, and her colleagues, and wait till she hears from, God only knows.' He stood and looked out his window. 'I cannot imagine what her grandfather will think of all this.' He turned back to her. 'You knew Robbo Robertson?'

'He was my DCI when I first joined Homicide.'

'Of course.' He struggled to speak. 'What a bloody, bloody mess.'

Jo parked the Humber in her spot at the back of her block of flats. It only just made it between the lines. She double-checked the locks and walked to her front door. Sitting on her step was Detective Sergeant Deborah "Billy" Hughes. Jo stopped.

'Oh no, you've come to arrest me,' said Jo believing those words.

'My bum is frozen. Can we go inside? And what are you driving? Is that the Strange vehicle?'

Inside they sat with Jo dreading the conversation. Billy let fly. 'I'm doing DI Rose's dirty work. Knowing how you ignore orders, she politely requests you stay away from Homicide and your colleagues.'

'Including you?'

Billy ignored the smart alec question. 'Somebody wants you off the Force, Jo, probably wants you dead. Not surprising given the number of cases you've cracked. You're the victim of a well-planned sting.'

'I'm glad someone believes me.'

'Shut up and listen. There is DNA evidence at Forensics which supposedly links your car to DI Richelieu's body.' Jo swallowed. 'There's more. You know about Pierre's new will, well not only has the DI bequeathed you his palatial apartment, he's thrown in his share portfolio and a solid chunk of cash.' Jo felt she was being punched. 'The hit and run is now a major incident. Professional Standards are examining the file and may pass it to IBAC.'

Billy saw horror on Jo's face. The new facts were devastating.

'This has to be a joke,' she managed to say.

'We're pretty sure you'll be suspended on full pay which will continue even if you're arrested and charged, and at least up until you're committed for trial, *if* it goes that far.'

Billy couldn't see Jo's mind and stomach. Both were in turmoil.

'I'd contact the Association as soon as. I've already told them about the situation and they're expecting your call.'

Jo felt new tears. DS Hughes didn't mince her words but did all she could to support her struggling colleague.

'So, Senior, that's the latest. Put your head down. Give Homicide and your mates a wide berth. Be ready if heavies come knocking, and stay strong.' She paused and looked at Jo who returned her gaze. 'We, *I* want you and DI Richelieu to walk away intact. Copy that, Missy?'

Jo couldn't speak although the tears she shed spoke volumes.

That night she returned the Humber Super Snipe to the pathetic pathologist. Jo revealed the latest about Pierre and his new will.

'In a way,' said Gabrielle, 'you'll want the poor old bugger to die. You'll be as rich as Croesus.'

Jo argued. 'I thought your creed was "first do no harm".'

'Be practical, woman. Happy and rich wallops happy and poor.'

'So tell me, please, Doctor Strange ...'

'Sounding a bit formal aren't we?'

'What are Pierre's chances—medically speaking?'

Strange stopped joking. She shrugged. 'Spleen removed, multiple fractures, induced coma, almost certainly other issues we don't know about; he's starting from a long way back.'

She paused wondering if her frank assessment was causing her friend undue suffering.

'Please continue,' said Jo.

'And if he does survive, he'll be on sick leave for a long time. He may never work as a detective again, and as for his sex life, well, how shall I put this?'

'Don't.'

Another pause. Strange tried to guess Jo's thinking then worried. 'You're not planning on doing a Jane Eyre are you? You're a lawyer and detective. Trust me, nursing's not your bag, old girl.'

Jo wondered if, in her life, good news was banned. She stood to leave. 'Thanks for the car, Madam Pathologist. You're a saint.'

Gabrielle roared with laughter. 'Me? A saint? Now piss off and get your head down.'

The detective jogged home, all 1.9 kilometres.

34

NOTHING MAJOR HAPPENED OVERNIGHT. The injured DI remained critical. Nobody knocked on Jo's door. Colleagues rang and she worried. By speaking to them was she disobeying her boss? She found it difficult to sleep—again.

The weekend dawned and with it the day of the party for Rags. Jo killed time shopping at the Queen Victoria market. She spent an age looking for a doggie birthday present. Any savvy dog owner would have suggested a stick from the local park. Just tie a ribbon on it.

Walking from the station, her phone rang. 'Hello Michael,' she said.

'How is the law-abiding super cop?' he asked trying to put a brave face on a rotten situation.

'I've been better. Have you any news?'

'Some,' he said which Jo knew meant a lot. 'Are you still car-free?'

'I am and likely to remain so.'

'How about I drop over for a chat?'

'I'd love that, Michael. Can you give me an hour?'

'See you then.'

Vlad wanted confirmation he was no longer a Mob target. Could he even return to his family in Florida? He rang the number on the card.

'Homicide, DI Blunt,' said the voice.

'Oh hi,' said Vlad in his pseudo-Canadian accent. 'This is Vlad Davydenko. Can I speak to Detective Senior Constable Joanna Best please?'

Blunt's radar went ping. 'What's it about?'

'Oh, Detective Best and another female officer, I think her name was Hughes, came to my home regarding a homicide, and I was able to help. She told me to call with any new information.'

Blunt wondered how he could use this bloke to bury Best. 'She's not here. Can I take a message?'

'Well actually I was hoping to speak to her. Do you have her cell number?'

Blunt's mind raced. He knew giving out an officer's private number needed a seriously serious reason but he wanted to finish her off. 'Is this important?'

'Oh sure, it's really important.'

Blunt trod water seeking a plan. 'How is it really important?'

Vlad hesitated. 'Look, I was recently the target of an assassin sent from the US in the pay of the Mob. They killed some guy in North Melbourne by mistake. I was the target.'

'What's your name again?'

'Vlad Davydenko but you may know me as James Anderson or Mike Grosvenor.'

Blunt played along. 'Oh, now I know. You're the guy who was running heroin in Columbia.'

'What?'

'You heard.'

'No, it was cocaine in Venezuela.'

Blunt laughed still unable to think of a way to hurt Jo Best. 'Just testing. But I can't help you, mate. Detective Best is not here. Give her a call tomorrow.'

'But tomorrow's too late. I'm leaving the country. I'm flying home. Look all I wanna do is give her a giant bunch of roses. She saved my life. Please.'

Blunt paused, thinking. *How can I set up Best with this drug runner and get away with it?* 'Sorry, mate. No can do.'

'Look, if I give you the name of the florist, will you tell them her address? They'll need it to deliver the flowers anyway. Don't tell me, tell the florist.'

Blunt hesitated. Was this a way he could whack Best and get away with it?

'Okay,' he said, 'what's the name and number of the florist?'

Vlad thought on his feet. 'Ah, Colleen and she's an Irish girl at Kensington Flowers. I've got her number here somewhere.' He found his housemate's number and gave it to Blunt. 'I'll place the order and pay for the flowers if you'll give Colleen the address.'

'Okay but this a special favour.'

'Sure and I really appreciate it, buddy. You're a star.'

Blunt ended the call and pondered his next move. Vlad rang Colleen and asked for a favour. 'Just pretend to be a florist and get the cop's home address.'

'Please.'

'Pretty please,' he oozed.

Michael arrived with more bad news some of which Jo knew already.

'I'm not sure how to put this,' he said, 'but the largesse from DI Richelieu to your good self is not confined to his lean-to in East Melbourne. He's thrown in some savings and shares as well.'

'DS Hughes told me.' He looked surprised. 'But why has he done this?'

Michael shrugged. 'His only living relative, his mother is dead. He's made generous provision for his incarcerated wife, and he clearly loves a certain detective.'

Jo shook her head. 'It's as if Pierre's set me up as his killer.'

'And you'll not be surprised to learn that the Honourable Hooray Henry has some scheme going to milk money from Pierre. He calls himself Pierre's agent on any film or book deal from his adventures, *our* adventures in Paris.'

Jo fumed. 'What! He did bugger all.' She needed help. 'What should I do, Michael?'

'You need legal advice,' he said. 'Is there a police union?'

'I've already contacted the Association.'

'Then until we discover who drove that car, we sit tight.'

She grimaced. 'Thanks Michael. I don't want to know how you discover these things but I really appreciate it.' He gave his half smile and she changed tack. 'Listen, you remember Rags.'

'Woof, woof,' he replied.

'It's his birthday party tonight at the Carr's place. We've been invited and I won't take no for an answer.'

'You just want a lift,' he chided.

'And I was wondering if you could give me a lift.'

Another of his famous half-grins appeared. 'So what time does Cinderella require her coach?'

Michael didn't drive a Humber Super Snipe but a much smaller Alfa Romeo. It suited him—neat, compact, quick, impressive and classy. As he drove Jo to Mont Albert, she told him about possible interest from Professional Standards and IBAC. He said little and they opted for inane topics, anything to avoid the elephant in the room subject.

They arrived amid great fanfare. Jack and his father Hugh heard the tale about Grace climbing out of her wheelchair and walking to greet Jo. With Michael beside her, Jo was greeted with love and enthusiasm and the party began. Little Harry remembered how Michael rescued Rags one dark night when the pooch was spooked and ran away. Harry told the geek everything Rags had done, both good and naughty, since that rescue, and Michael listened like a champ.

Rags took a while to twig it was his birthday but once he read the cards, his barks became more excited and more frequent. He loved his cake although needed Harry to help with extinguishing candles.

Despite the hubbub and activity of the party, Jack made a point of telling Jo how sorry he was about DI Richelieu. He knew Jo and Pierre were close and wished she harboured those feelings for him. Then as he tried to compliment her, the doorbell rang.

Harry and Rags set off in a flash with grandfather, Hugh in tow. Rags was rapt to see even more guests at his party.

'Good evening,' said the first of two suited middle-aged men. 'Is Detective Senior Constable Joanna Best in this house?'

'She is,' said Hugh. 'Please come in.'

Harry was desperate to help. He raced into the lounge room. Everyone was silent. 'Detective Jo, some men want to see you. I hope you don't have to go to work.'

A silence bomb went off. Jo's heart bashed against her chest as her stomach groaned. The birthday cake she consumed with delight was keen to reappear. The two men, guided by Hugh, stood in the open double doorway. Hugh, Peg and Jack wondered who on Earth they were whereas Jo and Michael had a pretty good idea.

The men knew what Jo looked like and stared at her as they held out their ID. The senior of the duo spoke.

'Detective Senior Constable Joanna Best, we're from the Independent Broad-based Anti-corruption Commission, and want to interview you under caution. Will you come with us now, please?'

This wasn't an invitation to a tea party. There was no RSVP required. The Carrs were stunned. Grace began to cry thinking it was something bad. Harry went to Jo taking her hand in both of his.

The visitors moved into the hallway keeping their eyes on Jo. 'Now Senior Constable,' said the IBAC officer.

Michael wanted to help. 'Jo, do you want me to come with you?'

She shook her head then looked at the Carr adults. 'Sorry to break up the party, folks.' She struggled to stay professional.

All three adults instantly dismissed the need for any apology. Jo moved to Grace and kissed her head. Harry held Rags, both of whom seemed confused and worried. Jo picked up her bag, patted the boy and the birthday boy, nodded to the Carr adults and Michael then led the IBAC boys out of the house.

Hugh closed the door, Peg took Grace, Harry and Rags to the kitchen, and Michael did his best to explain the situation to Jack and his Dad. Many questions and answers later, Michael excused himself and left. The Carrs were in shock.

The IBAC officers were used to interviewing people, many of whom interviewed people for a living. Clever police officers were unlikely to fall for any tricks and Jo was curious to know how they found her.

'It's our job to find people, Detective. And now we've found you, we'll take your phone please.' She gave it to them.

They reached IBAC HQ in the CBD. Jo declined the opportunity to have anyone represent her. The interview began and Jo kept telling herself to pause before answering. It was useless telling herself to be calm because her nerves were busy with fear and disbelief.

She was asked about the damage to her vehicle, the DNA material found thereon, and the bequests in the changed will of DI Richelieu. She played a perfectly straight bat. She heard about the hit and run incident by phone, and knew nothing of the new will until after the accident. She dreaded questions about her personal relationship with the dashing DI and stuck to the line about them being professional colleagues only. She thought she did okay.

But this was only round one. Jo knew they were looking for holes in her story. Any contradiction, any vague or disingenuous answer would be noted and studied before round two.

After an hour, the IBAC team called it a day.

'At the moment, Detective Senior Constable, this case is one of attempted murder. Should DI Richelieu die, as you know it will be upgraded to a case of homicide. Is there anything you wish to add before we end this interview?'

'No, sir,' she said in the same flat and sombre tone.

She was not arrested, her now scrutinised phone was returned, and she was released but warned to remain in Melbourne and to be available for further interviews. She was not to contact anyone connected to the incident. She declined the offer of an IBAC vehicle to drive her home. In Collins Street, she rang Michael Chan. Without hesitation he agreed to her request for a lift. She wandered up to St Patrick's Cathedral and Michael and his Alfa kept her waiting three minutes, tops.

He wanted to know about her health, particularly her mental health. He didn't ask about the interview leaving her to raise the subject. They reached Clifton Hill before she elaborated.

'This is serious, Michael. IBAC have me in the frame. They reckon there's only one suspect and unless I can discover who attacked Pierre, no-one else will.'

'I can have a go. Alan will help me.'

In the dark she smiled. She put her hand on his arm. 'You'll always be my friend, Michael. I'd love you to become my hero.'

He went all faux coy and spoke with a Texan accent. 'Oh shucks, ma'am, you sure do talk purdy.' Her smile hid her depression.

They arrived at her flat. He kept the motor running. 'I'm in your hands, Jo. If you want to talk, play pin the tail on the donkey or go hunting for lost dogs, just say the word.'

She appreciated his kindness and whacky humour. 'Thanks Michael, but I need to crash.' She leant across and kissed his cheek. He would have preferred something longer and stronger or an invitation to come inside but no, she was out and gone. He watched her open her front door. She turned and blew him a kiss, and he drove away.

Both failed to notice two females sitting in a car in the darkest part of the street.

189

35

MICHAEL WORRIED and when he arrived home, made a call. 'Ring Rowdy Laudi, I'm retired,' said the strange person who answered.

Gabrielle's answer puzzled him but he persevered. 'Good evening, Doctor. It's Michael Chan, Jo Best's friend.'

Strange switched to serious mode in an instant. 'What's happened?'

Michael gave a synopsis of the IBAC arrest and interview. Gabrielle gave a short critique laced with multiple effing adjectives.

'I was hoping, Doctor, you might call Jo, just to check she's okay.'

'Of course, I'll do it now. And thanks for all you've done for her, Michael. Goodnight.'

Inside her flat, Jo let out a restrained scream. It was a mix of rage, frustration and sorrow. She loved her job and thought she loved Pierre. Now he clung to life and she was the only suspect in his attempted murder. He could die and so too her life as a police officer.

She found her only bottle of brandy, and grabbed a glass. She froze and decided. No, she would fight this whole sordid situation stone cold sober. She put away the brandy and someone knocked on her door.

Bloody Michael, she thought. *No, it'll be Billy Hughes.*

'Hello,' called a voice Jo didn't know. It sounded American.

Jo peered through her spy hole and saw a well-dressed woman, 40s, short hair, with a purse on a chain across her largish abdomen.

'Detective Best, my name is Nancy Richelieu. I'm from Boston, Massachusetts. I'm the step-sister of Detective Pierre Richelieu. May I speak with you please?'

Jo hesitated. This has to be a con. In Paris, Pierre was scammed by a woman claiming to be his step-sister. *Is this her?*

'Detective Best? Are you there?'

Jo's mobile rang. She decided the woman at her door was more important. Her phone went to Voice Mail and Gabrielle worried. She left a brief message asking Jo to return the call as soon as she heard it.

Jo spoke from behind the door. 'How did you find me?'

'Oh it's a long story. Pierre's lawyer has been in contact with Pierre's father, my father for years. The lawyer in Paris contacted my father about Pierre's arrest. Then when Pierre's lawyer heard about his accident, he told my father who asked me to fly to Australia.'

'So who are you again?'

'My name is Nancy Richelieu. My father is Pierre's father. And I really would like to speak with you, Detective Best.'

'What about?'

She sounded surprised. 'What about? Why Pierre and his accident of course. I understand you work with him and helped with his recent troubles in France.' There was a pause. 'Please Ms Best, I know it's late and I promise I won't stay long. Please.'

Jo felt confusion and her gut reaction was to keep her door locked. 'I'm sorry; I'm not allowed to talk to anyone.'

'Pardon me?'

'I'm being investigated by IBAC and have been told to say nothing.'

'Oh please Ms Best. I'm not the police. I'm Pierre's flesh and blood. His father, my father is dying, and I need to explain why his father has not spoken to his son these last nearly forty years. Please Ms Best.'

This was different. Pierre's father left his wife and son when Pierre was a toddler. Now, if this woman is speaking the truth, both men are close to death, and here is the best, perhaps the only chance for some sort of reconciliation. *I can't prevent this family reunion.* Fighting a nagging thought to send the woman away, Jo unlocked her door.

The Yank had a solid frame. So much so a second woman was able to crouch behind her and hide. When Jo opened her door, this second woman sprang from hiding pointing a handgun at Jo. The American forced Jo inside. From her purse, Nancy produced her own handgun. Jo had ignored her nagging suspicions and was now about to pay the price. Would that be with her life?

The door was closed, Jo dropped on her sofa, and the two women separated making it impossible for Jo to attack both at once. The visitors sneered and Nancy had a double first in mockery.

'So, Ms Best, I believe y'got y'self in a little darn mess here.'

Jo opted for the calm response. Having two enraged women each pointing a deadly weapon didn't leave her with much choice.

'Actually I'm glad you're here,' said Jo in a flat voice.

'Oh yeah,' sneered Miss Boston, 'and why is that?'

'I want to meet whoever tried to murder my brave colleague.'

Both intruders laughed. The second woman spoke with a French accent. 'Not tried to murder, *did* murder as 'e will not survive.'

Jo couldn't help returning serve with sarcasm. 'Oh, so you're French.' She spoke with a terrible French accent. 'And are you per'aps 'is French sister?'

The French woman snapped back. 'No. I am 'is French wife.'

Jo couldn't speak. Surely this was another lie. She recovered.

'Really? So has the psychiatric facility let you out on day leave?'

'You ignorant bitch, I 'ave been out for weeks.'

This was another reply which packed a punch. Jo's mind spun. Facing fanatics with guns was scary. Facing fanatics making outrageous claims while pointing guns got one close to panicking.

'So is this a sister-in-law holiday Down Under or a business trip to kill a decent human being who happens to be a bloody good cop?'

The American, Nancy, her real name, took over. 'You deserve to know why you're about to die, by your own hand.' Jo felt worse, if that were possible. 'My father, Pierre's father, has got religion in his old age. Jesus has pricked his conscience and the hypocrite has re-written his will in favour of the son he ignored for decades.'

'Ah, so this *is* all about money,' said Jo staring at the American. 'One Timothy, six ten.'

'What is she saying?' demanded Margaux. 'Qu'est ce qu'elle dit?'

'Stick to English,' ordered Nancy.

Jo dropped all pretence of civility. 'Well if you're insisting on American English, we may as well speak French.'

The Yank smiled. 'I like a woman with balls. Make the most of it, bitch. You've got it coming.'

Jo knew her only chance was to keep the women talking. 'So Monsieur Richelieu Senior bequeathed to his already wealthy son even more of the folding stuff. Good luck, Pierre.'

'*Bad* luck, Pierre,' said Nancy, 'and seriously bad luck, Joanna. Letting Pierre into your panties in the hope he'd let you into his will has backfired. Killing the goose that laid the golden egg means you get diddly squat, and Pierre's whopping share of his father's estate will pass to his poor, heartbroken widow.'

Margaux grinned and gave Jo a wiggly finger wave with the hand not holding her gun. 'My 'usband is stupid,' she said. 'Pierre gave my brother power of attorney over my affairs. We hired expert lawyers to appeal my manslaughter conviction, and expert psychiatrists to support my now normal mental 'ealth. My appeal was successful and I 'ave been out for almost a month and stupide Pierre 'as no idea. The man keeps paying my brother for my specialist treatment which no longer 'appens. Pierre is proof that money *does* grow on trees.'

Jo quizzed her. 'I'm curious. How does a convicted murderer get access to Australia?'

'What, you 'ave never 'eard of a false passport?'

Jo shook her head. 'Pierre never told me you were so lovely.'

'Knowing Pierre, I am surprised 'e ever mentioned me.'

That hurt. Doubly so because it was true.

'So now you see our ingenious scheme,' said Nancy. 'We've been tailing you for days. Step one, we kill Pierre using a stolen car. Step two, we frame you for his murder by damaging your vehicle and planting DNA we collected from his house in Paris. And step three, in a fit of depression and shame, we help you commit suicide, which of course, removes you from Pierre's will. Heir today, gone tomorrow.'

Margaux laughed. 'Oh très drôle, sister-in-law. And everything 'appens 'ere in 'er apartment. It's brilliant, n'est-ce pas?'

'Oui, n'est-ce pas,' said Jo, 'and naturellement and s'il vous plaît me old sheila.'

'Right, enough,' snapped Nancy and moved towards Jo. 'Sit still Joanna and we'll make this as quick as possible.'

Jo's sarcasm and stirring sank. Her body had a mind of its own. Nancy knelt on the sofa and held her gun with both hands. She edged towards Jo. Margaux moved towards the door, out of the line of fire. Jo would have been glad to be sacked from Victoria Police rather than murdered but sometimes you don't always get what you want.

'Why don't you close your eyes, Joanna,' said Nancy exhibiting a snippet of human kindness, totally out of character for so evil a person. Jo took her advice. She could hear and feel Nancy moving along the sofa. She dreaded the explosion and hoped it would be instantaneous.

The barrel of the gun touched her temple. It was gentle but cold. Even with her eyes closed, Jo could clearly see Nancy's finger on the trigger. She sensed it being squeezed. What a way to die.

The calm before the storm was shattered as a loud banging sound scared the shit out of all three women as a fourth female let rip.

'Come on, girly, open this bloody door.' Gabrielle Strange couldn't raise her favourite detective, which was unusual in itself. When you throw in the fact the Senior Constable was being investigated by IBAC on suspicion of attempted murder, it was easy for the pathologist to worry. She would never forgive herself if she stayed home and the talented young woman did herself a mischief. Hence the door belting and the demand for admission.

Nancy hopped up still pointing her gun at Jo. 'Keep her covered,' whispered Nancy. 'If she tries anything, shoot her.' Margaux moved closer to Jo but not too close. Nancy moved to the door and paused.

More savage door knocking from a new seriously worried pathologist. 'Come on Detective. It's me, Florence fucking Nightingale.'

Strange worried even more when the door was opened and a woman pointing a firearm confronted the medico.

'Come in, slowly and quietly, or I will kill you,' said Nancy.

'Well,' said Gabrielle, 'since you put it like that; how do you do?'

She entered, the door was closed and Gabrielle took in the scene.

'Good evening, Doctor,' said Jo.

'Don't you ever answer y'phone?' she replied. 'And you might have told me you were entertaining a couple of fruit loops.'

'Shut it,' snapped Nancy waving her gun. 'Over there.'

Gabrielle sat in the single armchair. 'I take it black, no sugar.'

Nancy spoke to Margaux. 'Watch the lard-ass. If she moves, shoot her. And once we fix the cop, we'll finish her anyway.'

'Fix her?' said Strange. 'Is that some form of criminal argot?'

Nancy snapped. 'Another word and I'll kill you first.'

'Leave it, Doctor,' said Jo. 'With me dead, they may let you go.'

'Smart advice,' said Nancy as she resumed her position on the sofa. 'Eyes closed, Detective, and we'll help you commit suicide.'

'Suicide?' interrupted Strange causing Nancy to spin round and Margaux to cop an attack of nervous trigger finger.

'I'm warning you, bitch; shut it,' spat Nancy.

'But that's not how you commit suicide.' Strange's claim intrigued Nancy. 'If you want to be sure the pathologist reckons she topped herself, you'll need the right angle of entry.'

'What would you know?' demanded Nancy.

'She's the police pathologist,' said Jo still keen to keep them talking.

'That's me,' said Gabrielle. 'I've seen more suicides by shooting than you've had hot dinners, which, by the look of you, would be several and then some.'

Nancy ignored the insults believing Gabrielle knew what she was talking about. 'So tell me how to shoot her to make it look like suicide.'

'What, from over here?'

'Yes.'

'You'll get it wrong. Let me demonstrate. I'm a professional. I can guide your hand to the perfect position. You'll waste the pig and whoever does the autopsy will swear it was suicide.'

Jo's brain kept telling her it was a dream.

'Okay,' said Nancy, 'but move very, very slowly.'

'Slowly? I can't even *spell* fast.' She groaned as she rose and headed to the sofa. Jo cried silently unable to comprehend what might happen.

'Stop,' said Nancy and Gabrielle did.

'You sure this'll work?' asked Margaux more worried than anyone.

'It'll work. Get the car. We need to be out of here before the neighbours ring the cops.'

'We should use the silencer.'

Nancy snapped. 'I told you. Suicides don't use a silencer? Now go.'

Margaux moved to the door watching the others, and pointing her gun at Gabrielle.

'Tell me how to make it a suicide,' said Nancy, pointing her gun at Jo's temple.

'Too far away,' said Gabrielle. 'Powder burns are the key.' Nancy moved the gun a couple of inches. 'Now tip it upwards.' Gabrielle made her hand a gun. 'Like this. Suicides always point like this.' Nancy tilted the gun. 'Higher.' Jo's breathing sounded loud.

Margaux reached the door, and not wanting to watch the execution, started to open it.

'You're nearly correct,' said Gabrielle ready to lunge at Nancy who prepared to pull the trigger. She didn't because a huge roar erupted, and a man hurled himself at Margaux knocking her flat on her back.

Everything happened in fast motion, almost simultaneously. Nancy panicked, swivelled and pointed the gun at Gabrielle who froze. The intruder grabbed Margaux's gun and raised it to shoot Nancy who swivelled and shot the intruder. He fell and before Margaux could get up and grab her gun, Gabrielle dropped on her. Ouch.

Nancy spun round to kill Jo who gave the Bostonian bitch a backhanded throat chop. Her Eve's orange came under heavy fire. She choked, clutched her throat and dropped her gun. Jo snatched it and Margaux's, and the credits began to roll.

'Well done, Detective,' said Gabrielle. 'Who's your martyred knight in shining armour?'

Jo looked closer at Vlad, the drug runner with the now crimson shirt. 'He's a crim from the US who fled to Oz to get away from the Mob.' She felt for his absent pulse. 'He survived one American assassin but not another. He deserves a medal. He died to save our lives.'

'Yours,' said Gabrielle. 'They would have missed me, I'm so slim.'

Jo wanted to laugh and cry and scream and cheer. She cuffed the gasping Nancy, and asked Gabrielle to remain in situ atop the French con woman and killer, Pierre's secretive missus. Both intruders complained, their misery on fire. Jo reported the shooting.

Irony dominated the scene. DI Callum Blunt tried to ruin Jo Best by getting the American cocaine dealer further involved in her life. By doing so, he saved Jo's life. With masses of roses, Vlad drove to Jo's twice to find her not home. He gave it one more try and heard the threats inside. About to hammer on the door, it opened thanks to Margaux. Blunt's action saved Jo's life and uncovered the criminals responsible for Pierre's horrific accident. The grinding of teeth from DIs Steele and Blunt could be heard in outer space. Alastair Dean went quiet and Elly Rose and Billy Hughes, et al. went loud.

As Jo and Gabrielle waited for the cavalry, a machine got excited in the ward at St Vincent's Hospital where DI Richelieu clung to life. Medical staff hurried to the patient.

To be continued.

The DCI Robertson Mysteries

Somebody Murdered Maggie is a crime fiction novella. A young mother is murdered in her kitchen. Her toddler son is crying in the next room. Whodunit? There's a laundry list of suspects. Then a motorcyclist crashes and dies. Some strange woman reckons it's murder. Really? DCI John 'Robbo' Robertson heads the Victoria Police Homicide Squad and is about to retire. Can he crack the cases before he leaves? Can you solve the murders before the police? Can Robbo's six-year-old granddaughter Joanna Best help her Pop crack the case? Surely not. Download *Somebody Murdered Maggie* now. It's free.

www.cenfoxbooks.com

It's the prequel to the Detective Joanna Best novels, and it's free.

Tricky Conscience

Do you have a conscience? Does it work? Melbourne scientist, Bernie Slim, creates a drug designed to kick-start a conscience. Surely this *Moral Compass Pill* is science fiction. It's secretly given to ordinary people with unexpected results. When a heavy criminal is tricked into taking the drug, serious trouble looms. When a public figure pops the pill, it's no longer a secret. A leading politician, Mafia boss, and Big Pharma CEO fight for the formula. Bernie's in strife. Can the drug and Bernie survive? What would happen if cops, crooks and politicians followed their conscience?

Tricky.

Noodles for Shakespeare

It's *Pygmalion* and *Educating Rita* Down Under. In 1975, the Communists captured Saigon. A family of six flee, with their youngest, Thanh, aged two. It's terrifying. In Melbourne, Australia, English Lit teacher, David, introduces Shakespeare using the wit of Groucho Marx. David retires and hits a brick wall. Broke and alone, he rents a shoebox in Footscray surrounded by Vietnamese. His neighbour is the now adult Thanh who escaped decades ago. She only speaks Vietnamese. He offers to teach her English, or rather Elizabethan English. She rattles off *verily, forsooth* and *skimble-skamble, my Lord*. Their relationship develops. Has the young Vietnamese woman fallen for her senior Aussie teacher? With weird family members interfering, can Thanh succeed? Will her love for David bring happiness? And will The Bard ever get the same recognition as Groucho Marx?

A Plum Job

It's 1940. Germany is smashing through the Low Countries and the British, Belgian and French forces are trapped at Dunkirk. The Nazis are off to Gay Paree. Louise Wellesley, a gorgeous, aristocratic young Englishwoman is desperate to act. But Society demands women of her class go to finishing school, the Buck House Deb Ball, and remain at home waiting for Mr Right. Such young ladies definitely do not cavort semi-naked on the wicked stage. But war brings change. People lie. Rules are broken. So when you're in a foreign country and living by your wits while facing torture from the French police, Resistance, Gestapo and a double-agent, you'd better remember your lines, act out of your skin, and never ever bump into the furniture. And it helps if your new best friend is Edith Piaf.

Cassocked Savage

Patrick Brontë was a poor, Irish redhead—a brilliant Cambridge graduate and a priest for 50+ years. His daughters, Charlotte, Emily and Anne, were lauded; he was lambasted. Why? Why say he chopped chairs, cut clothes and made his kids vegetarians? Why say he banned newspapers and took pot shots at headstones? Why tell lies? Well actually the gun and the graveyard bit *is* true. But the other stuff? Was he really a cassocked savage? Patrick's been given a raw deal. Was he not the reason his daughters were so darn creative? Did not their love of literature and writing come from their old man? It's time for the truth, Patrick.

www.ingramcontent.com/pod-product-compliance
Lightning Source LLC
Chambersburg PA
CBHW071111100726
47908CB00008B/2344